MW01463085

IZZY'S
Adventure

A message for the four friends in this story: thank you.

I.L.

Table of Contents

The Dragon Fight 1
One Unexpected Mission 4
The Ravine 12
Dwarves 22
Ride the Dragons 34
The Fight 48

The Serpent of Tears 59
Firestriker 62
A Constellation and a Prophecy 65
A New Adventure 70
Caves of Serpents 80
Hole Too Deep 101
World Record for the Largest Serpent 114
Lunch (Breakfast? Dinner?) Break 129
The Stranger 136
A Battle With A Princess 144
A Lonely Prisoner 150
Betrayal 158
Blue Spark 163

The Land of Flowers **172**

    A Mysterious Message..*175*

    Riding Through the Clouds..*180*

    The Flower Palace *186*

    King Sky's Speech...*201*

    Invisible Arrows and Serpents *212*

    A Confusing Mess *229*

    Magmastone *239*

    The Hope Flower..*254*

The Dragon Fight

The Dragon Fight

The Dragon Fight

Once upon a time, in a land far, far away, in a place long forgotten, there was a small town by the seashore. The town was run by the mayor, who worked for Queen Sola, the queen of Esmeraldas. They lived a happy life, fishing and building, until one day, an evil dragon moved to the mountains that held large caves on the other side of the town.

The first sign of the dragon was the large shadows that dropped on them from high above during broad daylight, when the sun was in the middle of the sky. The second sign was that some of the townsfolk that fixed and built the windmills saw the large shape flying high above their village casting the shadows, swooping high and diving low. The third time were the farmers' crops on the edge of the town, closest to the mountains, that had been mysteriously singed. Although everyone was honest, from living a peaceful life, nobody turned themselves in as the troublemaker....

One Unexpected Mission

Izzy was a quiet girl who had a few friends: Chloe, Angela, Sara, and Kelsey. They lived in a cluster of houses closest to the mountains, near the farmers' fields that had been burned.

The five girls had varying personalities: Izzy was shy but loved to read, Kelsey enjoyed gymnastics, Angela liked to climb to the tops of houses to stargaze at night, Chloe loved to go into town and enter art competitions, and Sara often helped her family by babysitting her younger brother. The five girls were all around the age of ten.

Their mothers let them enjoy the tall grass and colorful flowers blooming near the mountains in spring during picnics, but forbid them from crossing the narrow ravine that was the border between the first tall, snow-topped mountain peak. They all knew it was because of the dragon and didn't object to the rule.

Izzy was sitting on the roof of Angela's house, reading a book. She liked to read outside because of the silence and the fresh air but at a place where she wouldn't be disturbed. Angela's roof was the perfect place to sit because Angela had installed a small, comfortable wall on both sides of the house's roof to be symmetrical to lean against while she stargazed at night.

Since Angela was going to the plaza of the town that was housed in the middle of the village to buy some more film for her camera that she used to take breathtaking pictures of the stars, the roof was quiet and available for Izzy.

Skimming through the contents of the book, Izzy silently flipped through each page, enjoying the thrilling stories of villagers, the daring quests of heroes, and the tales of the challengers to the heirs of the royal thrones.

"Hey, Izzy!" a voice called down from below Izzy, startling her.

"Oh my gosh," Izzy grumbled, setting down the book. "Can't a person get peace for at least a few minutes?"

Angela, who had spoken underneath her, gave Izzy a concerned look. "Are you feeling okay? I've left the house for nearly an hour."

Izzy sighed. "Just some issues with Mister Lord of Time. Okay, never mind. If you're interrupting me, something important must be going on. What is it?" Angela tried not to interrupt anyone while they were doing something important (to them, at least), because she never wanted to be interrupted while she was stargazing, so she only did it when there was important news that she really wanted to share. Well, also when she was really, really excited about something.

"Guess what?" Angela asked cheerfully. "The mayor is sending a group of townspeople to find and kill the dragon! He says that if more crops get singed, a lot of our food source would be depleted, and we'd have to survive on meat and fish. He also says that if more shadows frighten the villagers, they'll think that this area isn't safe, and people will move out of the town, and we won't have a decent population. He says now is the time for action."

Izzy sighed and leaned over the edge of the roof, trying to conquer her fear of heights. "Who's going?" she asked. She herself was way too nervous and scared and a little acrophobic to journey into the mountains, locate a dragon, and kill it without dying.

"Me, Chloe, Sara, Kelsey, and... you!" Angela exclaimed happily. "Isn't that amazing?"

Izzy nearly jumped straight off the roof as she gawked at Angela. "Excuse me? Did I hear you correctly?"

Angela rolled her eyes. "Come on, Izzy... we'll get free time! By ourselves! The mayor said the finest bakers in the village made some yummy food that we'll bring on the trip, too!"

Izzy sighed. *Anyone can persuade me with a bucket of chocolate ice cream,* she thought. *I guess I have a weakness. Does ice cream count as a weakness?* "Fine. Do the others know that we're going yet?"

Angela nodded energetically. "Yup, they do. I told them just before you. They're packing right now. You should pack, too, you know."

Izzy sighed again. It really bothered her that the mayor had arranged for her to go into the mountains on a dangerous trip without asking her first and considering her opinion. But the mayor was blunt like that, and sometimes it came in handy, after all. *I guess so, anyways.* "Okay," she told Angela. "Come over to my house at sunset." Angela nodded and darted off to who knows where.

Izzy grabbed her book and then carefully descended the wooden ladder that leaned against the right wall of Angela's house, the bars creaking a little in disagreement. Angela had told her that it had lasted before her great-grandfather's time, so it probably wouldn't break under Izzy's weight. Nevertheless, Izzy jumped off half a foot early, but luckily landed on her feet.

She walked towards her house, sandwiching her book in between her arm and her side. Her house was on a different street than Angela's, but the same as Sara's. Kelsey and Chloe lived on the same street as Angela, so she often invited them over for stargazing opportunities.

Izzy opened the door of her house and looked around. Nobody was in the kitchen, living room, or dining room. Nobody was on the staircase. No telltale footsteps came from above her. *Nobody's home.* Izzy's mom was probably out shopping, and her younger brother, Andy, was probably playing soccer or tag with his friends in the grass field.

She found a violet backpack in her closet and began packing. She stuffed in three days' time of clothes, the book she had been reading on Angela's roof, a traveling journal where she recorded all her travels, a couple of Angela's beautiful starry pictures, and some pens, pencils, and paper. *Hopefully, the mayor will have had prepared some other stuff—like special tools—for us.*

She was zipping up the suitcase when the front door swung open and knocked against the opposite wall with a thump. "I'm home!" Andy announced, walking in with his soccer ball in his left hand. "Hey, Izzy, what are you packing for?"

"First of all, don't open the door so hard," she scolded. Then she sighed. *He's going to be so disappointed he won't be able to go.* "Second, me and my friends are going to, um… go fight a dragon in the mountains."

"Can I come?" Andy asked excitedly, dropping the soccer ball. He kicked the white-and-black ball and it crashed into a cabinet with a bang. "I'll be super helpful and stuff!"

Izzy rolled her eyes. "No, you are not going to come," she said. *At least, I think not.*

"Aw, man!" Andy pouted, glaring at her. "I want to come!" He picked up the soccer ball and ran out of the house, slamming the front door behind him. Having a little brother is so hard, Izzy reflected.

Izzy kneeled down and zipped up the rest of the backpack and placed it on a chair in front of the dining table. Then she pulled out the book from her backpack and leaned against the wall to read.

Reading made Izzy forget reality; where she was supposed to be, why she was supposed to be there, and what she was supposed to do. Instead, she watched heroes and villains walk their own roads to their destiny from the sky and noticed mysterious figures watching them too. It was like glass; it reflected off the light, remembering what reality was, but watching the glow of the rainbow dance, too. It could only be shattered when—

"Hey, Izzy!" Izzy looked up from the book and saw Chloe, the unspoken leader of the group. She wasn't shy and was good at leadership, so she obviously qualified for the position of leader. "How are you doing? Did you pack yet?"

"Yup," Izzy replied, a little startled by the rush of questions. "Is it sunset yet?"

Chloe laughed. "Nope! I came here because the mayor asked for all of us to be at a meeting at his house."

Izzy quickly shoved a bookmark in her book and stuffed it into her backpack, zipping it up afterwards. "About what, exactly?"

Chloe grinned. "About the trip, of course!"

A few minutes later, Chloe and Izzy met up with Sara, Kelsey, and Angela at the mayor's house. It was exactly like the other houses, made of wood and stone, but it had a flat roof, the doorway was surrounded with stone embedded in the walls, and the house represented a box. It was near the plaza—only a few houses away, in fact.

"So... are we just supposed to wait here or something?" Kelsey asked, doing a cartwheel while making a bored facial expression. Angela looked like she was trying to stifle a giggle.

Chloe checked her pink watch that she had around her wrist. "Yeah, for a few more seconds," she answered. "Then the mayor is supposedly going to come out of his house and wish us a good afternoon."

Izzy was going to say something sarcastic, but then at the exact moment Chloe finished her last sentence, the mayor opened the wooden door and said, "Good afternoon, girls. Please come in."

"I told you," Izzy heard Chloe hiss to Sara as they entered the mayor's house.

Inside the mayor's house's first room that they came in was decorated with a few comfortable couches and chairs, a dark green carpet, a small wooden table, and a staircase that led to the second floor.

Kelsey sat in a chair that was next to the one that Angela sat in. Chloe, Sara, and Izzy all sat in a single couch next to Kelsey's chair. The mayor sat in a chair on the other side of the wooden table.

"So, as you are aware of, you are going on a trip to fight a dragon," the mayor began. Jeez, he makes it sound easy, Izzy thought bitterly. "Our village's townspeople will provide you with as many resources as they can, and you can carry efficiently. However, there are many things that you need, and they are all in different places, at different areas of the town. So, I will ask you to split up and get these supplies. Then, you may return home."

"Okay," Chloe said. "Who goes with who and where?"

"Chloe, you will head to Artist Malia's house and pick up some mapping supplies. The maps will show you were to go before the ravine, and a little bit beyond. Then, you will map the landscape yourselves."

Chloe nodded in acknowledgement. "Who next?"

"Sara and Kelsey, you two will go to the weaponsmith's and the ironsmith's houses and take the survival tools for the journey. Izzy and Angela, you'll head to Farmer Fall's house and pick up the food he's prepared for you, then go to the baker's corner and take some of the pastries they've made for you there. Alright?" The mayor opened the door again as all five girls nodded in unison. *That's kind of creepy,* Izzy noticed. "Go."

Izzy spent the next half hour of her life bringing food supplies from Farmer Fall's farm to their houses and from the baker's corner to their houses. To be honest, it was really quite tiring. She and Angela were relieved when there was nothing left to carry. They met their friends at Chloe's house, where the other three girls of the group were in Chloe's backyard.

"So, when are we leaving for our trip?" Izzy asked Chloe, who was reading a schedule for the millionth time.

"'Today, pickup for supplies,'" Chloe read aloud. "'Evening, sleep.' Well, *that's* kind of obvious. 'Tomorrow morning, heading off.' That's the schedule the mayor has given us. Also, he doesn't want *all* the townspeople to know about our... trip, so he's asking for us to leave at sunrise. Fine with you, Angela? You know, with all your stargazing and stuff?"

"Yes," Angela replied, putting a few bottles of orange juice into a teal-colored bag. "That's fine with me. There's supposed to be a new moon tonight, so there'll be more stars in the sky. I'm not missing this stargazing opportunity, but I guess I'll just go to sleep really early tonight."

Chloe shrugged. "Sure. Whatever you want to do."

The Ravine

Izzy heaved her violet backpack on her shoulders and curled her arms around the straps. She walked through the town, enjoying the silence embedded in the air. She'd never seen the village like this. But then again, she'd never seen it at sunrise.

The beautiful, glowing colors of the rising sun blinded her, reminding Izzy that she had to meet the other girls at the area of the ravine closest to the mountain peaks as fast as possible. There were so many colors—purple, pink, yellow, and orange. She wanted to stop and take a picture, but she had to hurry. Otherwise, the townspeople would question her endlessly, and she'd never get a chance to go on the journey.

In a few minutes, she'd reached the edge of the ravine. "Hi," she greeted the other girls. "So, have you guys thought about how we'll cross this ravine?"

The narrow cliffside stretched at a taller point on the side that Izzy and her friends were on and dipped a little to a lower point at the other side of the ravine. There was a thick tree stump on the other side with many rings that told the tale of a long life, betraying its old age. Symmetrical to the to the stump, on the girls' side, was a young birch tree that had a seemingly steady trunk and green leaves the color of flourishing grass.

"Does anybody have, like, a rock we can use or something?" Chloe asked, gazing over the edge of the ravine into the dark, misty depths of who knows what.

Sara spotted a smooth, gray pebble in the grass and picked it up. She opened her fist. "Here," she offered to Chloe.

Chloe delicately picked up the pebble and examined it. "Cool," was all she said before she tossed it into the ravine. They watched it fall, fall, and fall until it was lost in the dark, out of their sight... but they never heard it reach the bottom.

It was quiet for a few moments.

"That's deep," Angela finally said, breaking the silence. "I don't like the way it's dark and stuff. Nighttime might be dark, but there's always the shine of the stars or the moon... sometimes both."

Nice metaphor, Izzy thought, but she didn't bother saying it aloud.

"So... climbing down and then back up on the other side is obviously off the list," Chloe said, drumming her fingers on her palms. "We'll just have to find a way to cross it, then. Who has an idea of what we should do?"

Kelsey slowly raised her hand. "Walk... across... the... ravine... and... when we... come to... a thin part... we... jump across," she said really slowly. It sounded like a zombie with a major confusion problem. *I'd be hesitant, too, if I had to say that aloud,* Izzy thought. *But then again, I'd be hesitant to suggest* anything.

Chloe was quiet. "No," she finally decided. "That would take too long." *Some other ways might take longer,* Izzy retorted quietly, trying to douse her anger.

"I've got an idea," Angela offered. "We can use the old tie-a-rope-to-an-arrow trick. Somebody can shoot the arrow across and make it go in the tree stump."

"Hm," Chloe said. "That just might work. Who's a good shot with a bow?"

Silence.

"Me," Izzy piped up timidly, although it sounded more like a question than a statement.

"Okay," Chloe said, not hesitating for a moment. "Who has a rope?"

Angela took off her pink backpack, zipped open the backpack, and fished out a long, sturdy-looking rope. "Here," she answered, handing it to Chloe, who took it and grabbed an arrow from her own backpack. She tied the rope on the arrow, just before the fletching.

"Okay. Shoot this to the other side. Try to get it on the stump, or at least *in* the stump," Chloe instructed Izzy. "Understand? Take it."

Izzy nodded and grabbed the arrow. It felt fragile in her hand, like something that would snap if she tried to crush it. *Are we really depending on this?* she wondered.

She took out her bow from her backpack and notched the arrow in it, aiming for the side of the tree stump. Hoping for the best, she released it, and it flew through the air and embedded itself in the wood.

Kelsey was the first to celebrate. "Yay!" she cried, throwing her hands in the air. "Okay, what now?"

"We need someone brave enough to jump across and grab the rope while not falling in the ravine and hopefully not smashing into the side," Chloe answered immediately without hesitation.

Izzy scratched her chin. "Um... you sure about that?" she asked Chloe. "I mean... it *does* seem awfully, um, *risky*."

Chloe rolled her eyes. "Duh!"

"*Okay*," Izzy said.

"I'll do it," Kelsey offered. Chloe gave a nod, Izzy covered her eyes, and Kelsey jumped across. It seemed like she wouldn't make it, but then her foot caught on a rock ledge, and she grabbed the rope.

"Okay, Kelsey, now you climb up!" Chloe shouted.

Izzy couldn't look. "Did she fall?" she muttered.

"No, she didn't," Sara said. "At least, not *yet*."

Angela frowned at her and Sara shrugged her shoulders like, *What? I didn't do anything!*

"Oh, *good*," Izzy mumbled.

Meanwhile, Kelsey had somehow managed to clamber up the rope and had just reached the area of land aboveground. "Yay!" she cried, dropping the rope on the grass. "I did it!"

With a sigh of relief, Izzy lowered her hands and asked Chloe, "What next?"

"Kelsey, now you throw the rope over to me!" Chloe yelled to Kelsey. "That way, we can tie it around this birch tree here!"

"Okay!" Kelsey shouted back, picking up the knotted rope in both of her hands. "Throwing it on three! One! Two! *Three!*"

She threw the rope, and much to Izzy's surprise, it sailed across the ravine and landed in Chloe's outstretched arms. It had just reached the end of its limit, and Kelsey was trying to keep the arrow from falling off the stump.

"How do we get across, exactly?" Angela asked. "I get the rope and all, but are we supposed to crash into the cliffside and then climb up?"

Chloe rolled her eyes in impatience. "No, no, no. I'm going to tie the rope to this birch tree right here, and we can kind of... *swing* across," she explained.

Now it was *Angela's* turn to roll her eyes. "That sounds like an even more dangerous plan than the one I just said... but never mind." To everyone's surprise, she added, "I'll go first."

"Okay..." Chloe said uncertainly, tying the rope around the young birch tree. "Just be careful...."

Angela gave her a nod and began swinging across. She wasn't particularly good at monkey bars or climbing walls, but she had practice when she'd climbed up all the roofs in the town for a school project titled "The Best Stargazing Roof in Town."

She made her way across the rope and called back when she was on the other side. "I'm across! Who's next?"

Chloe went next, then Sara, and finally Izzy. None of them noticed the wary shadow that trailed behind them, crossing the rope after the last girl—Izzy—had turned her back on it, its grip slipping perilously before it regained a steady hold. No one noticed it sneaking a sandwich away from the basket of food they'd brought with them. No one noticed it prowling in the shadows, just a few feet from the group.

As the last girl, Izzy, crossed the ravine, they were all officially outside of their hometown, the only place they'd been in all their lives. She felt nervous and excited at the same time. Nervous because she'd never been away from the village before, and excited because she was going to have an adventure with her friends.

A tall mountain guarded the horizon in front of them, daring them to climb up and possibly get to the next mountain behind it, or slip off and crash to their doom. Izzy felt her nerves begin to rouse. *I'm scared,* she thought. *Very scared.*

"We're on our own now," Chloe said, glancing up from the blank map she held in both hands. "No one has come this far yet."

"Incredible," Izzy commented dryly.

"Which means now, it's *our* duty to map this place down," Chloe continued, ignoring Izzy. "Otherwise, people from the town a million years later will *still* be trying to map it."

"Awesome," Angela said.

"Kind of," Kelsey offered.

"Sure," Sara agreed.

"Irrational math numbers are terrible," Izzy replied. Chloe frowned at her. "What?"

"Never mind," Chloe muttered, waving a hand at the snow-topped mountains. "Let's just continue on."

The Dragon Fight

"Alright," Sara said.

"And the adventure begins!" Angela announced cheerfully, skipping ahead. She bent down to examine a patch of white snow. "Hey guys, look! I don't think we've actually *seen* snow in the village before, right?"

Izzy kneeled down beside her and peered at the snow curiously. "Yeah, I don't think so," she replied. "This looks new to me. Well, there *were* pictures in books, but that doesn't count."

"Yeah," Kelsey said, pinching some in between two fingers.

"I think I should put some in a vial," Sara said, dropping her backpack down from her shoulders and zipping it open.

Izzy's jaw dropped. "You have a *vial?*" she cried, spinning around to stare at Sara, still on her knees. "And you never *told* me?"

Sara shrugged awkwardly. "You never asked," she responded.

Izzy sighed.

Sara took out a cylinder glass vial and carefully scooped up some snow with it. Then she twisted the light gray cap and tightened it some more. After that, she set it back in her backpack, zipped it up, and hefted it over her shoulders again.

"Pit stop's over," Chloe announced, marching on top of the snow that Angela and Izzy were looking at. "There's plenty of the white stuff in the mountains, so you'd better get going!"

Angela and Izzy stood up as Sara studied the mountainside. "Looks like there's a clear path over there," Sara said, pointing to a narrow ledge on the side of the mountain. It went left, then turned a corner and disappeared,

The Dragon Fight

out of sight. The ledge was terribly thin, and below it, there was nothing but a steep mountainside dappled with snow and tall, stony crags that reached for the sky.

"Clear path?" Izzy echoed. "That sounds more like a path to your snowy doom."

"Well, do you see any *other* ways that *aren't* paths to snowy dooms?" Sara retorted, crossing her arms. "And plus, I think it's Chloe's decision if we're going to go that way, not yours."

Good point, Izzy thought. *Both of them.* "Okay, fine," Izzy said, looking up at the cloudless blue sky. She cupped one of her hands on her forehead to shield her eyes from the bright sunlight.

The sun was about a sixth of the way up into the sky. *There's still plenty of time before we reach the dragon's lair,* Izzy thought. Then she shivered, despite the warmth of the sunny day. *How are we—five ordinary, normal girls—going to defeat a real dragon?*

"Chloe?" Kelsey was asking Chloe. "Should we go on the pathway that Sara spotted?"

Chloe tapped her chin. "I think so," she finally said after a lengthy pause. "It's precarious and dangerous, but that seems like the only way we can go."

"Come on," Izzy complained. "I'm *afraid* of *heights*, you know!"

Chloe ignored her. "Time to go, people. Is everybody ready?"

"Wait a sec," Angela said. "Can I have the map, Chloe?"

She shrugged. "Sure," she replied, handing the blank piece of paper to Angela. "Are you going to begin mapping the area?"

"That's exactly what I'm going to do," Angela said, beaming. *"That's precisely what I'm going to do,"* Izzy thought, changing Angela's spoken sentence to a slightly more eloquent phrase.

"Okay, but don't take long," Chloe said, tapping her feet on the grassy ground. "I'm going to go scouting ahead, just before the ledge. Kelsey, wanna come with me?"

Kelsey was almost jumping with anticipation. "You got it, Chloe!"

They left their backpacks on the ground, and then the two set off towards the narrow ledge, leaving Angela, Sara, and Izzy to map the area out.

Sara found a mostly flat rock embedded into the ground to use as a table, and Izzy discovered a loose tree stump nearby, hidden by the tall grass, that she and Angela managed to haul over to the rock to use as a seat.

The stump was wide enough for two people to sit on, so Sara and Angela sat down, and Izzy remained standing. They all deposited their backpacks by Chloe's and Kelsey's, but not before Angela snatched a pencil from her bunny-themed one.

While they got everything set up, no one noticed the dark shape lurking at the front of the mountain, hidden by a thin shadow. It glanced up at the girls twice, but otherwise, staying where it was, watching, waiting... waiting for the perfect time.

Angela began by drawing a quarter of a circle in the top left corner of the map. "That's the town," she explained, tapping the eraser of her pencil on it. She wrote the words *Town* in the quarter circle, officially marking it. However, the rest of the map was still blank.

"Are you going to draw the mountains?" Izzy asked impatiently. "Also, when I can *I* have a turn on the stump?"

"Soon," Sara said. "Soon, Izzy."

Dwarves

The sun was almost a quarter of the way up into the sky before Kelsey and Chloe returned. "Guys," Kelsey said, tapping Angela's shoulder. "We're back!"

Wow, Izzy thought, jumping up from her place on the stump. *She startled me.* "Brought back any useful news?" she asked. "It's almost midday. We should get going soon."

"Yes, Miss Impatient," Chloe said, rolling her eyes. "We went along the path for a while before we came to a *really* long section of snow that looked like it was challenging us. Then we went back."

"The point is," Kelsey said quickly, "is that we can go that way. That's what Chloe means."

"Right," Chloe confirmed.

"Sounds good to me," Angela agreed. "Mapping this place is getting boring, anyway."

"It's okay, I guess," Sara relented. "But it would be better if my feet wouldn't get wet... although it's probably the only option."

"What Sara said," Izzy replied.

The Dragon Fight

The dark figure started in surprise, then settled back into the shadows, preparing to follow the girls on their adventure through the mountains.

Angela rolled up the map and grabbed her pencil and stuffed it in her backpack, but kept the map out. "It'll probably be useful," she explained when Chloe inquired about it.

The girls walked the way to the ledge, the shadowed shape creeping after them, and then they stopped. "There'll probably be some very dangerous areas in the snow," Chloe warned them. "Kelsey demonstrated that when she stepped on a thin layer of snow and almost fell into a cave."

"Yeah," Kelsey added.

"Rule 1: tread carefully," Izzy said sarcastically.

Angela nudged her. "What?"

"Never mind," Angela said.

The five girls set off on the high, narrow ledge path, trying to keep up a steady pace once they reached the snow, which turned out to be knee-high, and sometimes went up all the way to their waists.

"This... is... so... hard," Sara gasped. "How... are... you... holding... up?" She lifted up her knee and put it as far ahead of her as she could in the snowdrifts.

"I... don't... think... Angela... and... Kelsey... are... very... well," Chloe huffed back. "And... I'm... not... very... well...."

"Neither... am... I," Izzy puffed out. "I... hope... we'll... arrive... at... the... caves... soon—anything... to... get... out... of... this... horrible... snow...."

23

Izzy suspected the dragon lived in one of the mountains' caves, and she had no idea what dangers were held in the caves. There was the dragon, of course, but what about other things? She had a pretty good grade in bow-shooting at school, but she had no idea how much they'd need that skill in the caves that dotted the mountains.

Kelsey spotted a cluster of rocks up ahead. "Guys, I think we're nearing a cave!" she exclaimed excitedly, quickly forcing each foot in front of the other.

"Cool!" Angela said.

"What did you say?" Kelsey asked, turning back around to look at her.

"That's cool," Angela said. She glanced down at the pure white snow, then looked back up. "In fact, so is this snow. It's actually getting *colder*, if it's not my imagination."

"They might actually be," Izzy said thoughtfully. "Maybe if we're closer to the caves, the colder the snow is, somehow. Maybe it's a weak defense if a sheep or something is trying to find shelter in the caves."

"A *sheep*?" Sara asked in disbelief. "Do you *actually* think that?"

"Uh, maybe," Izzy answered, shrugging.

"Stop chitchatting and get—" Chloe snapped, then got abruptly cut off by Kelsey. She'd somehow ran ahead and was poking her head inside the cave.

"Guys, I'm in!" she squealed, her voice slightly muted. "And it looks, um... very dusty!"

The other girls climbed after her and they all went inside, not noticing the same dark, humanoid figure sneaking up behind them and settling in a corner of the stone-walled cave.

"Huh," Izzy said as she glanced around. "There doesn't seem to be any signs of life here."

"Stop right there," a low, rumbling voice growled menacingly. All five of the girls froze. *I just jinxed myself,* Izzy thought. *I need to remind myself to never jinx myself again.* "You're in our territory."

Wait, Izzy thought. *"Our"?*

All five girls grew rigid as small creatures that looked like dwarves and gnomes from fairy tales surrounded them. They only went up to the girls' elbows, but what stopped them from attacking the creatures were the weapons they carried. Despite their size, they wielded heavy weapons that looked as big and sharp as metal axes.

One of the creatures that was slightly bigger than all the rest marched towards them. "What are you doing in the caves of my people?" he snapped. He had a nicely ironed green shirt and brown pants that were covered in dust and chips of rock. On his head, he had a few bits of brown hair, but otherwise, he was bald.

"I'm guessing we're in the cavepeople's territory now," Izzy told Chloe.

She rolled her eyes. "Not very helpful *now*," she snarked. She turned towards the elbow-high creature who'd spoken up. "Sorry... we didn't mean to intrude. We're from the village, the one near the ocean."

The human-like-yet-not-human creature visibly relaxed, and his companions (*his people?* Izzy wondered) backed away from the five girls, making a friendly perimeter instead. "Thank goodness," he said, obviously relieved. "I thought you were spies for the dragon." As he spoke the words "the dragon," a shiver came over the room. Izzy shuddered. "I am the dwarves' mayor, Mayor Dwaggen."

So not cavepeople after all, Izzy thought, surprised.

"What dragon were you talking about?" Chloe questioned, exchanging excited looks with the other girls. "We think a dragon has been terrorizing our village, and that's why we're in the mountains: to get rid of the dragon."

Mayor Dwarf began nodding thoughtfully, but then he seemed to spot something. "Guards—get that shadow!" he yelled, pointing at the dark shape that had followed Izzy and the rest of the girls all the way to the mountains. "He's been sitting there, watching our conversation!"

In a moment, all of the dwarves except for Mayor Dwaggen went for the shadow. It yelped in alarm and tried to get away, but the astonishingly nimble dwarves grabbed it and dragged it into some sunlight streaming in, revealing who it was.

"It's *Andy!*" Izzy shrieked, jumping up from her standing position, making Angela start and lean a little way away from her. "Andy, *what* are you doing here and *why* did you *follow us?*" She spiraled from very shocked to *very angry* in a matter of seconds. *Quickest record of changing emotions,* she thought before her attention went back to Andy.

"I wanted to go," he muttered. "I followed you. You left the rope behind over the ravine and it was easy to hide in the shadows." As he spoke, he couldn't hide a mischievous smirk that kept getting wider and wider.

Izzy facepalmed. "Mom would *kill* me if anything happened to you," she groaned. Sara watched with a slightly amused expression, while Angela looked like she was outright trying to not burst into giggles. Izzy poked her head outside the cave, where the sun was beginning to set. "But since it's starting to get dark, I guess you *can* stay with us for the night...."

Mayor Dwaggen had his people make a comfortable sleeping area for the five girls in the cave. The dwarves couldn't make five beds quickly, so they settled for a blanket on the ground and a blanket above that for each of the girls.

Before they went to sleep, Mayor Dwaggen approached the group and said, "I think you'll have trouble fighting the dragon, so we have prepared some... weapons and helpers for you."

Kelsey gasped. "*Already?!* But we've only been here for half an hour!" she exclaimed.

Mayor Dwaggen smiled. "Us dwarves, in addition to having an underground civilization, are miners. We don't just live in caves; we hollow out our own openings." He paused, then continued. "Right now, what you see is about only one-sixth of our population. The others are still underground."

Chloe facepalmed. "I... am... very... confused...."

Mayor Dwaggen smiled again. "On a different subject," he said, "my miners have crafted unique and powerful weapons for you to use. Including *him*," he added, pointing at Andy, whose face immediately lit up like a lightbulb.

"Where are they?" Izzy asked, glancing around. *Is there really magic in this world?* she wondered, then slapped herself internally. *Of course there is, Izzy! Have you forgotten about all the books about magic you've read in the library?*

Okay, well, what I meant was "Will I actually be able to possess magic?" she asked herself more than a little doubtfully.

Maybe, her mind replied. *Maybe not. That depends if you're able to stand still and not keep asking me questions that Mayor Dwaggen will answer.*

"Follow me," the dwarf said, walking over to a cave wall where shadows stretched across it, beckoning for the girls and Andy to follow. They did.

"We came from this door," Mayor Dwarf explained, knocking on a door that was about as high as Izzy. Now she knew why she wasn't able to see it: it was shrouded in darkness and blended in almost perfectly with the gray colors of the stone. "On the other side of the door, there's some wide wooden stairs that lead down into the place we call home."

"Are we going to go through it?" Kelsey asked excitedly.

What's behind that door? Izzy wondered.

"Yes," Mayor Dwaggen replied. He opened the gray door and walked through, gesturing for the girls to follow him.

When Izzy stepped through, she was almost blinded by a burst of yellow light. In the cave, with only the sun as a source of light, it was dark, as the sun was beginning to set. However, in the room with the wide wooden stairs, yellow crystals embedded in the smooth stone ceiling emitted soft glows that lit up the whole room.

Izzy blinked. *That's so bright!* she thought.

"Down here is where the weapons—your staffs—are," Mayor Dwaggen explained, walking down the steps. The girls followed him, while Andy bounced down the steps energetically after Izzy.

The Dragon Fight

"Are the weapons staffs?" Chloe asked curiously.

"Yes, they are. Each of the staffs have powers found in the wild," Mayor Dwaggen said as they walked down the wide wooden stairs. "For example, one can shoot lightning and summon thunder. Another can control vines and summon plants. But they also have defense motives as well; one can protect you from freezing, and another won't let you drown."

"Awesome!" Kelsey exclaimed. Angela and Sara nodded in agreement.

"Cool!" Chloe said.

"Um... powerful?" Izzy said uncertainly. *Hey, I know that's a weird word to describe some weapons,* she thought defensively, *but all the other good ones were used already.*

Mayor Dwaggen rolled his eyes. "Whatever you want to describe them with, I suppose," he said. "That isn't my decision to decide upon."

They descended down the staircase for a few more moments before they reached the bottom, where a hallway with walls of stone was dug. Doors dotted the passageway; all of them were wooden except for a stone door, which was only visible by a painted black outline. This door was the one that Mayor Dwaggen pushed open and said, "Here are your staffs."

Izzy waited until Chloe, Angela, Sara, Kelsey, and Andy had entered the room before she went in herself. It was a simple cube-shaped space with gray walls, but there were six stone pedestals in the center of the room, lined up in a row, and each pedestal had a staff on it.

Dominating the first pedestal and with the orange letters *AL* for Andy on it was a gray staff with a darker gray storm cloud sitting on top. There was an orange staff with a red flame on it that had a *CC* for Chloe in

29

light pink. A deep blue raindrop sat atop a sky-blue staff, the letters *AX* embedded in gold for Angela. With the silver letters *SL* on it for Sara, a white staff with a pale blue ice cube on top rested on the fourth pedestal. Another staff was pale gold with a transparent, shimmering crystal on it with the letters *KT* on it for Kelsey. The last one was dark green and had an almost-black leaf sitting on it with the letters *IL* written for Izzy on it in ivory.

"Nice!" Angela exclaimed, gazing at her staff. "I like the little droplet of water on it. Oh, and the golden letters!"

"Mine looks cool, I guess," Sara said, touching the ice cube.

"Literally!" Izzy joked. *Okay, that was a failed attempt,* Izzy thought as Sara didn't crack a smile.

"What, uh, *powers* do they have?" Chloe asked Mayor Dwaggen. "I know it's supposed to be kind of obvious, but we don't exactly *know*...."

Their dwarf guide nodded patiently. "Andy's staff is storm type, yours is fire type, Sara's is ice type, Kelsey's is underground type, Angela's is water type, and Izzy's is earth type," he told them, using violent hand motions as part of his explanation. "Each staff can summon creatures of their type, and you'll have be able to control the creature using spoken commands."

"Er, and how exactly do we use their power?" Chloe questioned. "I mean... there's no *buttons* or anything...."

"Ah... for *those*, you need *these* powerful creatures," Mayor Dwarf said with an excited smile. *It's like he's a kindergartener,* Izzy thought with wry amusement. "Follow me."

Mayor Dwarf led them out of the room the staffs were in and back into the hallway. Then he proceeded to go to the *very back* of the hallway, which proved to be a *very long* time. Izzy was almost falling asleep when Mayor Dwarf opened the door at the end and ushered them inside.

"Wow..." Angela breathed, staring up at the magnificent sight.

"Amazing..." Chloe whispered, her eyes seemingly locked to what she was watching.

"*Awesome!*" Andy yelled at the top of his lungs, jumping around wildly. Everyone—including Mayor Dwaggen—flinched when the sound pierced their eardrums. *I thought jumping around was* Kelsey's *job,* Izzy thought, still disgruntled about Andy's following them.

Inside the room were what looked to be *dragons*. Dragons that were at least ten times bigger than any of the girls (or Andy). There was a fiery orange dragon with red-hot eyes and a pale pink saddle on it, a sea-blue dragon with dark blue eyes and a golden saddle, a white dragon with light blue eyes and a silver saddle on it, a golden dragon with gray diamond-shaped eyes and a purple saddle on it, a dark green dragon with almost-black eyes that had a black saddle, and last but not least, a dark gray dragon with bright yellow eyes and an orange saddle on it.

"These will be your dragon companions," Mayor Dwaggen explained proudly. "The orange dragon is Lava, the blue dragon is Whirlpool, the white dragon is Ice, the golden dragon is Jewel, the green dragon is Leaf, and the gray dragon is Storm. They have to be near the staffs for the magic to work—you just need to hold the staff and think about what you want to do with it." Pausing for breath, he added, "Each of these dragons also have excellent tracking, eyesight, and sniffing skills. We've trained them especially so that they're very smart."

Sara was gazing wondrously at Ice. "Wow," she murmured. "If you're saying that these dragons are like that, it seems like Ice can help us cross those thick snowdrifts."

"Possibly—these dragons are called the Withering Wings," Mayor Dwaggen said proudly. "They are mysterious and powerful to legendary, but we miners know how and where to get these dragons and train them into obedient steeds."

"Um... I've got a question," Izzy said. "How are we going to get the dragons out of the mountain? They *definitely* won't fit through the doorway...."

Mayor Dwaggen grinned, jogging to the wall on the other side of the room. Izzy didn't say it out loud, of course, but she thought it looked quite strange, for a creature as small as him to be seen jogging. *I mean, seriously?* she thought. Mayor Dwaggen pressed a bumpy gray button on the bumpy gray wall that blended in amazingly. So that was why Izzy hadn't seen it before.

For a second, nothing happened, and Izzy was confused. *Why doesn't it do anything?*

Then, there was a low rumbling sound, and the wall opposite of the dragons slowly creaked upwards to reveal the snowy wonderland—ice spikes, caves, mountains, and more, all part of the new terrain that Izzy still wasn't used to, even after almost a half day of trekking in it.

"We're on the edge of the mountainside," Mayor Dwaggen explained, "so I had some of my workers install a moving door for the dragons."

Izzy noticed that the sky was already ink-black instead of the cloudless blue in the afternoon, and she suddenly felt very tired. "Um... can we go to sleep?" she asked. "I'm tired. Very tired."

Mayor Dwaggen smiled warmly. "Of course. In the morning, you'll head along to the caves. There's a wise old man on the cave up and diagonal, so if you manage to get some advice from him, it's about as good as a dead dragon."

"Er, thanks," Chloe said. "And if you don't mind, we'll be off to bed now."

Ride the Dragons

The next day, the six warriors-in-training were discussing battle plans to fight the dragon, sitting crisscross at a low table with the map spread out on it in the cave where they'd first 'met' Mayor Dwarf and his people.

"Well...." Chloe trailed off, lost in thought, drumming her fingers on her knees. "We have to see what everyone's good at if we want to make a proper plan, so... report cards, anyone...?"

The girls and boy dug into their backpack, suitcase, or pocket, and put down a rectangular shaped piece of paper on the table with the map on it. These were their report cards and their grades:

Sara

Report Card ~ Subjects, Grades, and Comments from Teachers (Combat School)

Sword Fighting

Grade: A

Comments from Mr. Slicer: "Good at ducking, dodging, and avoiding other blows, and is quick and nimble, but has to work on offensive/attacking moves."

Bow Shooting

Grade: B

Comments from Ms. Stream: "Sara pulls back the string very well, but she has to focus on aiming at her target."

Kelsey

Report Card ~ Subjects, Grades, and Comments from Teachers (Combat School)

Sword Fighting

Grade: A+

Comments from Mr. Slicer: "Fighting is flawless."

Bow Shooting

Grade: B+

Comments from Ms. Stream: "Kelsey's shooting is amazing, but she has to pay attention during class."

Chloe

Report Card ~ Subjects, Grades, and Comments from Teachers (Combat School)

Sword Fighting

Grade: A

Comments from Mr. Slicer: "Amazing at agility. Good at dodging and the spinning technique."

Bow Shooting

Grade: B+

Comments from Ms. Stream: "Chloe is great at pulling back the bowstring, but she has to work on her aim."

Angela

Report Card ~ Subjects, Grades, and Comments from Teachers (Combat School)

Sword Fighting

Grade: B

Comments from Mr. Slicer: "Definitely needs a little work. Okay at the thrusting move."

Bow Shooting

Grade: A

Comments from Ms. Stream: "Angela is amazing at shooting, although she could use a little work on pulling back the bowstring."

Andy

Report Card ~ Subjects, Grades, and Comments from Teachers (Combat School)

Sword Fighting

Grade: A+

Comments from Mr. Slicer: "Amazing at sword fighting. Can do all the advanced moves—unusual for a third-grader."

Bow Shooting

Grade: B+

Comments from Ms. Stream: "Andy has to work on his aim."

Izzy

The Dragon Fight

Report Cards ~ Subjects, Grades, and Comments from Teachers (Combat School)

Sword Fighting

Grade: C

Comments from Mr. Slicer: "The worst sword fighting student I've trained in fifty years."

Bow Shooting

Grade: A+

Comments from Ms. Stream: "Izzy is above your average bow shooter. Her aim is flawless, but she has to work a little on pulling back the string."

Chloe stared at Izzy's report card, clearly in shock. "How come your sword fighting skills are so bad?" she asked, tearing her gaze from the paper and looking at Izzy.

Izzy shrugged. "Well, that hunk of metal that's called a sword always seemed so heavy. It seemed a lot easier to lift some string and a bundle of wood."

Kelsey was reading over Angela's card. "Good point," she commented. "So... what's the battle plan?"

Chloe quickly skimmed the report cards. "Kelsey, Andy, and I will fight directly near the dragon, seeing as we have the best sword fighting skills—not you, Sara, because we need more people at the back," she added quickly to Sara's insistent inquiring look. "We'll stay at the front of the group with swords and the staffs. Angela, Izzy, and Sara will shoot the dragon with arrows. Mayor Dwarf didn't say the staffs had a certain range, so I think you guys can use those too."

"But how are we going to avoid shooting you, Andy, and Kelsey?" Izzy asked worriedly. She was good at shooting, but a sword fighter's lightning-fast moves could easily make her arrows hit the wrong target. *I'm not bad at using a bow!* she thought defensively. *Look, I'm only in the fourth grade, okay?*

"We can borrow some rock from the dwarves and make a small wall," Chloe suggested, not answering Izzy's question for some reason. *Ugh*, Izzy thought. *But then again, maybe Chloe has something else that's more important to think about than my obviously unimportant question.* "After all, they must have some leftover stone, after mining underground for so long...." For a second the look on her face turned wistful. "I wish I could stay here and observe these guys. *Seriously.*"

"Let's get going," Angela said, grabbing all the report cards and putting them in her light pink-with-yellow-stripes backpack. "I'll give the cards back to you when we get back to the town."

After saying thank you and goodbye and thank you again to the dwarves, they set off for the cave that the wise old man inhabited, according to Mayor Dwaggen (and whoever had made the maps). The miners gave them a clear crystal that looked like any other and told them that the minute the man saw it, he would accept them as friends, not enemies, for many of them, like hunters or dragons, roamed the ice-topped mountains. (Many *enemies*, like hunters or dragons, roamed the ice-topped mountains, not many *friends*, like hunters or dragons, roamed the ice-topped mountains. If it were the other way around, then it would be completely absurd.)

The group was puzzled but took their word for it. The clear crystal was now safely nestled in Chloe's pocket.

According to the dwarves' calculations, which they had assured the group that they were nearly entirely accurate, it would take about an hour to arrive at the cave on foot. They knew they had a long hike ahead of them, and they weren't looking forward to it. *Especially* Andy.

Which, naturally, made Izzy very annoyed.

"Can't you slowpokes go faster?" Andy complained, trudging the fastest he could go. Izzy knew her brother well; he liked to brag, act like he was the best, and pretend that he wasn't tired unless they were alone and there was no one in sight.

"Come back down and stop complaining," Chloe snapped. Andy came back down and stopped complaining. *That is a wonder,* Izzy thought, amazed. *Can Andy now be ordered around by* me*, too?*

Chloe glanced at Izzy, smiling. "He's like the spitting image of Claire," Chloe told her. Claire was Chloe's sister and a few years younger than Andy. However, they were both alike in soul.

"The *literal* spitting image of Claire?" Izzy asked, curious to see which one Chloe meant. "The image of Claire spitting, or the image of as if Andy is Claire?"

Chloe frowned, her smile gone. "The second one, of course!"

Kelsey snorted but quickly turned it into a cough. "Say... can we ride the dragons?" she asked. The Withering Wings were trailing behind them, chatting amongst themselves.

"Which vacation spot do you like best?" Storm asked.

Ice blew a breath of icy air and huffed, "Icebergs, of course! Isn't it obvious?"

Ice, of course, had a very icy temper, as Storm had a stormy one, Leaf had a soft one, Lava had a spirited, fiery one, Whirlpool a bubbly one, and Jewel had a hard, stony one. *Most* of the time they didn't let their anger get the better of them, but Izzy had been listening (read: *eavesdropping*) on them long enough to realize that they *did* treat each other like siblings—which meant that they *argued* like siblings.

"I would definitely go to the bubbling volcanos..." Lava said dreamily, the tip of her tail whooshing in the air. The sound reminded Izzy of an arrow whistling into the sky.

"Bubbles?" Whirlpool asked excitedly. "My favorite vacation spot is the Bubbling Village! You have to try the dragon tub! It's full of water and it's really big, and there's a bunch of new saddles and new wing conditioner and fang cleaner and...."

As the water dragon droned on and on, Jewel hissed in Lava's ear, "Great. Now you've set off Whirlpool's blabbing trap!"

"I didn't expect her to talk so much!" Lava growled back. Izzy noticed her tail was *thrashing* now. *How curious,* she thought, keeping it to herself. *I really don't want to anger Lava right now.*

"Great idea," Chloe said, finally answering Kelsey's prior question. "Mayor Dwaggen said they were extra-special Withering Wings that they had extra-special training. If we ask them to bring us to a certain location, I'm sure they will."

Will they, though? Izzy wondered.

The Dragon Fight

"Especially if we ask Whirlpool to visit the Bubbling Village," Izzy said, shooting a glance at Angela. *Hey! It's not my fault I'm being funny!*

Angela shrugged, looking helpless. "Not my fault she's so talkative." Angela sighed. "Well, she's certainly *bubbly*...."

"Great joke," Kelsey said, "but we have a mountain to climb up. Hey, Jewel, can I ride you up? It's really boring...."

Jewel sniffed and growled, "Sure... as long as you can get Whirlpool to shut up. She's really annoying me."

"Stop talking, Whirlpool," Angela told her dragon sternly. "Now let me ride you up that mountain. Stop at that cave, see? That one? Okay, let's go."

Izzy climbed onto Leaf's enormous back that shined and shimmered continuously from her shiny green scales. Leaf was humming a summer tune to herself. The school taught the summer tunes, the winter tunes, the autumn tunes, and the spring tunes to all the students, so the summer tune was easy for Izzy to remember. But the autumn tune was her favorite.

The summer tune went like this: "Fresh and full of ferns and flowers, this is when cold old winter cowers; bright and sunny and master of fun, come out and enjoy the summer sun...."

There were more words than that, but right now Izzy wasn't focused on repeating the summer tune over and over again until it got stuck in her head. Instead, she was focused on riding Leaf up the mountain.

Leaf was an earth dragon, which meant she could use her earth powers to help aid her up the mountain. She pulled up a few sturdy vines from the ground and made a tree-trunk platform high in the sky, jumped on it, and took off.

The Dragon Fight

Izzy's first feeling about riding dragons were fear. That was when she realized that the dwarves had made the dragons like horses; they'd put saddles and bridles. Of course, she suspected that they knew they couldn't control a dragon with a bridle, but instead put it on for holding, just in case you felt like you were going to plunge down, down, and down—and then splat on the ground like a soggy pancake. *I don't eat pancakes, anyway,* Izzy thought, hoping she wouldn't splat on the ground like a soggy pancake.

She gripped the black bridle and braced herself for the quick ascent. It was faster than she thought; Leaf spread her large wings that were nearly as wide as the tallest mountain from height, preparing to soar into the sky.

Leaf took off and soared above the mountain peaks, making Izzy wonder if the cave was really so far away. "Where are we going?" Izzy asked.

"The cave," Leaf replied in a soothing growl. Izzy had no idea if a growl could really be soothing or calm, but she'd read somewhere in a dragon dictionary that a growl for a dragon was the equivalent of a whisper. So maybe Leaf meant it quietly?

The view from Leaf's back was magnificent. Snow-topped mountains stretched as far as the eye could see, and ice spikes took up the space in between the magnificent cones. Clouds were just a few flaps overhead and Izzy saw the other girls (well, also the boy) riding their dragons in the same direction Leaf was flying. *Okay, at least I know she's going to the right place,* Izzy told herself.

That comfort vanished in thin air when they came to a mountain that was directly below them; the dragons tucked in their wings and shot straight down. For a second, Izzy thought that they had broken free of their loyalty and had planned to plummet their owners to death. Then she recognized the technique from the famous book *How Dragons Fly* and tightly clasped onto Leaf's neck scales and closed her eyes, bracing herself for impact.

The Dragon Fight

Within a few seconds, Leaf was on the ground, padding towards the cave entrance with her dark green eyes shining with pride. *Probably because of her show-off landing,* Izzy reasoned, although she didn't bother saying it out loud.

The entrance to the cave looked like it had been wedged open by a dwarf. It was a small crack, and Izzy estimated that they could just fit through it if they squeezed themselves between the ridges of rock and ducked down even lower.

They hopped off their dragons, giving them a pat on the shoulder blades. "Stay here while we're gone, okay?" Izzy told Leaf. "It's fine to play hit-your-friends-with-a-snowball," she added once she saw a bored look in Leaf's eyes, afraid that her dragon would fly away to the other side of the world.

Leaf gave another soothing growl in acknowledgement and hopped off to play hit-your-friends-with-a-snowball with the other Withering Wings. Izzy turned towards Chloe, Angela, Sara, Kelsey, and Andy.

"Let's get through that hole," Chloe said once she saw she had Izzy's attention.

They each squeezed through the narrow gap, the first ones giving advice like, "Grab that spike to get some momentum!" or "Careful to avoid that nasty poke!"

When they all got to the inside of the cave, brushing off bits of rock and dust, they looked forward. There was the old wise man, sitting... in a pile of rose petal leaves. He cracked open his eyelids to reveal irises so yellow that they seemed like the sun themselves. He had a fine crop of light gray hair that thankfully hadn't started falling out yet. *By that, I mean that I'm glad he's not bald,* Izzy thought, relieved. *Otherwise, this would be too much out of a fantasy story.*

The Dragon Fight

She ignored the fact that Mayor Dwaggen had been very close to bald.

Chloe stepped forward and handed him the crystal. "We've come to ask you a question," she said, her voice ringing through the cave.

"Quiet now, youngster," the old man rasped with a croaky edge. "What shall you ask me today?" The way he said it made it seem like they would ask him again one day. *But will we?* Izzy wondered. *Can he see the future so clearly he knows we'll come back someday?*

"What do you know of the dragon that lives in the highest peak of these mountains?" Chloe inquired. Izzy noticed a slight tone of impatience. *That would be understandable,* she thought. *I'm a little impatient right now, too, although I'm an impatient person from nature.*

"Ah," the old man said, his seemingly dry throat rasping uncomfortably as he spoke. "The dragon is a fine magenta color and has, oh, golden eyes. Has the power... hypnotizing...." His yellow eyes seemed far away as he said the last few mumbled words.

"Excuse me? Uh, what was that?" Chloe asked, looking confused.

The old man shook his head. "I apologize for my... ramblings," he responded. "The dragon can hypnotize... allies... of yours... with one look from the eye."

The six children were silent, waiting for the next sentence that would be breathed out of the old man.

"That is all," he said, closing his sun-like eyes once more. "I am glad to see you. Good luck battling the dragon. You... will need it."

The Dragon Fight

His ominous words sounded in heroes' minds as they exited the cave through the narrow gap and started hiking up the mountain once more, this time to their battle which they awaited, full of suspense, fear, and anticipation.

It had been a few good minutes when the group realized they didn't know how far it was to the dragon's cave. "Now what?" Kelsey muttered in a not-so-good tone.

"We can ask the dragons," Izzy suggested. "They could fly above the mountains and estimate."

Chloe shrugged. "Any way's fine if we get there quickly," she huffed, her breath a little visible puff of air in the frost. "This place is really cold. Lava!"

The fire dragon was immediately hovering above Chloe's head, sending off bright orange sparks and volcano-hot heat. "You called?" she asked sweetly. A spark landed on Chloe's hair and set fire to her head. Reacting quickly, Angela immediately threw some snow on top of it, stopping the fire but soaking Chloe.

"You're terrible," Chloe grumbled unhappily to her dragon, brushing off the remaining solid snow and patting down her cold, wet hair. "Thanks, Angela." Angela nodded, looking happy to have been acknowledged.

Lava gave her a bright smile. "It was an accident!" she replied cheerfully. "Sorry about that!"

Chloe sighed and rolled her eyes. "Anyways, can you tell us how long it'll take to the dragon's cave?" she asked.

Lava flapped her wings in a stretch and yawned. "On those puny human feet, probably sixteen hours," she said, tipping her head to the sky.

Izzy followed her fiery red eyes and saw that the sky was beginning to turn into shades of orange, pink, and purple, and the sun was nearly on the horizon.

"The sun's beginning to set," Izzy told the others. "We'll never make it to the dragon's lair before dark. Let's take our dragons." She thought the phrase 'dragon's lair' sounded really cool, but apparently her friends didn't, and neither did Andy, who just shrugged.

Sara sighed and said, "Just don't have that dropper move at the end, okay, Ice?" The white dragon appeared at Sara's side, her pale blue eyes shimmering solemnly.

"If you say so, Sara...."

Taking their dragons, according to Jewel's calculations, would brush off at least nine hours. They soared over the landscape, taking in the beautiful views that were twice as pretty because of the setting sun.

Gazing over the land on a dragon's back was Izzy's dream. But gazing over the land on a dragon's back while thinking of battling an evil dragon with chances of death was not really Izzy's dream.

Yeah... that's far from what my dream is, she thought. *But hey! I can still admire the view, right?*

"The world is beautiful," Izzy breathed.

Ice, with Sara on her back, overheard her. "This is beautiful?" she scoffed, twisting her head around to look at Izzy. "The Northern Lights in Fairbanks, Alaska, are totally prettier than this puny display."

Sara sighed. "Why do you dragons have to say the word 'puny' so much?" she grumbled in an annoyed tone. "It's very distracting."

Ice huffed out an icy breath that chilled a clump of air (don't ask why) and it froze into solid ice and fell towards the ground, shattering with a chilling shriek when it reached the bottom. "That's the word that describes humans," she snarled, flapping her wings and gaining a burst of speed that propelled her further.

"That's that, then," Izzy said aloud to no one in particular.

The Fight

They made it to the dragon's cave in exactly six hours and fifty-three minutes. The entrance of the cave was wide and large, the perfect size for a dragon five times as large as any of the group's Withering Wings. Polished spikes, worn by age and weather, hung from the ceiling and jutted out of the floor, forming a mouth-like appearance with sharp, shiny, smiling teeth.

"I'm getting the creeps," Angela said, shuddering. "Half of cold, half of the feeling of evilness."

Chloe rolled her eyes. "Come on, Angela," Chloe chided. "There's nothing to be afraid of. C'mon, let's go in...."

The group of inexperienced explorers entered the cave, oblivious about the dangers of a very particular Gigantic Giant dragon.

"This cave is beautiful," Angela breathed, forgetting all about what Chloe had said before they'd headed into the cave. *'Beautiful' is an understatement*, Izzy thought, gazing around the cave in miraculous wonder. *How can such beauty grow in a cave of all places? Why can't it be out in the open?*

Crystals as shiny as the sun and as transparent as water itself was on every wall of the cave, only a few bits of drab gray rock peeking through the beautiful spikes. There was sea-green, sky blue, lilac purple, bright yellow, and so many more different colors that it was nearly indescribable. The entrance let in the dying colors of the sun which bounced off the outside shell of the crystals and reflected off every colorful spire. But the girls could see it was somehow storing the light inside of it into a small ball of light, layer by layer, that continued to burn fiercely. The outer shell expanded as the ball of light grew bigger.

As the group of adventurers traveled farther and farther down the cave, the light somehow grew brighter and brighter, as if there was a different light source that was more powerful than the sun. They also became more numerous, too, and soon it seemed like the cave itself was made out of these fantastic crystals, not the dull gray rock that most caves were.

Finally, they came to the end of the cave. Expecting there to be a sleeping dragon or something, all of the children were shocked to discover that there was nothing—just a dead end.

"But this is where the dragon is supposed to be!" Izzy protested to no person in particular. "The map said that the dragon lived here, and the dwarves said it too!"

"Now, calm down a little, Izzy—" Chloe was broken off by a large rumbling noise coming from the back wall. "Wait a second...."

The back wall was the only slab of uncovered dark gray rock they'd seen for a while. Everyone—including Chloe—was speechless as they realized this. The rumbling continued to get louder, like a train was rushing towards them at the speed of light.

With a humongous roar, the back wall split apart to reveal a magenta-scaled Gigantic Giant dragon. She had a long tail with no arrow shape on the end, but instead a large round ball with spikes adorning it, giving it a resemblance to the ancient dinosaur Ankylosaurus. She was easily five times bigger than the Withering Wings. Looking back on the rock wall, Izzy realized it was extremely thin, about five times as thick as her fingernails' height. A dragon, especially a Gigantic Giant, would've easily been able to crumble it with a flick of its paws.

"You dare to challenge me, do you?!" the magenta dragon roared. The group made sure not to look into the dragon's hypnotizing eyes, which, according to the wise old man, could hypnotize them.

"Yes! We do!" Chloe replied bravely, standing tall, her posture strong. "You terrorized our village until we couldn't take any more. If you continue to do this, we have to stop you. What's your answer?"

The dragon suddenly looked tired. "Dragons are smart, and they have to use it for something," she sighed. Then she drew up and showed her teeth in a brilliant, flashy white smile. "And I will never stop doing that. We are Gigantic Giants. And we fight for ourselves." Pausing for the smallest fraction of a second, she roared, "Give me all you got, cowards!"

Kelsey immediately set to work building a small but sturdy stone wall, grabbing pieces of stone and nimbly placing them together. Izzy and Sara were shooting arrows that bounced harmlessly off the dragon's thick scale armor, making a ping sound every time one hit its mark. Angela was holding her water staff and shooting bubbles that exploded with magic each time one hit. Andy and Chloe were darting around, fast as an insect, as they used their magic on the dragon. Fire sparks and lightning bolts were teaming up to set fire to the dragon.

Kelsey finished building the wall as Izzy, Sara, and Angela ducked behind it, saving them from a gruesome death from the dragon's spiky-ball tail that swept over their heads, missing by a fraction of an inch. *Close call,* Izzy thought, breathing a sigh of relief. Very *close call.*

The Dragon Fight

"Okay, gotta go," Kelsey blabbed quickly, pulling out her pale golden staff and darting away. "The others need my help."

So far, trying to beat the dragon with the power from the staffs wasn't working... until Izzy remembered something. The dwarves had said that they could summon creatures of their elements, right...?

Only one way to find out.

"Chloe!" Izzy called, stopping pinging the dragon with arrows for a second, grabbing another one and reloading her bow.

Chloe made a fire near the dragon's feet that stopped as soon as the dragon stepped on it. She poured a bucketful of the gooey lava on top of the dragon's head that disappeared after the dragon reared up and touched it. "What?!" she yelled over the drama.

"Try and summon a Lava Laugher!"

Lava Laughers were dragons that were about half the size of a Gigantic Giant and lived in active volcanos. Normally, encountering a Lava Laugher during a serious battle was certainly a hundred-percent death for you—unless it was on *your* side. Izzy remembered Mayor Dwarf saying that they'd also have full power over the creatures they summoned with their staffs.

Chloe saw Izzy's plan straight through as if it were as clear as glass. "Lava Laugher, here we come!" Chloe shouted, flicking her wrist so her staff soared up in the air and then she caught it in midair. *How did she do that?!*

Suddenly, there was a red Lava Laugher with green eyes—one of the common types—standing behind the Gigantic Giant that was fighting Kelsey and Andy. "Breathe!" Chloe yelled to the Lava Laugher as the Gigantic Giant almost swept her off her feet using its long tail.

The Dragon Fight

Izzy recalled from her books that a Lava Laugher's breath was most unusual indeed. Instead of breathing out breaths of fire, which most fire dragons spewed out, a Lava Laugher's mouth shot out *lava*—not just *any* hot lava, though. It was Extreme Hot Lava, the hottest known lava in the entire universe. Izzy knew Extreme Hot Lava could melt any dragon's scales—*except for a Gigantic Giant's,* Izzy suddenly remembered, realizing the flaw in her plan. *But the Lava Laugher can still distract the dragon.*

The Lava Laugher blew out a huge breath, and Extreme Hot Lava soared through the air and landed on the magenta dragon's back. As the dragon was distracted by the sudden heat on its scales, Andy vaulted on top of the dragon and struck a lightning bolt in the place where the dragon's body and neck connected. Even from here, Izzy could see the crack. The magenta beauty howled in pain.

"Aim for the crack!" Andy shouted. What happened next was like slow motion to Izzy. The Gigantic Giant twisted its head around and looked, with its gold eyes, straight into Andy's horrified dark brown ones. In a flash, Andy's moving shape had turned to stone right before Izzy's very eyes.

She screamed in horror.

The dragon roared in triumph.

At that roar, Andy's stone body turned back into his regular self. Izzy breathed a sigh of relief. The wise old man had been wrong when he said that the dragon had hypnotizing powers....

... or so she thought.

As Andy lifted his head up, his formerly excited eyes had turned into cold spheres of gold, just like the Gigantic Giant's. The wise old man had not been wrong after all.

The Dragon Fight

"Don't look into his eyes!" Izzy shouted hysterically. She had no grasp on reality right now. She had a million questions buzzing in her brain. *Will Andy stay like this forever? Will he ever change back into his normal self? Will my mom kill me once she finds out that Andy came on a perilous life-threatening quest and turned evil during a battle?*

So she had no idea that Kelsey had gotten hold of Andy's staff. She had no idea that Andy had pulled out the sharpest sword he owned. She had no memory that he called it the Slicer, after his sword fighting teacher, Mr. Slicer. She had no idea that Kelsey had struck a lightning bolt in the center of the Gigantic Giant's scale armor gap and the dragon was slowly weakening.

But she did notice that as the dragon became slower and weaker, the crystals of the cave behind them were glowing brighter and brighter. She wondered what it was about as the main part of her brain still worried about Andy. *Perhaps the crystals suck in light and power? Then how did they originate in the first place?*

She could think up many ways for light-and-power-sucking crystals to be created, but right now she was focusing—or rather, fearfully watching—the battle with the dragon.

Chloe shouted, "Aim for the gap!" Then she ducked under the dragon's sweeping tail and raced towards her, her sword up and ready for a fight.

The Lava Laugher breathed a bucketful of its lava in the gap and the dragon shrieked in pain. With her spike-covered tail, the Gigantic Giant smashed the Lava Laugher to the ground, the red-scaled dragon hardly a fly to her.

Angela summoned some water dragons with her blue staff. Bubble Blasters used bubbles as everything: homes, weapons, force fields, and more.

The Dragon Fight

They preferred to live peacefully underwater, but they were large, almost half the size of a Gigantic Giant.

The group of dark-blue-scaled dragons blasted a pale blue sphere around the evil dragon's magenta head and added water and seaweed in it. Izzy fuzzily recalled that Gigantic Giants could breathe underwater, which meant it wouldn't drown, but it would distract the dragon for a bit because it couldn't see anything through the churning mass of saltwater and underwater plants.

Kelsey smacked her staff against her knee, and in a second, there was a Rock Reacher next to her. Rock Dragons, as Izzy had read from books on dragons, were generally timid and shy, but some that came from cold places like ice mountains or hot places like the volcanos were fierce and battled each other over for territory. They used rock-related objects as weapons and could lift them easily with their mind or their body. *If you don't have a metal detector,* Izzy had told Sara once, *a Rock Reacher will very well do the detector's job and more,* because Rock Reachers were large, as big as a Bubble Blaster, they could *dig for whatever you were searching for, too! And* they didn't have a fear of avalanches, because they could breathe in tight areas and they had scales so hard that even a volcano's lava wouldn't be able to set it on fire.

The gray-colored dragon hurtled boulder after boulder with its mind at the Gigantic Giant, loud sounds of smashing being audible as the rocks crumbled at the dragon. But its effort wasn't wasted, though. The momentum of the rocks pushed the Gigantic Giant in every direction, left, right, forward, and back.

Izzy's heart pounded in her chest, as loud as a drumbeat, as Kelsey threw the storm staff at Chloe, who was trying to defend herself from Andy without hurting him or getting injuries from him herself. For some reason, the sight of his storm staff made Andy freeze for a second, and Chloe got the

The Dragon Fight

time to leap onto the dragon's back as it stumbled this way and that from the Rock Reacher.

Sara summoned a Brightice Breather behind the dragon, startling Chloe a little bit. Brightice Breathers were bright-blue-scaled dragons that lived in lakes and flooded caves underground in the ice spike mountains. Their breath was ice that chilled you to the bone. Like the Lava Laugher's hottest lava breath, their ice breath was the coldest feeling on Earth.

The Brightice Breather blew ice on the dragon's bubble-helmet that completely covered it like barnacles, and then it danced right in front of the dragon, teasing it by breathing little breaths of ice on its toes.

Izzy realized that Chloe was tying one of the ropes that the village had given them into a lasso. Why was she doing that? Izzy caught sight of Chloe's foot slipping off one of the dragon's jutting-out scales and she saw that she was in extreme danger of falling off and getting trampled to death by the dragon's roaring stomps. *Oh, so that's why,* Izzy thought in a frozen manner, still too horrified to do anything but watch.

Chloe shot Angela a look of panic as both her feet slipped off. In slow motion, Chloe threw the lasso around the dragon's neck, but it couldn't stay because the bubble-helmet was too long. Just as Chloe was slipping off, Angela shot a star-streaked arrow at the rope that pinned the lasso to the dragon. Chloe breathed a sigh of relief and climbed back on, not bothering to remove the arrow.

But Izzy did notice something strange about the arrow. It had *stars* spinning around it. Surely...?

It was, however. Angela had Starstruck Arrows? Where'd she even *get* those from?

55

The Dragon Fight

Starstruck Arrows were the most powerful arrows ever invented (to Izzy's knowledge, anyways). They had the sharpest point, the perfect length, and everything else. But they could only be shot by a 'creature driven by friendship.' Starstruck Arrows could pierce anything, even dragon armor. But then…?

Izzy tore her gaze back to where Angela had shot the arrow and, sure enough, she saw that there was a gash. The Gigantic Giant roared in pain and tried to buck Chloe off her back but failed. Chloe held onto the rope tight with one of her hands and held the storm staff and her fire staff in her other hand.

Chloe tied the rope around her left wrist and grabbed the storm staff with her left hand and summoned a few lightning bolts. One hit the crack Andy had made, and the other few hit the dragon on random spots.

The lightning bolts struck true to their targets and made the dragon slump to the ground. Before she closed her golden eyes for the last time, she stared straight at Izzy and whispered, "My name is Firestriker."

As the Gigantic Giant bled her life out, Andy froze again and turned to stone. But this time, Izzy hoped it was for a *good* reason instead of a bad one.

As the once-powerful, gold-eyed, and magenta-scaled dragon died, Andy's stone statue slowly unfroze back into him. He collapsed onto the ground, too bewildered to speak, and Izzy rushed over and hugged him.

But they didn't notice the crystals grow brighter each time more of the dragon's blood leaked onto the ground.

The Dragon Fight

The six heroes had come back from their adventure. The dwarves had told them they could keep the staffs and dragons; besides, they weren't the type to go on adventures and battle evil dragons—they mostly just mined underground. They had thanked them and wished them luck for running into precious gemstones.

One thing still bothered Izzy, though. Why had the dragon told them her name while she was dying? What did the name 'Firestriker' have to do with this? She felt the urge to tell the mayor and she trusted it. She always trusted her instincts.

So that afternoon, three days after the battle with the dragon, she knocked on the mayor's door.

She waited.

And waited.

And waited....

... until it seemed like the mayor wouldn't open his door. But he did.

"Ah, Izzy," he said, glancing at her from inside his house. "What's up?"

"The dragon said her name before she died," Izzy said bluntly, deciding to just get straight to the point. "She said it was Firestriker."

Izzy didn't know if it was just her or not, but suddenly the mayor paled a bit, then grew rosy again so quickly she had no idea if it really happened. "Hm... 'Firestriker'? No, that doesn't ring any bells," he muttered. "Nothing important, Izzy. Off on your way."

Izzy knew the mayor must be hiding something, but she decided not to question him right now. She was exhausted after the battle, and what she *really* wanted to do was go take a nap under her bedcovers, not interrogate the town leader about something that might've been just her imagination.

She turned away.

That was a secret.

To be discovered...

... another day.

The Serpent of Tears

The Serpent of Tears

She had heard of the tales of the large snake-like creatures that slithered through the caves at the bottom of the narrow ravine, but she had never imagined that they had evil intentions. They had a mind set to destroy all humans, a brain smart enough to calculate distance and disactivate traps, a body flexible enough to go through any amount of training.

And now, they were about to wage war on them... all because a dragon told them to.

Firestriker

Izzy was searching through her impressive collection of books, hoping to figure out what the dragon had meant when she'd said her name was 'Firestriker.' The name had made a weird response on the mayor she'd told him, and she wanted to figure out what it meant. After all, the world had many secrets. Didn't she have the right to find out just *one* of them?

She was currently on a page that had a couple of pictures of the dragons that lived in the mountains, but none of them fit the image of the dragon she and her friends had battled last time, in the cave highest of the mountain range.

"Nope, nope, nope," she muttered. "No... *ugh*."

She closed her book and hurried out of her room and then out the front door. She was hoping to find Chloe at the town square, or maybe Sara at her house. Sara's younger brother, Andy, needed to be taken care of while her parents went shopping.

Her shoes crunched lightly on the pebbles that were scattered along the smooth stone path. This path led all the way around the village, making an uneven circle, connecting all the houses. It snaked in the village in some places to reach the houses that were more *inside* the town.

Reaching a cinnamon-brown house with a white doorstep and a pale red carpet that read *Welcome!*, Izzy climbed up the steps and rang the doorbell, which was activated by a simple gray button.

The yellow wooden door creaked open, and Sara stood in the doorway. "Hi!" Izzy greeted her friend enthusiastically. "What's up?"

"Andy," Sara replied. "He just scribbled over all of my best drawings! He's so, so, *so* annoying. I need a break...." She took a deep breath. "Can you babysit him while I try and find out what the word means?"

Izzy nodded. "Sure! I haven't had any luck so far, so... why not?"

Sara sighed and walked past Izzy. She inhaled a big breath of fresh air and replied, "You'll regret that... he's like somebody made up of pure annoyance."

Izzy stepped into Sara's house, closing the door behind her. She walked to the living room, which was decorated with two couches, a table, and a small desk in a corner with a chair, which had a jar of pencils and pens on it. A stack of paper was on one corner of the desk, and in the middle were a few drawings that Izzy guessed Sara had made. A black crayon was next to the drawings, and at least five scratches made by the crayon were on each otherwise admiring picture.

Andy was sitting on the chair, doodling on a piece of paper. "What are you drawing?" Izzy asked, walking towards him.

Andy looked up. "I'm drawing a mushroom," he replied. "Wanna see?" He picked up his piece of paper and Izzy walked closer to get a look.

Andy had drawn a circle and then a stem sprouting out of the bottom that was too thick at the top and too thin near the bottom. The entire thing was filled with brown crayon that was *much* too dark. In other words, Izzy thought it was horrific.

"Like it?" Andy asked eagerly. "I practiced a *lot*." He pointed towards a recycling bin near the kitchen that was overflowing with pieces of paper. Even from here, Izzy could see that each page had a scribbled fail of what looked like a slice of dark brown cheese.

"Um... yeah," Izzy said, trying to hide her smile. "So, what else can you draw?"

Just then, Angela burst through the door. "Hey—Izzy—I think I've—found out—what—the word—means!" she wheezed, gasping for breath.

"Whoa, whoa, Angela," Izzy exclaimed, rushing over to her friend and helping her down to a chair. "Why so breathless?"

"I think I found out what that dragon, Firestriker, meant," Angela replied, catching her breath. "I'll show you. Come over to my house at midnight."

Izzy had no idea what she would see, but all she could do was to promise that she would be at Angela's house at midnight tonight.

Why midnight?

A Constellation and a Prophecy

Izzy climbed up the wooden ladder that led to the roof of Angela's house, the wooden creation creaking and groaning under her weight. Izzy knew from Angela that this ladder had been passed on from generation to generation in her family, and she would get it when she was old enough.

"Hey, Angela," she said once she'd reached the roof. "So, what did you want to show me?"

Angela was sitting against one of the bricks that jutted up from the roof. "I found a constellation that looks like Firestriker," Angela explained. She pointed up at a small cluster of stars that Izzy hadn't noticed before, not ever. "It seems like they appeared there, above my house, as soon as we defeated Firestriker."

Izzy frowned. "Huh, weird."

Angela grabbed a notebook from behind one of the bricks. "Here, I sketched it out," Angela said, flipping to a page that was marked clearly with a neon green sticky note. "It isn't the best drawing ever, but it should give you a good idea of what it looks like. It'll only come out at the strike of dawn."

Izzy took the notebook and gazed at it wondrously. Angela had drawn tiny stars with faint lines connecting them to show her what the real form looked like.

The drawing was a large dragon (at least Izzy assumed it was large, since it took up half of the page) breathing out a blast of fire. Inside the blast of fire, there were words written below in a handwriting that seemed related to cursive, that was apparently not part of the constellation:

The dawn can bring up the hottest fire,

With their power they grow higher,

But with only those tears can they make,

The following words: the largest lake.

Wait... 'the dawn can bring up the hottest fire, with their power they grow higher, but with only those tears can they make, the following words: the largest lake'?

Izzy couldn't believe her eyes. "Angela, did *you* write this?"

Angela looked over Izzy's shoulders, and her eyes grew as wide as a squirrel's that had spotted a mountain made of nuts. "No, I didn't!" she exclaimed, looking both shocked and surprised. "How did *that* get on there?"

She grabbed a pencil from her pocket and began erasing it. "There, that should do it." But once she took the pencil away from the notebook, the words reappeared!

"Well, I guess you can't erase them," Izzy said, trying to be helpful. "At least we won't forget it...."

Angela sighed and frowned. *There is* way *too much frowning going on today,* Izzy thought. *Like, too much.* "Well, I guess so," Angela replied. "And I'm *also* betting that this has something to do with those constellations, because, well, otherwise, why would they be here, and not on some other page?"

"Yeah," Izzy said, hoping to come up with more answers but only creating more questions, "and what do they mean?"

"Well, I guess that means we're going to tell Chloe, Sara, and Kelsey about this, then," Angela said.

"I'm *really* getting tired of all this running about," Izzy muttered, handing the notebook back to Angela, who took it and shoved it back behind one of the bricks.

"So, what's this all about?" Chloe asked, fingering the rough bark of the log.

The log had been cut from a tree about a century ago and placed in a secluded clearing fifteen minutes' walk away from the closest house in the village. Trees crowded around the edges of the dew-laden, grass-filled clearing, an invisible force keeping them back. Sunlight poured through the circular hole above that was aimed at the clear blue sky, and small beams of the bright light filtered through the thick green tree leaves.

Bracken, moss, and mushrooms carpeted the forest floor, so abundant that Izzy could spot a giant cluster of brown mushrooms just a few feet away from the clearing. If Izzy hadn't known better, she would've thought it was a pine forest or something.

"We found strange writing in my notebook," Angela began, then was cut off by Izzy.

"But first, we have to explain the constellation to you," Izzy interrupted, giving Angela a slight nudge.

"Right, right," Angela said hurriedly. "So, this is the constellation."

She opened her notebook, flipped to the page with the green sticky note, and held it up so Chloe, Sara, and Kesley could see it.

"What's the writing in the middle of the dragon's breath?" Kelsey asked, squinting to read it. "*The dawn can bring up the—*"

"I'm getting to it, okay?" Angela said impatiently. "Anyways, that's the writing that I told you guys about earlier. I think it's a prophecy."

Izzy shot Angela a look, but she didn't say anything. *Isn't that a bit straightforward?* she wondered.

Chloe flicked at a bright green leaf that had fallen on the log. "What do you think it means?" she asked. "After all, prophecies are always confusing...."

"Which 'tears' is it talking about?" Sara asked, speaking up for the first time. *Well, she's pretty quiet,* Izzy reflected. *No surprise there.*

Angela shrugged. "I don't know. I probably know as much as you guys do, anyways."

"Maybe we have to find a pond filled with ancient water?" Kelsey suggested.

"But then it wouldn't be *tears*," Chloe countered, who always had a knack for knocking down ideas. But she was equally skilled at bringing up new ones. "Maybe we have to find, like, a creature or something and get tears from *that*."

"Good idea," Izzy replied. "That could possibly work. But two creatures couldn't create the same exact tears, because it said, *'with only those tears',* which means that we're talking about *one* creature in the *entire world* here."

"Right," Sara said, looking lost in thought.

"But how does this connect to Firestriker?" Kelsey asked. "It's confusing."

It's supposed *to be confusing, Kelsey,* Izzy thought, but she didn't bother saying it aloud. "Another dragon could've done it," she suggested. "Because Firestriker was a dragon, and aren't all dragons, like, family or something?"

"Probably not," Chloe argued. "They've probably got so many generations that there are, um... maybe three billion families?"

"Great!" Angela said. "*Then* how are we supposed to figure this out?"

"I don't know," Izzy replied, "but an idea better come soon."

A New Adventure

Izzy was strolling through the streets with Angela, out to get a few mini cakes for snacks. At the moment, they were debating on which store to go to.

"Let's go to Mandy's," Angela said. "She has the *best* cakes."

"But Carol's has awesome chocolate frosting on her cakes," Izzy complained. "And chocolate is my *favorite*."

As quiet as she was, Izzy was very stubborn, so eventually she got her way, and they were heading to Carol's.

"What do you want?" Izzy asked, pulling out a few coins from her pocket and jingling them in her cupped hand. "Carol's *is* cheaper."

"A cupcake," Angela replied. "Classic vanilla."

"Which one?" Izzy asked, handing her a menu wrapped in a plastic folder. "There's the Cream Cupcake, the Snowflake, the Blender, and the Snow Mountain Giant."

"Hm... I'll take the Cream Cupcake, since it has lots of vanilla," Angela decided. "Is the Snowflake really a snowflake?"

"Nope," Izzy answered. "It just has a lot of ice cubes. I love Snowflakes. I'm getting one."

The Serpent of Tears

"How much will it cost altogether?" Angela asked, fingering the menu.

"About a dollar and sixty-three cents," Izzy replied. "Super cheap, right?"

"Wow," Angela said, looking amazed. "Mandy's is never *that* cheap. How do they stay in business and not get bankrupt?"

Izzy rolled her eyes. "They get a lot of customers—*that's* why."

They walked into the store, and Izzy handed a one-dollar bill, two quarters, two nickels, and three pennies to the guy at the counter. "A Cream Cupcake and a Snowflake, please," Izzy said, but before the guy could punch the order in the machine, a man burst through the door and hunched over, panting. Izzy recognized him as Frederick, the guy who managed all the town security systems and often volunteered to patrol the ravine.

"What are you here for?" the guy at the counter asked. "Ice cream?" *Would Frederick really run that quickly for ice cream?* Izzy wondered, suspicious. *It has to be something else, right?*

"No," Frederick replied, huffing and puffing. "There's been a serpent spotted at the ravine. Inside it, in fact. It even attacked our workers without warning."

Izzy shared an excited glance with Angela. *This could be it!* she thought, her pulse racing excitedly.

The guy at the counter looked scared and quickly hurried towards the back of the store where he was no longer visible. The people who were sitting at a table nearby, a woman and a young girl, stared at Frederick like he was an alien from outer space who'd just landed in a UFO.

"The mayor has ordered a lockdown for the village," Frederick continued, catching his breath. "But he says he wants to meet the people who went beyond the borders of the ravine last year to meet in the town square."

Angela glanced at Izzy. "I think we should go now, right?" she asked her friend, trying to sound casual. "We should get ready for the... *lockdown*."

"One dollar and sixty-three cents wasted," Izzy complained as they dashed out of Carol's ice cream shop. "At least I'm faster than you," she added as she overtook Angela, who just glanced at her with a faint smile.

"Girls, I want you to fight these serpents that have been dwelling in the ravine," the mayor said. "Your trip to the mountains to kill Firestriker has proved that you are ready for another adventure."

The five girls and the mayor were once again seated in his simple home. Izzy sat next to Kelsey on a soft turquoise couch with thick cushions, Angela and Sara were seated on a dark maroon couch designed the same way as Izzy's and Kelsey's, Chloe sat on a light gray couch with soft pillows, and the mayor reclined comfortably on a deep green armchair with a matching thick pillow that nearly took up half of the seating space.

"How do we know that those things have been in the ravine for millions of years?" Sara asked, who never went on a mission, only if it was dire. "How do we know that *we're* not the ones intruding on *them*?"

"The serpents *have* lived in the ravine for thousands of years, generation after generation," the mayor confirmed. "However, they haven't been a nuisance to us, and we haven't done anything to them. Kind of a mutual let's-leave-you-alone thing."

"So then what *has* been going on?" Izzy asked. "Are they getting more aggressive or something?"

"Today, they attacked a farmer while he was harvesting his crops," the mayor explained. "Once rescued, he was terrified, but was capable of telling us that the giant serpents were hissing '*Dragonsss, dragonsss*' before he was wheeled to the hospital. I'm thinking that you could work with that."

Chloe glanced at Izzy. "Yup, I'm sure we can do that. Are we excused?"

"You are," the mayor replied as he stood up, and, without another word, opened the seemingly heavy wooden door with little effort and ushered the girls outside.

"Add '*Bring the dragons*' to the list," Chloe decided.

They were sitting in the same clearing as they had when Angela and Izzy had first shared the prophecy and the constellation with the others, and Chloe was having Izzy write down things they needed to remember for the trip.

Izzy scrawled '*Bring the dragons*' neatly on one line of the lined paper, adding a bulletin point at the beginning. Her handwriting couldn't beat Chloe's, but since she was suggesting most of the ideas, and Izzy the least, it was the best they could do.

"Good idea," Sara commented. "Ice, Lava, Jewel, Leaf, Whirlpool, and—"

"Wait a second," Kelsey interrupted. "Is Andrew even going on the trip with us? I mean, last time he came without our invitation, so... just checking."

"Let's vote," Chloe proposed. "Raise your hand if you want Andrew to go."

The vote was unanimous for Andrew to go. *I guess he was a big help last time, even if he* did *get hypnotized,* Izzy recalled.

"Well, that's that," Chloe said with a sigh. "Anyways, continuing! Sara, what were you saying?"

Sara cleared her throat. "Ice, Lava, Jewel, Leaf, Whirlpool, and Storm will certainly be helpful if we engage in battle against the serpents," she said. "But our staffs would be equally useful, too."

"I stashed them in my basement, but I'm sure I can dig them out again," Angela suggested brightly. Chloe nodded approvingly.

"I'll go to the dragon stables to fetch the dragons," Kelsey offered. "But I need someone to come with me."

"I'll go," Izzy volunteered. "I'll get to see Leaf again. It's strange not to see her a lot anymore."

The dragon had a gentle nature, unlike the other dragons. Izzy fuzzily remembered Mayor Dwaggen, the leader of the dwarves that had been extremely helpful on their journey to defeat Firestriker, saying that Lava had a somewhat fiery attitude, Ice a coldhearted one, Whirlpool's was bubbly, Jewel had a personality as hard as stone, and Storm's was cloudy, and, well, *stormy,* ironically. In fact, as Izzy kept reflecting on those specific terms used for describing their attitudes, they were *all* ironic.

I wonder how I didn't know that before, Izzy thought. *Or did I, and I forgot it? I really have no idea.*

"Sounds good," Kelsey replied.

"What else?" Angela asked.

"Weapons is a must," Chloe decided. "In addition to our staffs, I think each of us should wield at least one other weapon, including Andrew," she added after Izzy wrote down *'And Andrew'* in parentheses.

"I'm bringing my bow and my Starstruck Arrows," Angela said confidently.

"How did you get those arrows, anyways?" Izzy asked.

"Oh, I picked them up from the dwarves," Angela replied casually. *Casually* and *vaguely,* Izzy thought suspiciously.

"I'm bringing my bow," Izzy said. "I'm a failure at sword fighting. Anybody could beat me."

"A C, right?" Chloe asked, smirking. Izzy slapped her on the arm. "Ow," Chloe muttered. "No need for *that,* okay?"

"I'm packing my bow *and* my sword," Sara said. "I got a B in Mr. Slicer's class, and an A+ in Ms. Stream's."

"I'm definitely bringing my sword," Kelsey said. "And speaking of a sword, I got an upgrade!" She pulled a shiny silver blade from her backpack. "It's a Full Moon sword. I hauled it up while I was fishing."

"Lucky!" Chloe said. "I'm bringing an electric spear I bought at the weaponsmith's. It'll *shock* you." She paused. "Like the pun?"

"It's great," Izzy replied sarcastically.

"Is Andrew going to bring something other than his lightning staff?" Angela asked. "Just checking."

"I'll make sure he brings the Slicer," Izzy confirmed, tapping her knees impatiently.

"Then that's all set," Chloe said. "I'll meet you guys all at the edge of the ravine tomorrow evening. Remember, this is supposed to be a *secret* mission."

"I hope Andrew can keep a secret," Izzy muttered as they exited the somewhat peaceful clearing and left the brown log.

Izzy ran as fast as she could after Kelsey, following her to the dragon stables, aware of the *crunch* sound they made when they stepped on dry leaves, the sun shining straight at them with no branches or rocks to block the way. *I should've brought sunglasses,* Izzy thought frustratedly, squinting to keep the blinding sunshine out of her eyes.

"I can't believe the dragons can live out here, especially Whirlpool," Kelsey complained, slowing down so Izzy could catch up.

"Have you no sympathy for *me?*" a grumpy voice growled. "How disrespectful."

Izzy whirled around to find herself face-to-face with Ice, Sara's dragon. "Uh, whoops," Kelsey stammered. "Sorry!"

"Water's not the only element that doesn't thrive in sunshine," Ice complained. "It's so uncomfortable, I'd rather be in the chilly ice winds of the mountains."

"Of course you would," a sarcastic voice sounded behind Kelsey. She whipped around, and there stood Jewel, her gold scales gleaming in the sunlight. Izzy and Kelsey both quickly closed their eyes, then slowly opened them, adjusting to the blinding burst of dazzling sparkles dancing on Jewel's scales. "Ice would *love* to be in the winds when I'd rather bathe in a cool pool of underground water."

"Hey, hey, there's the elements talking," Izzy said, trying to cool down the heated conversation. "It's obvious that you like where you want to go, okay? Point made."

Ice blew a chilly breath over Izzy, making her shiver, and then growled, "Well, what's up, anyways? You don't always visit us here in these boring fields."

"We're going on another adventure," Kelsey said, saving Izzy from having to speak. "We need to bring you."

Jewel and Ice immediately looked very interested. "What kind of adventure?" Ice asked. "A freezing, chilly, snowy adventure?"

"Nope, unfortunately," Kelsey replied. "A slithery adventure. I'd take ice over giant serpents any day."

"Sounds creepy," Jewel answered. "I'm up for it, though."

"I'll check with the others," Ice added.

Soon, they had rounded up all the dragons, from Lava to Whirlpool, and they headed back to the town. The sun was slowly dipping down, casting pink, orange, and yellow colors across the once bright blue sky.

"I think we can make it to the ravine before evening," Kelsey said, checking her digital watch. "*If* we keep walking at this snail pace."

"How about we pick it up?" Izzy suggested. "We could ride Jewel and Leaf."

Storm yawned and flapped her large wings a few times, blasting a cool wave of wind over the two girls. "I could use a little wing stretch," she admitted. "Couldn't hurt."

Kelsey got on Jewel, Izzy got on Leaf, and they soared over the village that was completely oblivious to the majestic, mystical creatures flying over it. Izzy thought that it was pretty funny that the other people in the town had no idea that dragons were living in a stable just at the edge of the village in the Peaceful Plains. They landed at the ravine where Andy, Angela, Sara, and Chloe were waiting for them.

"Where *exactly* are we going?" Whirlpool asked. Izzy could practically see her bubbly personality being filled to the top. *Now it's overflowing,* Izzy thought to herself. *And it's spilling everywhere.*

"Into this ravine, actually," Chloe replied, pointing a finger into the narrow mass of black darkness. "We're going to fight—or at least drive off, anyways—some evil serpents!"

"Great," Whirlpool mumbled. "I'm claustrophobic." *Now her personality's popped,* Izzy thought. *Nice pun, Izzy....*

"Everybody got their supplies?" Chloe asked. "I want to make sure everybody's prepared."

"We've all got ours, Chloe," Izzy said, rolling her eyes. "You triple-checked earlier, and you double-checked even earlier, and you checked *even earlier*."

Chloe glared at Izzy. "Well, don't blame *me* for making sure our team has everything it needs."

Izzy rolled her eyes again, but she didn't say anything.

"So, ready to set off?" Chloe asked, facing Andrew, Angela, Sara, Izzy, and Kelsey. "Ready to explore unknown dangers, dangle off cliffs, get chomped by giant snakes, and possibly die a very painful death?"

"Jeez, Chloe, enough with the negative talk," Andrew grumbled. "I could live without that being told to me."

"And plus, I'm pretty sure that's not an accurate summary," Izzy added.

Little did they know how close Chloe was to estimating what their trip would be like.

Caves of Serpents

Darkness hovered around the girls, the boy, and the dragons, floating over them like a fog of blackness. It was so dark that Izzy could only see the faint outline of her hand when she held it up a few inches away from her face, and she could barely distinguish the silhouettes of Andrew, the girls, and the dragons from the darkness.

"Anybody having the same problem I have?" Angela called from the darkness. Her voice echoed multiple times, ringing through the narrow passageway they were walking in.

After descending the steep walls of the ravine, they'd picked a random corridor out of six ways to go. So far, it had been darkness, darkness, and darkness. *Yup,* Izzy thought dryly. *Totally exciting. Jewel might actually be the only one who's enjoying this.*

The underground-type dragon was scouting the walls, golden eyes searching hungrily for flickers of sparkling stones. "You know we can get rich, right?" Jewel asked as she scouted for gems behind the group, falling behind. "We can sell the—"

At that very moment, Jewel walked straight into the solid rock wall, not looking where she was going. Jewel huffed and caught up to the group. "Well, maybe not... I guess my plan has a slight flaw in it."

"I think there's a turn up ahead," Chloe said, squinting into the darkness. "Could you bring out a flashlight or something, Lava?"

Lava grinned. "You asked the right dragon." She began to radiate rapidly increasing heat, and as her heat meter rose, her scales gleamed brighter and brighter until it seemed like a fire was inside Lava herself. "Nice, huh? Right now it's burning."

"Very convenient," Chloe replied, walking on and not blinking an eye, while Izzy stared at Lava in awe, her mouth gaping in astonishment. "Turn, everyone!"

"I have a bad feeling about this," Sara muttered to Izzy as they turned.

She was right, and as soon as they rounded the corner, glowing red eyes popped out from the darkness in pairs, obviously signaling the serpents. Estimating their size from the width and length of their eyes, Izzy guessed that they were about half as thick as the dragons, and as long as two of the dragons stacked on top of each other were tall. *Creepy,* she thought, shuddering. Without warning, the serpents lunged at them, and for the first time, Izzy caught a glimpse of one of them.

It was about as thick and long as she estimated, with red eyes the size of pancakes, and dark green scales that didn't even have a single sparkle like Lava's did. Darker red stripes in their eyes made them actually seem like pancakes—the stripes were the syrup—except they were red. *I don't eat pancakes, anyways,* Izzy thought, feeling terrified. There were six of the large snakes there.

"Finally, the dragonsss have come," a serpent hissed. Izzy noticed that it was slightly bigger than the other, and with a larger gleam of combined rage and sinisterness in its eye. *Maybe that's the leader,* she thought. *Or should it be obvious?*

"We're the Withering Wings," Lava growled bravely. "Why do you have a sudden interest in destroying humankind?"

"We are not sssearching waysss to dessstroy humankind," the big serpent answered, stretching out the s's. He sounded insulted, and even a little regretful. *I wonder why,* Izzy thought suspiciously. "We are here becaussse thisss dragon named Firessstriker told usss to."

Izzy audibly gasped out loud, which she probably shouldn't've done. Although she didn't see anybody else react as she did, she saw that Chloe and Angela both had their hands over their mouths in shock, and Andrew's eyes went wide for the same reason.

"Well, what are you here for?" Lava continued. Izzy thought she detected a little annoyance in the fire dragon's voice. *I can understand that,* Izzy thought.

"The reassson we are here is becaussse Firessstriker has told usss to dessstroy everyone in the town," the serpent replied. "Ssshe sssaid to essspecially get the five girlsss with the dragonsss. And *essspecially* the boy with the ssstormy dragon." It turned, its eyes glinting evilly, towards Chloe, Angela, Sara, Izzy, Kelsey, and Andy. "And it looksss like they are here."

Immediately, three of the serpents lunged at the girls and the boy, including the lead serpent. The other three surrounded the dragons, daring them to attack. "Get in a crevice!" Chloe shouted as she struck a serpent in the head with her electric spear. The spear itself didn't even do a dent, but a shock ran through the serpent, freezing it place.

"Bulls-eye!" Angela yelled as she shot a Starstruck Arrow at a serpent and hit it right in the center of its eye. "Look out, Sara!"

Sara spun around and hit a serpent in the side of its scaly face, which distracted it long enough for her to use its dazed head as a springboard and jump over, through a small hole in the side that seemed to be the only entrance, into a small indent in the cave's wall that seemed half-buried, where Angela was shooting Starstruck Arrows. A large crack in the rock allowed Angela to see, attack with her arrows, and hear what others were saying.

Izzy launched an arrow at a serpent that was hissing at Chloe, who had her back turned to it. The arrow miraculously found a crack in the serpent's scaly armor, and it howled in pain, giving Chloe an obvious warning that there was a serpent sneaking up behind her.

Nearby, Andrew was trying to get to the dragons, slashing at them angrily with Slicer, and bravely pushing his way through the masses of fallen scales. "C'mon! Fight!" he yelled to the Withering Wings, hitting a serpent into tomorrow with the handle of his sword.

Storm took that as the signal, and with a fearsome roar that echoed through the caverns, called upon the largest sounds of thunder she could bring up. Lava darted out of the circle of the serpents, making them hiss in annoyance, and blew breaths of fire straight into their faces, making their hisses turn into coughs and sputters. Whirlpool, seeing that Chloe was trying to ride a serpent, Andrew was on Storm, and that Izzy could swim pretty well, allowed wave after wave of water to surge into the cavern with powerful speed, pushing the serpents under the tossing waves, their red eyes screaming with anger.

Izzy gasped for breath as she emerged on the top of one wave, and then was pulled under by another. "Help—me—"

"Coming!" Leaf shouted as she dived into the water. "Here, Izzy, hop on me!"

The Serpent of Tears

Izzy could barely distinguish Leaf's dark green shape from the churning water, much less make her way to it, but she tried her best. Natural forces pulled her right and left, giving her scratches that stung, but she pushed through them and swam over to Leaf, grabbing the bridle that was placed on the Withering Wing along with the saddle, and pulled, signaling that Leaf should take off as fast as she could. Izzy was very much afraid of the fact that underwater serpents could (and would) bite her and gobble her up.

They lifted off, slowly at first, since the bubble-infested water slowed Leaf down, but gradually gained speed as the earth dragon flew out of the churning waves. They soared high into the cavern, and Leaf nearly missed some long, sharp stalactites that poked out from the uneven, rocky roof.

"Be careful where you're going," Izzy muttered, clinging onto Leaf for dear life as the skillful dragon weaved her way through the spikes. Izzy counted four serpents flopping in the waves and one hissing angrily on a dry platform on the other side of the cavern from Angela's and Sara's hideout. Chloe was clinging to it, but Izzy couldn't spot the last serpent. *Maybe it drowned?* she thought hopefully.

"Hey, could I have a hand?" Chloe yelled as she tossed her lasso over the serpent's thick neck. It found its mark, and Chloe heaved herself onto the serpent's back as it hissed and thrashed around, trying to buck Chloe off.

"Down there," Izzy directed Leaf, pointing to where Chloe was struggling with the serpent. The earth dragon dived down, and landed on the serpent's back behind Chloe, her claws extended. The serpent howled in pain as Leaf's needle-sharp claws sank into its scales.

"Thanks," Chloe panted, hopping off the serpent as it hissed its final word and fell, limp. Izzy nearly threw up because she was standing in front of a giant serpent carcass, but amazingly, she managed not to. "Let's go get to the others. Lava!"

The fiery orange dragon had been spewing large amounts of lava everywhere, dropping some on a serpent's head, and making some appear in another one's way, but she flew right over when Chloe called for her. "Okay, hop on," Lava said, and Chloe complied.

They flew over the watery mass of serpents, Izzy shooting an arrow now and then, carefully aiming and timing her angles so that they hit the serpents right on. Chloe had the magical staffs, so she used hers to create Lava Laughers all over the place and slowly quench the water that Whirlpool had unleashed and gave the earth staff to Izzy.

Izzy created a Leaf Laugher, about as big as the Withering Wings, with pale green scales and brown eyes the color of bark. It was one of the common types, which were the rival cousins of the Lava Laughers, which spewed tangling vines that trapped even the strongest of enemies instead of Extreme Hot Lava. Izzy remembered reading a passage somewhere in a dragon guidebook that the vines worked as high-tech nets, springing up from the ground when stepped on and weaving themselves with astonishing speed into a cage with thick bars, making the Leaf Laughers nearly as dangerous as the Lava Laughers.

Andrew and Storm circled above the pool of thrashing water below, probably scouting the area for serpents. The boy spotted Izzy and Chloe on Leaf and Lava and gave them an enthusiastic warning. "Hey, this battle is *awesome!* And by the way, there's a serpent behind you!"

The last serpent that Izzy hadn't seen—the sixth one—had somehow curled itself up into the roof and onto the stalactites that hung over Leaf and Lava *right now*. "Nice last-minute warning!" Chloe shouted sarcastically to

Andrew as she lunged out of the way of the serpent's razor-sharp teeth, nearly falling off Lava and into the churning water below in the process.

"Sorry!" Andrew yelled—*a little cheerfully,* Izzy thought, annoyed—back to them. Then he apparently spotted a serpent down in the water below because he called for Storm to dive, and then they were lost in the swirling mass of waves below.

"A little help here?" Chloe called as she clung to one of Lava's legs, a slight push away from falling to her perilous doom and splashing into the serpent-infested waters below. Lava was desperately trying to turn around and breathe a blast of fire onto the serpent without dropping Chloe, carefully moving only about an inch each time. It looked hilarious, to be honest, but Izzy didn't want Chloe to plummet about three thousand feet down into the cold water, so she helped.

The Leaf Laugher which she'd summoned earlier trapped the serpent in a cage on Lava's back, allowing Lava to move with no fear of the serpent reaching downwards and pushing Chloe off her leg. However, *that* problem wasn't solved. And by 'that' problem, Izzy meant that Chloe could still plunge into the water that probably had three serpents in it. It was a very possible situation, actually, now that she thought about it.

"Hang on!" Izzy called to Chloe. "Let me climb over to you. Leaf, hover next to Lava." The earth-type dragon complied, flying smoothly over to where Lava was hovering. Izzy quickly got on her hands and knees and crawled over to Lava, unfortunately aware of the long drop underneath the two scaly dragons, grabbed Chloe's hand, and, with much effort, pulled her up.

"You're heavy," Izzy panted, gasping for breath.

"Gee, thanks," Chloe replied dryly, rolling her eyes. "Anyways...." She pointed to the serpent that was trying to wriggle its way out of the Leaf Laugher's cage. In fact, the Leaf Laugher looked like it was close to laughing right now... *for real.* "Can I get rid of that guy? The serpent?"

"Sure," Izzy answered.

Chloe ran back over onto Lava and stabbed her electric spear into the serpent. Instantly, its red eyes went wide, and then it went limp. A slightly smelly stank rose from it, and Chloe ran back to Leaf with her hand pinching her nose.

"Terrible smell," Chloe gasped as soon as Leaf had taken flight and they were halfway across the cavern. "I wouldn't've offered to kill it if I'd known that."

Izzy sniffed the air. "I can't smell anything now, and I barely smelled anything over there."

"Well, yeah, but you were a whole dragon away!" Chloe complained. "I was right next to it. The stench was *killer.*"

Izzy rolled her eyes. "Anyways, let's go, Leaf." Pausing for a moment to survey the ground below, something struck Izzy terrifyingly. "Hey, have you seen Kelsey anywhere?"

Chloe's eyes went wide. "I think so, actually. I saw her get pulled under by the waves... but she had her Full Moon sword. Maybe she can hold out long enough?"

As if hearing her very thoughts, Izzy heard a shout way below them. "Hey! Can I get a ride?"

She dropped onto her stomach and looked below her, risking falling off if Chloe gave her a little nudge. "Hey! Kelsey?" she called, lurching back and forth as Leaf flew around the cavern in perfect circles.

"I'm down here!" her friend shouted back. "There's a serpent right—" Her voice was suddenly cut off as Izzy saw her head vanish beneath the waves.

"Leaf!" Izzy yelled, almost unable to control herself from diving off the earth dragon and into the leaping waves below. "Dive down and get Kelsey!"

Leaf did a spinning dive in a complex fashion that would've probably earned her a 10 out of 10 in a dragon flying show, Izzy and Chloe clinging on for dear life. "Hey, Leaf, could you go a little slower?!" Izzy shouted. "I would be very—"

She was cut off when they reached the water, and instead of hovering over it like Izzy expected her to do, Leaf dived straight in as Chloe and Izzy tried to take a deep breath and ended up gulping in a mouthful of water instead.

Izzy saw Kelsey struggling in the waves under one of the serpents that had dropped into the water. Trying to muster up some strength, she swam over to the serpent and stabbed it in the back with her earth staff, hoping to buy Kelsey some free time.

Kelsey sliced at the serpent with her Full Moon sword, the blade glowing gently in the dark water. Particles mixed with the once clear water, and the mist blocked Izzy's eyes from seeing what was going on. Had the serpent surprise-attacked Kelsey? Was she okay?

Izzy began to panic as her supply of air was being used up; there was so much fog that she couldn't tell which way was up or down. Risking it, she blew some bubbles out of the corner of her mouth, and, feeling faint, saw that the bubbles were going to her right. *Okay, that way, then.*

Spinning her arms in circles, she propelled herself up to the surface, where she took a big breath of fresh air. *Okay, maybe not so fresh,* she thought to herself, a little disgusted. *There's kind of a smell.*

"Hey! Leaf! Where are you?" Izzy called. "Is Kelsey okay?" She treaded water while waiting for a response, occasionally getting lifted up by a wave.

The earth dragon swooped down from wherever she was and skimmed the edge of the water with her talons. "Kelsey's good. She slashed down that serpent with a few strikes of her sword. I never knew blades could be so powerful."

Izzy heaved herself out of the water and onto Leaf's damp, scaly back. It wasn't the ideal setting for her, especially when she was wet, but where else could she go without being chomped by serpents? For all she knew, there were still two serpents in the green-blood-infested water....

"Hey!" she heard Andrew shout from across the cavern, his voice echoing. "I got the serpents in the water!"

Okay, well, maybe not... Izzy thought. *I guess those guys are no more.*

"I killed the last serpent a few minutes ago while I was trying to get the dragons to fight!"

"Nice," Izzy called back, not really paying attention. "Where's Kelsey? Angela and Sara?"

"In the little hole! I saw them there. For some reason, it didn't flood," Andy replied back.

"Thank goodness," Izzy muttered under her breath. "Okay, thanks! Leaf, fly over to the little hole." Leaf complied, flapping her monstrous wings to where Angela, Sara, and Kelsey were huddled.

"Why did Whirlpool even summon all that water?" Kelsey was complaining to Angela. "I nearly *drowned* in there! With a serpent!"

"*Sorry*," Angela huffed back. "It isn't *my* fault she's too creative to do something extra from my orders...."

Kelsey rolled her eyes but said nothing in response.

"Hey, guys!" Sara said excitedly. "Izzy's here!" She seemed tired of all the debating. Izzy could sympathize her. She didn't want to be stuck in a cramped space with two arguing people while a flood raged outside, either.

Kelsey scrambled up from her spot on the damp rock. "How's the battle going?" She glanced at Angela for a second, but then she averted her gaze.

"All the serpents are dead," Izzy replied flatly. "It's time to continue exploring the caves."

"And who knows what else might wait in the deeper caverns," Angela added with a shudder.

They traveled on wearily, keeping an alert watch. Jewel hung behind to scout for gems and enemies that might be on their tail, and Lava trotted ahead to look for serpents that might be ahead of them and preparing for an ambush.

"Spotted anything?" Kelsey asked her dragon, whose eyes were trained on the stony walls of the cavern.

"Nothing of value," the dragon replied. "A small patch of citrine, though it's not worth very much."

"I meant something other than gems, Jewel," Kelsey replied, rolling her eyes. "Gems can't attack us. Serpents can."

"No, other than the citrine, I didn't find anything," Jewel said, looking disappointed for a moment. "Nothing dangerous, anyways."

They continued on, stopping occasionally to get a report from Jewel and Lava. Nothing came up as urgent until Lava told them that she'd spotted what looked like a serpent's scaly green tail whisking around a corner. They'd come to a crossroad with an option to go left, which was the way the serpent tail was spotted, or they could continue forward.

"Let's vote for which way to go," Chloe suggested.

"Sounds like a good plan," Angela agreed. "Okay, I'll count the votes."

"Raise your hand—or paw—if you want to go forward," Chloe said. Izzy, Leaf, Ice, and Sara voted to go forward.

"Raise your hand or your paw if you want to go left," Chloe said, then raised her hand. Beside her, Angela, Lava, Whirlpool, Jewel, and Kelsey wanted to go left.

"Six against four," Angela said, counting the tally marks she'd scratched in the soft clay floor of the cave. "The winner is the left tunnel."

Ugh, Izzy thought in her mind. *Why do so many people want to go to the tunnel where Lava saw the serpent's tail? We're bound to get into* some *kind of trouble....*

Sara gave her a look that said, *Jeez, why are we doing this?* Izzy had to stifle a laugh.

"Okay," Chloe said. "I'll keep watch ahead with Lava. I'll run back to you guys if we spot any serpents, and Lava will slow them down. Kelsey, stay behind with Jewel, and come back if you see any serpents. Jewel should be able to hold them off for a moment."

Kelsey nodded. "Fine with me."

"And with me, too," Jewel added.

"Angela, Sara, Izzy, and the rest of the dragons, you guys can stay in the middle group and look out for anything else. Who knows if a serpent might unexpectedly pop up through a hole in the floor?" Chloe made a little laugh.

"Okay," Sara said, not even cracking a smile.

"Well, then let's continue with our exploration!" Chloe said cheerfully, jogging ahead with Lava. Jewel and Kelsey began to walk slower and slower than the others until they were *way* back. *We're all set,* Izzy told herself. *Nothing to worry about.*

Suddenly, a loud hissing noise began ahead of them. The hissing grew louder and louder as they continued forward. About one minute after the hissing began, Chloe ran back to them.

"There's a giant nest of serpents up ahead," she gasped as soon she was in earshot. "I think it's the main group. Lava is spying on them. There's no way she can take all of them down by herself."

"About how many of them are there?" Izzy asked, feeling worried. *Maybe this* is *something to worry about....*

"Maybe, like, I don't know, three hundred of the devils?" Chloe responded. "But that's just a guess from a quick glance, though. But seriously! The floor was literally carpeted in the serpents."

Kelsey, who had previously been quiet, suddenly said, out of the blue, "I haven't thought about what this trip has to do with the prophecy yet. Do you think it's a connection, or just a coincidence?"

Izzy, struggling to pull it up from the depths of her mediocre memory, recalled the ominous, four-lined message:

The dawn can bring up the hottest fire,

With their power they grow higher,

But with only those tears can they make,

The following words: the largest lake.

"What does a fire born from the dawn have to do with serpents?" Angela asked.

"Prophecies are always confusing," Kelsey replied. "But they're not once someone sheds even a *little* light on it. For example, the serpents could be related to the tears. Izzy?"

Izzy generally knew the most out of the six about magical and mystical creatures, though, for example, Chloe had been doing tons of research on angels, in case she encountered one on their quests, and she knew *a lot* about them by now.

"There's a type of water serpent, and a fire serpent, I think," she replied, getting used to being called on for being a walking, talking dictionary of magical creatures. "They could be related to either the fire or the tears, though these are evil serpents, so I don't think they could produce tears, fire, or be related to those elements."

"Okay," Angela said, scrunching up her face and looking baffled.

"Anyways," Izzy continued, "there could be a possible chance of them capturing a water serpent or a fire serpent, however, so it *could* possibly be, uh... *possible*."

"What are these evil serpents called?" Andrew asked curiously, suddenly popping into the conversation.

"They're devil serpents, the evil serpents," Izzy answered. "They have both lungs and gills, which means they can live on land or underwater, *and* it means that they're part-fish *and* part-mammal."

Chloe shuddered. "So creepy."

"So, what's the connection between the prophecy and the devil serpents?" Kelsey asked. "Things don't pop up into our lives for *nothing*. There's got to be a reason."

"Maybe some serpents could've made tears?" Angela suggested. "Because the devil serpents had captured then?"

"Well, then it would be *one* serpent, if that's the case. The prophecy said *only those tears*, which means it's a unique serpent," Izzy countered.

"Can we just get moving?" Chloe asked, looking slightly annoyed. "It's kind of... *meaningless* if we do nothing and just stand around talking."

"Fine," Izzy replied, annoyed. *We can figure out stuff from talking and thinking!* "But what are we going to do with all those serpents?"

"Something important must be hidden in that cavern if there's so many serpents," Angela said thoughtfully.

"*And* something that we don't have. Not a lot of, anyways," Izzy added eagerly.

"It could be whatever produces the tears, or the tears themselves," Kelsey said.

"But we're going to have to fight a big battle first," Chloe said grimly. It wasn't like her to douse high spirits, but they *did* have to face the truth. And the truth was that they had to fight a big battle.

Izzy peeked around a sharp slab of stone. The number of serpents astonished her to no limit. It was just like Chloe had described. Serpents lined the walls and the floors, creating a dark greenish look.

Overall, it creeped her out. A *lot*.

Their red eyes darted from left to right, up and down, filled with anger and evil. The smell of slightly damp but hard scales filled the cavern, fitting in with their smooth movements. *Are we really going to battle these serpents?* Izzy wondered fearfully. Six serpents had been hard, and now there was at least—definitely more—than *three hundred* in a cramped space. Izzy was slightly claustrophobic, but she was confident she could deal with that problem later.

The Serpent of Tears

"Ready?" Chloe asked her friends and Izzy's brother. "We're about to take on about four hundred serpents. Think about it. Six dragons and six people against *all those* serpents. Do we even have a chance? At least we can go down fighting and not... you know... fall off a cliff."

"Great way to crush our spirits, Chloe," Kelsey muttered, hefting her Full Moon sword. "'Wow, we're going to die! Let's at *least* die heroically!'" She glared at Chloe. "I'd rather survive."

"Well, yeah," Chloe admitted. "But we should—well, never mind... let's go!"

Without another word, or at least a fierce-sounding battle cry, she charged into the cavern, slashing at the devil serpents with her sword in one hand and shocking serpents with her electric spear in the other hand.

"Jeez, she's going to kill herself in there!" Angela shouted, racing after her with her bow in one hand and her quiver full of Starstruck Arrows on her back. "Come on!"

Izzy's heart pounded in her chest as she ran forward and shot four arrows in different directions. It didn't really matter on aim, because the cavern was carpeted in serpents. Those four arrows met their targets, and four serpents went down.

Meanwhile, Angela had shot her way to Chloe, and she called for Whirlpool. "Hey! I need a dragon here!"

Whirlpool swooped down obediently, and Angela whispered something in the dragon's ear. Izzy thought she saw a little grin on Whirlpool's face before she took flight into the air, soaring away.

Chloe ducked as a serpent lunged at her, then stabbed it in the belly, the serpent to flop lifelessly onto the ground. Izzy cringed as she shot three more arrows, making her eyes avoid the gruesome sight. *I could've lived without that.*

A shout from the pair's direction made Izzy look back. A serpent was attacking Angela, coiling around her like a boa constrictor. *It's probably going to squeeze her to death,* Izzy thought, horrified. And since Angela only got a B in sword fighting class, and Izzy only a C, they couldn't really fight with close combat.

But Angela tried.

She took some of her Starstruck Arrows and turned them into makeshift daggers, stabbing the serpent's scaly armor furiously. Izzy almost couldn't believe it when the arrows held and didn't snap to pieces. She was even *more* surprised when the arrows made a small cut in the serpent's scales.

Izzy stuck out her tongue in disgust and looked away. "Ew," she muttered.

I thought the serpents would be on us by now, Izzy thought. *Some of them have attacked us, but not the majority yet. What's keeping them back?*

When she lifted her gaze skyward—or rather, *roofward*— she saw.

The six dragons—Storm, Ice, Whirlpool, Lava, Jewel, and Leaf—were blasting the serpents from above with their elemental powers.

Storm called down a lightning bolt that struck a serpent, shocking it. Ice made icicles as sharp as the blade of a knife rain down onto the serpents' scaley backs. Whirlpool, instead of deciding to flood the cavern again, created a shallow pool of water that went up to the girls' ankles, then made a super-crazy tsunami in not-so-super-crazy water. Lava blasted the serpents from above with plummeting lava, causing the serpents to hiss as heat surrounded their scales and burned them up into red-eyed crisps. Jewel was doing almost nothing, but she was occasionally causing a small earthquake, and sometimes having a giant slab of rock pop up from the ground and suffocate a serpent. Leaf was throwing trap vines around, the vines that Leaf Laughers coughed out.

It was chaos.

A serpent suddenly knocked into Izzy, making her yelp in surprise. "Eek! Hey, Leaf, come down here!" Izzy shouted as part of the tsunami pushed her into the serpent. "Come on—*AAAAH!*"

Leaf swooped down and sunk her shiny silver claws into the serpent, causing it to emit a high-pitched hissing noise for a brief moment before it went limp, dead.

Izzy gagged and looked away. "Seriously, Leaf, you know I can't stand the sight of... *that*. Next time, can you kill it some other way? Like, throwing it in the tsunami or something?"

Leaf nodded while grinning mischievously. "But the expression on your face was hilarious. How about one more time?" the earth dragon pleaded.

Izzy sighed and rolled her eyes. "Fine. But just *one* more time," she muttered as Leaf took flight again into the air to continue blasting vine nets at the serpents, trapping them so that Angela had easy targets.

She notched another arrow and shot off two more in rapid succession, hitting two serpents, but only taking one down. However, Andrew stabbed the serpent with the Slicer, and *then* the serpent finally went down. As usual, Andrew was riding on Storm, and the two made a magnificent fighting pair.

"Hey, Kelsey! Serpent behind you!" Izzy yelled, letting an arrow fly into a serpent's neck, making a cut that made the serpent hiss in annoyance.

Kelsey spun around and embedded her Full Moon sword in the serpent's scales, making it howl, and vaulted over the serpent's head as she stabbed it again in the neck, making it go limp. For what seemed like the millionth time that day, Izzy felt a little nauseous, and turned her head away.

After what seemed like hours and hours and *days* of fighting, stabbing, shooting, looking at dead serpent carcasses, and smelling a terrible stench, only three serpents were left, fighting for their lives.

Leaf had been bitten in all four legs by a serpent each, so she'd retreated back to the echoing tunnels that had led them here in the first place, along with Whirlpool, who was a little light-headed after a particularly large serpent had nearly squeezed her to death, and Jewel, who had been 'knocked out of the sky,' as Andrew had said, by a sneaky serpent that had crawled up to the roof and had made her fall in the middle of a cluster of serpents that had injured her badly. Izzy hoped the rock dragon was okay.

"Tell us where the 'tears' come from!" Chloe was demanding of the serpents.

The three looked at each other with red eyes that glowed with hate and evil. "No, never," they hissed together, making Izzy shudder. *How can they communicate so easily?* she wondered. *Do they use telepathy?*

"*Tell us* already!" Chloe shouted at the trio of serpents, hefting her electric spear threateningly. "Tell us, or we'll kill you!"

"We won't tell," the snake-like creatures hissed in unison again. "We have no idea what you are talking about. Ssso we can't tell, even if we wanted to."

Chloe glared at them. "*Tell us* or I'll cut your heads off, one by one!" she screamed. Izzy flinched. *Okay, I forgot that Chloe can be scary when she wants to be,* Izzy thought fearfully.

The serpents looked at each other. Finally, they turned their heads to look back at Chloe. "The water ssserpent that hasss causssed all our problemsss is at the bottom of the cave sssysssstem, the deepessst part of where we live."

Suddenly, they all lunged at Chloe at the same moment, baring their gleaming white teeth as sharp as a great white shark's. "Too bad you won't live another sssecond to sssee it!"

Just as Chloe had promised, she cut the heads of the serpents off, one by one, with her electric spear, giving them a good shock along the way. This time, Izzy was brave enough to stare at the mindless, chopped-off serpent heads before she had to look away.

"Time to continue searching for that water serpent that those guys confirmed," Chloe said, turning to look at the other eleven creatures there. "Bottommost cavern, here we come."

Hole Too Deep

Izzy wouldn't be surprised if they got lost in the gigantic cave system. *Really.* The tunnels winded downward and twisted skyward until Izzy completely lost her sense of direction. Currently, they were walking down a tunnel that sloped downwards, hoping that it led to the bottommost cavern. *With our luck, we'll be here for hours,* Izzy figured. It wasn't that Chloe was a bad leader or anything, of course. It was just that there were so many *options.*

"Another dead end," Chloe said once they reached a wall of rock standing in their way. "Let's go back." She turned to backtrack their steps, but Angela stopped her.

"Can we *please* get at least a fifteen-minute rest?" she implored. "You know we've been down here for, like, days? We need to take a break if we need to last longer."

Chloe stopped for a moment to consider that. "Fine," she sighed. "I *guess* we'll need it."

They all sat down, leaning against the chipped rock walls of the tunnel. Sara pulled out a bag of mini sandwiches and passed them around, giving two to each person (except for Izzy, who only took one since she hated sandwiches) and four to each dragon.

As Izzy took another hesitant bite of her sandwich (yes, she *really* didn't like sandwiches), Kelsey said, "Are we sure that these caves aren't *magical*? What if it's designed to lead us into a trap?"

Angela frowned. "Yeah... that *could* be possible, now that I think about it."

"Come on! We've got to keep going, even when things seem down," Chloe argued. "If we stop, then we won't *ever* have a chance of reaching the end. But if we continue, then it's half-half."

"Good point," Kelsey replied.

They finished up their snack of mini sandwiches and began backtracking, Jewel dragging them down by slowly—oh, *so slowly*—searching for gems hidden in the walls, her eyes darting back and forth for just a gleam of any precious stones.

"I guess it's back to guess-the-tunnels," Andrew said hopelessly. "I really wish we could do something else."

Izzy rolled her eyes. "Just close your mouth so we can get a little peace, okay?"

Andrew stuck his tongue out at her but closed his mouth.

After what seemed like ages of running, walking, and jogging down the rocky passageways, Chloe found something while she was scouting up ahead with Lava. "Guys!" she called. Her voice echoed in the empty underground tunnel. *Guys! Uys! Uys! Uys! Uys!* "Come over here! I found something!"

Izzy, Sara, and Kelsey ran forward to see what she'd found. The ground sloped upwards slightly, but otherwise it was smooth. Chloe gestured towards the end of the tunnel, but Izzy didn't see anything. "You told us to come all this way to see a *dead end?*" Izzy asked crossly. Her arms and legs ached from hours of running, and she felt like she could use a long break. Maybe take a nap, even.

"No," Chloe whispered. "Look." She stuck her hand out to the ground and put it in a secret tunnel. Izzy now realized why they couldn't see it before. The ground was going up, which meant that their prying eyes were trying to detect holes in the walls or ceiling, but never before had they thought to look to the *ground*. Now, staring at a hole that went as deep as the eye could see, Izzy wondered why the entrance was so secretive.

But the serpents must've thought that nobody was going to search for them.... Well, the past is in the past. Onwards into the future, Izzy thought dryly, without any enthusiasm. "Come over here, guys!" she called to Angela, Andrew, and the other five dragons. They all jogged over.

"How are we going to get down there?" Angela asked, peering into the dim hole. They'd been relying on Lava's steady glow and Jewel's sparkling golden eyes, so the bottom of the hole seemed pitch-black, and they had no idea how far it went down.

"We could climb down the hole," Sara suggested, running a hand over part of the smooth rock wall. "There wouldn't be many obstacles in our way if we did that, and we fit into the hole."

Chloe slid her hand over part of one of the rocky walls that made up the hole, nearly tipping over and into it. *Don't fall, Chloe,* Izzy thought, like her thinking that could prevent it.

"No," Chloe responded. "The walls are *too* smooth. We might fall down. And besides, the dragons don't fit, and they're an important part of our mission."

Izzy tapped her chin. "Maybe Leaf could make some vines sprout out of the side of the walls and make a vine ladder for us to climb down?" she suggested.

"That won't work, either," Chloe said. "There's absolutely *no* cracks in the rock that Leaf could make plants out of. I have an idea, though."

"What is it?" Izzy asked impatiently. *I want to see what's down there,* she thought. *We don't have time to waste.*

"Whirlpool should fill this hole with water," Chloe began, "and then we'd go in it, and then she'd slowly decrease the amount of water, and we'd sink lower and lower until we reached the bottom!" She beamed, obviously proud of herself (and oblivious to the fact that Izzy was rolling her eyes). "Isn't it great?"

"It's not great," Izzy said. "One, that doesn't solve the problem of the dragons not being small enough to fit through the hole. Two, what if something dangerous is down there, like a gigantic nest of serpents? The water will definitely get their attention, so they'll have the upper hand."

"Do *you* have something else?" Chloe countered. "As far as I know, this has been the best idea yet."

Izzy had to admit that Chloe was right. "Fine," she sighed. "But do we all know how to swim, though?" They had to consider that option, because it was possible that one of them could drown while going through that plan of action.

"I do, which is why I suggested it in the first place," Chloe said, huffing.

"I can swim..." Sara said. "But I don't like to do it."

"I can swim, but I'm not really fast. Although this isn't a race, so I guess I can do it," was Angela's response.

"Of course I can swim," Izzy said. "What about you, Kelsey?"

"I can," she said slowly.

"But this needs the skill of *treading water*, not swimming," Chloe said. "Can anybody here tread water? I *love* treading water, so of course I'm great at it."

"I can, but it wears me out," Izzy replied.

"I can do it, too, but I *hate* it and I'd rather do the bunny paddle," Angela huffed. Izzy thought about telling her that it was the *doggy* paddle, not the *bunny* paddle, but she brushed that thought away. There were more important things to do then argue about what type of paddle it really was.

"I can do it," Kelsey simply replied.

"I can," Sara said finally.

"Hey! Did everyone forget about *me?*" Andrew complained, marching up to the five girls. *I forgot about him, but of course I'm not admitting that,* Izzy thought, only slightly guilty. "I can tread water too, for your information."

Chloe rolled her eyes. "Okay, okay, thanks...."

Andy made a *humph* sound and turned away. Izzy knew him, though, and he would come around in a few minutes. The record so far as three minutes and eighteen seconds. *Will this be a new record?* Izzy thought with soundless dramatic noises.

"Whirlpool, are you ready?" Angela asked to her dragon.

The blue-speckled ocean-blue dragon nodded eagerly. "Yup!" Whirlpool responded cheerfully. "Totally, awesomely, totally—" She stopped for a second. "Wait, I already said totally, so I need to find another—"

She was interrupted by Chloe. "No time for that," the girl huffed. "Just fill the hole with water already."

Whirlpool pouted but she did as Chloe said. *Maybe even better,* Izzy thought... well, *thoughtfully*. The water was crystal-clear, shimmering and sparkling like the sun was reflecting on it. However, there was no sunlight in the dark caverns.

"Okay, Whirlpool, so the plan is too lower the water slowly—*very slowly*—after all of us have gotten in," Angela explained. "Then, we reach the bottom. End of plan. How does that sound?"

Whirlpool nodded enthusiastically, but then her excited smile turned into a confused frown. "But then how do us dragons get down there?" she asked, narrowing her blue eyes.

Angela glanced at Chloe. "Well, uh—um, you see—" she stammered nervously, looking back and forth between Whirlpool and Chloe.

"She means that you're not small enough to go down," Sara interrupted, who was not afraid of the truth. "We'd *love, love, love* your help, but you can't get down."

"Of *course* we can get down," Whirlpool said cheerfully, seeming to have gained back her eager attitude. "We can transform into creatures that are less powerful and crawl down there."

"*What?*" Izzy exclaimed. "You can *shape-shift?*"

Behind Whirlpool, Izzy saw Ice eye her, then whisper something into Lava's ear. *Gossip,* Izzy thought, annoyed. *Better ignore that.*

"Obviously," Whirlpool responded, and then it was *her* turn to look annoyed. "We'd be lesser dragons if we couldn't."

"So you guys can transform into other stuff?" Izzy asked, who was beginning to feel light-headed.

"Yeah," Jewel confirmed from the back of the group. It looked like to Izzy that she was still searching for sparkles in the hard rock walls.

"So do you mean you can transform into an ant and crawl down there?" Izzy said in disbelief. *If only we'd known that they could shape-shift... that would've been so helpful.... I wish I could travel back in time and use that knowledge,* Izzy thought longingly. *But we can totally use that in the future, so I won't linger over it.*

"Well, no," Whirlpool admitted. "Only Leaf can do that. But I can do a dolphin!"

"Um, how about a crab?" Angela asked.

"Sure," Whirlpool said, shrugging. "Whatever floats in your boat."

"All right," Chloe said. "Time to put Step 1 in action."

Step 1 wasn't actually that hard... in Izzy's eyes, anyways. All it required was Whirlpool to fill up the hole. Unfortunately, it proved itself to be *very, very* frustrating....

Whirlpool made a sweeping gesture with her front claws, looking tense, and water piled up in the hole. However, when Chloe reached out tentatively to touch it, her hand went straight through the water, never reaching a liquid barrier at all. Whirlpool relaxed, and the water suddenly became real, and the water suddenly began rapidly disappearing, the water level growing lower and lower.

"What's happening?" Chloe cried in alarm, staring down the hole. She looked very shocked and very alarmed.

"There's a large space underneath the hole, and the water has slipped in it. It's going to take a *long time* to fill it up," Whirlpool replied sourly, annoyed not by Chloe, but by the large space underneath the hole.

Izzy wrung her hands. "Can't we help?" she asked.

"Yeah," Andy said impatiently, pacing back and forth. "What can we do?"

"I can produce a bucket's worth of water every fifteen minutes; I can add that to the amount," Leaf offered.

"I can melt Ice's ice breath to make water," Lava volunteered.

Everyone turned to stare at Jewel, who just blinked. "What?" she asked. When Kelsey glared at her, she sighed. "Fine. I'll scout around for underwater pools." Izzy thought the rock dragon was tempted to add 'and jewels' but had stopped in case Kelsey decided to yell at her. Jewel padded away, her nose in the air.

In the end, it was decided that Whirlpool was going to continue making water down the hole, Leaf would make the water she could, and add it to Whirlpool's amount, and Ice would make an ice cube, and Lava would melt it into water, thus adding more of the clear liquid. The girls and the boy ran around, helping everyone pour the water down the hole. Chloe stayed by the hole's edge, watching the water level rise, slowly but steadily.

Whirlpool released another five buckets' worth of water into the hole, then stepped back to give Leaf a turn. The schedule was planned so that Whirlpool would continue to make water, but since her supply would run out *some* time, Leaf would add hers every fifteen minutes. The water that Lava and Ice made was filled into buckets by the six humans and poured into the hole as Leaf went, because hers wasn't a large amount.

Currently, Izzy was helping Ice and Lava fill up the two buckets that they had. Ice breathed her... well, *ice breath,* and as soon as the ice cube formed (this time it was about half the size of Izzy), Lava would melt it into water with her fiery breath.

The water would slope downwards until they reached the buckets, and it was Izzy's, Kelsey's, and Sara's job to make sure not even a single drop of water escaped the buckets. *When is this going to stop?* Izzy wondered, but as soon as the thought came, a shout echoed across the cavern. *Oh! That must be Jewel. Has she found an underground pool of water?*

"Hey, guys!" Jewel called. It sounded like she was a few yards away, and getting closer every second, judging by the steady pound of dragon footsteps. "I found an underground pool of water!" *Exactly what I was thinking,* Izzy thought, rolling her eyes to the irony.

"Really?" Kelsey called back excitedly. "Where is it?" She ran forward to Jewel, who was just in sight, rounding a corner. The two wandered off and out of sight.

Izzy sighed and pulled up her bucket. It was full to the brim, and the water around it was gone. Since the tunnel's floor was made entirely of solid rock, it was almost impossible for the water to leak through it. A few feet away, she saw Sara grabbing the handles of both her and Kelsey's buckets. *Leaning your work on other's shoulders isn't good,* Izzy thought.

Izzy and Sara came up to the hole to pour the water from the buckets in, and to see how far they'd gotten.

"How much more do you think we'll need?" Izzy asked Chloe, glancing at Whirlpool. The water dragon was slightly panting, and beads of sweat trickled down her scaly forehead. "It doesn't look like Whirlpool can hold out much longer."

Chloe squinted into the hole. To Izzy, it simply looked like a pit of pitch-black darkness. "Maybe three more rounds," Chloe replied. "I don't know. It's so dark down there that I can barely see anything."

"That was *just* what I was going to say," Andrew complained, walking over with a bucket filled with Leaf's water. He dumped the water in, and Izzy saw Chloe watching the falling water with her eyes before they heard a *splash* noise.

"What was that?" Izzy cried, alarmed.

"I don't know," Chloe answered, looking panicked. "Okay, uh... abandon hole?"

"It's *supposed* to be 'abandon ship,'" Izzy corrected. "But, well... this isn't a ship, so I guess this *is* an exception."

She, Andy, Sara, and Chloe jogged over to where Kelsey and Jewel were returning. The pair had big smiles on their faces.

"Where have you *been*?" Chloe huffed, putting her hands on her hips. "You know you've been gone for, like... half an hour?"

It probably hasn't been half an hour, Izzy thought, grinning on the inside and trying to stop smiling.

Kelsey and Jewel shared a look. "We found a big underground water pond," Kelsey explained. "We dug a tunnel all the way back to where we left a shred of blue cloth, and we climbed out of the tunnel here." She pointed down the tunnel. "We pushed a rock in the way of the water, but I think it's going to burst soon."

Chloe immediately took action. "Andrew, go back and get Angela and Storm, then come back," she ordered. "Jewel, Kelsey, Izzy, and Sara will come with me to figure out a way to get the water back to the hole without any of it spilling or dripping."

The four girls and the dragon ran over to where the water was battling the rock slowly. Izzy could see that the rock would probably give way in maybe... ten minutes? Fifteen? *I'm not a genius in physics,* she thought, slightly annoyed with herself.

"So, any ideas?" Chloe asked, clasping her hands together tightly. *Maybe too tightly.* Izzy noticed that her knuckles were growing a little white. *Yeah, definitely too tightly.*

"We could get Leaf to make, like, little plant bags made of large leaves," Kelsey suggested.

"No, that would take too long," Chloe said. "The hole is still pretty far away from here."

I've got to make the best idea this time, Izzy thought competitively. *I know it's not good, but... I am competitive. Time to face the truth.* "How about if Jewel made a slide-like thing that would pour the water over to the hole?" Izzy suggested.

Chloe tapped her chin. "I guess that would work," she admitted, then turned to Jewel. "Can you handle that?"

Jewel nodded, and for a moment Izzy thought she could detect a vibe of arrogance. "Of course," she replied.

"Then do it," Chloe countered, gesturing towards the rock. "That thing's going to move in—what? Maybe fifteen seconds—so hurry up."

"Fine," Jewel huffed. *It's obvious that she doesn't like to be rushed,* Izzy thought. *She probably does worse under pressure.* "I don't like to be rushed. I'll probably do worse under pressure," Jewel added. *Case solved,* Izzy thought sarcastically.

Jewel closed her eyes, took a deep breath, made a claw gesturing move, and... Izzy, Kelsey, Chloe, and Sara were absolutely amazed. Because... *nothing happened.*

Luckily, at that moment, Andrew came running towards them with Angela and Storm on his tail, but not *really* his tail, since people didn't *have* tails. Only those fake, plastic ones used for lizard costumes on Halloween. Anyways, the point was, it eased the awkwardness.

"I got Storm and Angela," Andrew panted, stopping to catch his breath.

"We're *so* proud of you," Izzy replied sarcastically. "Anyways, Angela, did Andrew give you an update on the way here?"

"Yup," Angela answered. "And Storm, too. It was actually a pretty good, very brief... *brief.*"

Izzy rolled her eyes at the pun. "So, anyways, Jewel was supposed to make a 'rock slide' from here to over where the hole is, but apparently it didn't work."

"Hey!" Jewel exclaimed, looking embarrassed. Izzy knew that dragons couldn't blush, but right now Jewel looked the equivalent of a dragon blushing. "I... just didn't do it correctly."

Kelsey gave Jewel a little nudge. "Then do it correctly this time, please," she said, looking very patient.

Jewel took a deep breath, did the same thing as she did before, and... *something* happened this time. A low wall of rock—about up to Izzy's knees—appeared on the ground of the cavern, a wall that would block the water from flowing right *if* it was released. And by the looks of the rock stopper, that was going to be pretty soon.

"Hurry up," Chloe said impatiently, walking over to where the rock looked like it was about to burst and pushing it further into the hole. "If we let all this water spill, then—"

She was interrupted by a slithering noise coming from further along the tunnel, coming from the direction of the hole. "W-what is *that?*" Izzy stuttered, suddenly being hit by a bad bout of I'm-really-nervous-about-fighting-more-serpents. "I-it sounds like t-there's a *s-serpent* coming along our way!"

World Record for the Largest Serpent

Everybody turned around slowly, their gaze landing on the largest serpent they'd seen today by far.

Even with half its body slithering on the floor, the serpent was still taller than the dragons—maybe three times as tall—and had menacing red eyes two times the size of large pancakes. Its scales looked like it used to be shiny, but now they were covered with dust, and time had made small dents in the serpent's armor.

"Do you dare venture down to my sssacred nessst?" the serpent hissed, its large red eyes glowing with anger and power. "I guard the sssecret that hasss not been revealed... for you mussst never know it."

I don't think we're going to have much of a chance in a battle, Izzy thought, averting her gaze from the gigantic serpent as it hissed again for no apparent reason. She was right. Andrew, Angela, Storm, Chloe, Sara, Jewel, Kelsey, and her had no chance in a fight between the seven of them and the giant serpent. *Is there a way we can get the other five dragons' attention without the serpent noticing? Also, those red thingies are starting to creep me out,* she added mentally as the giant snake-like creature's eyes stared at her.

Maybe I can use Morse code? Izzy wondered. *Do any of the dragons even know Morse code?* She wasn't sure about that, but Mayor Dwaggen, the, well... *dwarf* that had given them the six unique dragons had told them that they were super-smart, intelligent creatures. *Does that mean they know and are fluent in Morse code?* Izzy herself wasn't perfect at it—in fact, she was just *barely* passable in it. Could she remember it now, under pressure, and while a giant serpent with large, creepy red eyes was staring at her like she was going to be its next snack?

"Well, we're going to find that secret, whatever it is," Chloe shot back.

An expression of surprise flickered across the serpent's face for a moment, like it didn't expect its lunch to talk back, but it soon regained its serious look.

"You cannot venture down here," the serpent replied with a menacing grin. "Thisss sssecret hasss been kept for ssso long, no ssserpents remember a time when other creaturesss touched it. Or witnesssed itsss presence, in fact." The serpent's eyes glowed as it told the tale, unnerving Izzy. She shivered. *A lot, too.* "Many died trying. You, ssseven travelersss, will be among thossse who have fallen."

"How do you know?" Kelsey asked bravely. "We've gotten through your cavern of serpents."

"Oh, yesss," the serpent replied, its red eyes sparkling with mischief and humor. "There wasss nothing in that room, after all. It wasss not the point of it. It wasss sssupposssed to ssslow you down, and posssibly ssstop you from touching the ssserpentsss' sssecret."

"This guy is scaring me," Angela whispered into Izzy's ear. "How do we get out of this sticky situation before it eats us?"

Izzy took a deep breath and began tapping on the wall. *Okay, 'H' in Morse code is four short dots... right?* Izzy began to doubt herself as she tapped four short, quick taps on the stone wall.

"Well?" the serpent asked impatiently. Izzy didn't see *why* it was saying that; she thought it was for absolutely *no reason* at all.

"We'd like to go past you," Chloe huffed, glaring at the serpent and hefting her electric spear menacingly. Even a few feet away, Izzy could see the glowing, red-hot sparks that flew off it.

The serpent laughed, a cold and cruel laugh, like it was teasing its prey. *We probably* are *its prey,* Izzy thought, shuddering in fear. "You cannot kill me with sssuch a lower-ranked weapon," it hissed, showing its white fangs. They were long and smooth, but something about them seemed sinister. *Just like their owner.* "Ssserpentsss have been living long before weaponsss of even that power came into being. We can withsssstand their bite like a ssstalk of grasss."

Chloe glared at the serpent some more, but Izzy thought she could detect a bit of fear in her fiery gaze. "Then what *can* kill you?" she snarled. "I'd like to personally bring you down."

The serpent laughed again. "Oh, it is mossst hardessst to find," the serpent growled. "Found where nothing elssse isss found. Growsss where nothing elssse growsss. Where nothing elssse isss. It isss impossssible to find. For that matter, you won't even be alive to dissscover *it'sss* sssecret."

In a swift move, the gigantic serpent lunged at Chloe, but she was expecting it. With precise skill, she ducked below the serpent's scales and shoved the tip of her electric spear upwards. Izzy expected it to break through the serpent's scales like the other serpents, but this time, it only bounced off harmlessly.

Quickly, Izzy tapped the rest of the letters: *E*, *L*, and *P*. Together, the words spelled '*HELP*,' which, in fact, they desperately needed.

The Serpent of Tears

Meanwhile, Kelsey had leapt into the battle and hit the serpent on its back with her Full Moon sword, but again, like Chloe's spear, the scales somehow repelled the sword, and it went flying with astonishing speed into a small, rocky ditch. *I hope the other dragons get here soon,* Izzy thought.

Chloe zoomed out from underneath the enormous serpent's stomach and stabbed it right in the middle of the serpent's left eye with her electric spear. But as the electricity crackled up and down the spearhead, Izzy saw with her very own eyes that it did nothing. The serpent simply blinked, and the spear seemed to bounce off the eyeball. The force (Izzy didn't know that a giant serpent blinking could create force) sent Chloe flying into the same exact ditch as Kelsey's Full Moon sword.

"Come on!" Andrew hollered to his dragon, Storm. He swung himself onto the saddle that was on her back, and they soared to the heights of the cavern. The serpent reared up and began flicking his thick, forked tongue out at them, trying to knock them out of the sky, but Storm flew with swift precision and versatile skill, dodging each of the attacks. *I never imagined a dragon getting knocked out of the sky from a giant tongue,* Izzy thought with amusement. *But I have to admit, it's a good plan. Distracting the serpent will give us some time.*

Sara and Angela were firing arrows at the serpent, and Angela was sharing her Starstruck Arrows with Sara. Angela hit the serpent in the belly, and surprisingly, the giant serpent growled in pain.

"How did you find the arrowsss?" the serpent screamed as it flung its head about wildly. "They are sssacred to the culture of the ssserpentsss! How? How? *How?*"

Angela gave no audible reply, but she whispered something in Sara's ear. Sara nodded, a new expression of determination on her face, and began shooting arrows at the serpent's stomach along with Angela. *They've discovered a weakness, and they're using it to their advantage,* Izzy thought, watching the pair with her eyes. *Smart.*

Kelsey was running towards the ditch. *Her sword.* Suddenly, Izzy remembered that Chloe had fallen in there, too. *How could I be so clueless?* She ran towards the ditch, too, dodging out of the way of the serpent's tail as it swung wildly back and forth. *We could've cushioned Chloe's landing somehow!*

"Hey! Come on over here!" Kelsey yelled above the noise of the battle. She was at the ditch, peering over the edge.

"Coming!" Izzy shouted back, leaping over a rock. She skidded to a stop in front of the ditch, which was actually a slight dip in the ground. Chloe was sprawled out on the floor.

Only a few scratches and bruises blanketed her, but Izzy still felt a little dizzy staring at the sight in front of her.

"Eww," Izzy groaned, looking away. "Hey, Kelsey, could you do me a favor and bring Chloe back to where Angela and Sara are? I'm getting light-headed looking at her."

"Sure," Kelsey answered. Izzy heard some shuffling and scraping, and then she opened her eyes and followed Kelsey (who was somehow dragging Chloe along) back to the archers.

"Hey, can I shoot?" Izzy asked Angela. "And borrow some of those cool arrows?"

Angela grinned. *She seems to be enjoying herself,* Izzy noted. "Sure. Help yourself." She gestured towards a stack of Starstruck Arrows that were lying on the floor.

Izzy picked one up and notched her bow, aiming straight for the giant serpent's stomach. As she aimed, she surveyed the battlegrounds in a single moment.

Jewel had joined in on the action, and currently, she was making giant spearheads of rock jut out of the ground and strike the serpent right in its tail, mooring him to the stone. As Izzy watched, a column of stone zipped out of the ground and impaled the serpent right in the center of its tail. The serpent roared in pain—a loud, screechy, screaming roar—and hissed, "You will pay for thisss... you will pay like the othersss before you. Even the bravessst of warriorsss can fall."

"Well, then this is going to be a first for you!" Jewel roared back with so much force Izzy flinched and her arrow struck the floor in front of the serpent instead of in its stomach.

"Be *quiet*, Jewel!" Izzy hollered. "I can't aim straight when you're screaming!"

"Um, you're actually screaming right now," Sara whispered in Izzy's ear.

"Oops," Izzy replied, her cheeks flushing in embarrassment. "Um... ignore that, I guess."

The serpent roared and lashed out at Storm and Andy. Storm swiftly dodged out of the way and Andrew stabbed the serpent in the scales under its eyes with the Slicer, his trusty sword.

As quick as lightning, the serpent grabbed the Slicer and snapped it in half like a toothpick. Andrew watched, with wide eyes, as the two halves of the adamant sword fall and clang against the floor.

"Looksss like you are defenssselesss now," the snake-like creature hissed, its large red eyes focusing menacingly on Andrew.

"Not quite!" Storm screeched as she called upon a lightning bolt. It hit the serpent on the head, flashing white and pulsing heat. Just as quick as it appeared, it vanished, and the only sign of the lightning bolt was the drifting smoke on top of the serpent's head. The scales were burned black and brown, like a cookie that had sat too long in the oven.

"*How dare you?*" the serpent screeched, fuming. "*I will get you for that!*"

Storm snickered cheekily, goading the serpent on. "Try and catch me!"

The serpent roared and lunged for Storm, its white fangs gleaming, but the storm-type dragon dodged and sliced a cut under the serpent's chin.

Just then, Whirlpool, Leaf, Lava, and Ice zipped into action.

Ice froze the lower half of the serpent, locking it into a position that made it look like it was about to flop to the floor. Whirlpool created a bubble helmet over the serpent's head, then added swirling seawater and varying ocean reeds in it, so that the water was *inside* the helmet instead of *outside*. Leaf made a large, thick vine sprout out of the ground and looped it around the serpent's neck. Lava created a giant, floating block of lava that she poured around the serpent, making its scales grow black and scorched. Ice blasted ice shards and hail at the serpent, slamming into its armor. Izzy ducked as an ice shard whizzed past her and would've struck where her head was and slammed into the wall.

Behind Angela, Chloe stirred. "Wha... what's going on?" she mumbled. "S-serpent... I—I remember... s-somebody was—they were—"

"Um, let's stop rambling for now," Angela said, glancing at Izzy. "We're trying to fight a dragon here. Andrew just lost his sword to its teeth."

"Fangs," Izzy corrected.

"Fine," Angela sighed. "*Fangs,* then. Andy just lost his sword to its *fangs.*" She put extra emphasis on the 'fangs' part.

Izzy rolled her eyes but didn't say anything.

Chloe's face turned into an expression of shock. "But I thought his sword was made of adamant!" she exclaimed, her eyes wide in surprise.

"It is," Izzy confirmed. "But can adamant survive a sixty-thousand-yard-high drop? And a gigantic serpent's super-sharp fangs?"

"I guess maybe not," Chloe admitted. "So, what can *I* do?"

Angela shared a look with Izzy. "You could help me fire arrows," Angela suggested. "I have a spare bow."

"*Or* you could ride on Lava and scream insults at the serpent," Izzy offered.

Chloe scrunched up her face. "Hm... I think I'll pick the insult one," she said. "I can't injure the serpent *physically,* but at least shouting insults at him will make me feel better."

Izzy shrugged, casting a glance at Angela. "Whatever floats in your boat," Izzy replied.

"Lava! Come here!" Chloe shouted.

The fire dragon looked surprised for a moment, then flew towards Chloe and landed softly. "Yes?" Lava asked, flapping her wings impatiently. "There's a giant serpent to take care of."

"Let me ride you," was Chloe's response.

Lava bowed and let Chloe climb on her back, then she took off and continued pouring floating stuff on the serpent's back. Lava, of course. Not Chloe. That would be absolutely absurd.

"So... what now?" Izzy asked Angela. She sat down on the rocky floor of the cavern. Running a hand over the smooth ground, she wondered how long it had been here, waiting for the serpents to inhabit it.

"I don't know," her friend replied. "Just sit here and wait? Shoot arrows?"

"I guess so," Izzy answered, grabbing her bow and a Starstruck Arrow. She notched the star-streaked arrow in the bow.

Aiming carefully, she fired an arrow in the underbelly of the serpent. The snake-like monster growled and slashed at Storm and Andy with its long white fangs. Those teeth were surprisingly good weapons, ripping through air like it was made from... well, *air*. The point was, Izzy had expected that the fangs would create more friction than it actually was. Did this serpent have magic that was even superior to science?

All magic is superior to science, Izzy reminded herself, laughing internally as she notched another arrow in her bow, her fingers aching.

It continued for hours—possibly half the day—but finally, the serpent was defeated. It gave one final, challenging roar to Leaf, who had killed it by scraping her claws across one of its eyeballs, then it *crumbled to dust* right in front of their eyes. It was possibly the most amazing sight Izzy had ever seen. The monstrousness of the serpent had shocked her, and so when it disappeared, it felt like the cavern was being made twice its size because so much space was open now.

As Andrew waded forward through the huge amount of dust to find the remains of his sword, he let out a gasp. His eyes still on what he was watching, he said, "Guys, you have to see this."

Izzy hurried over. "What is it?"

Andrew pointed to a particularly large clump of dust that rose above the others. "Look at that."

Izzy looked at it. In fact, she even *squinted* at it. But she could see nothing past the pale brown fog. "I can't see anything. Is this a trick?" she asked crossly.

"No," Andrew said. "Look closer."

She looked closer. Finally, she saw it.

"What? How is this possible?"

But she had to believe it. It was right in front of her eyes.

The two halves of Andrew's sword had cracked right in front of Izzy's eyes... and his, too. How was this possible? It was like they'd been connected again by some magical spell.

"How is this possible?" Andrew asked, staring at his sword. He picked it up and stuffed it in his backpack, careful to not accidentally make a hole in it. The backpack, of course, not the sword. If it were the sword, it would be absolutely absurd.

"I don't know," Izzy replied, frowning. Then something caught her eye. "Look!" She pointed further into the fog of dust, where they could barely see anything. "There's something in there!" She squinted and then frowned *again*. "No, that looks like a *bunch* of somethings. I'm going to check it out." She waded forward in the sea of dust, coughing as she inhaled it.

She reached forward with her hands and felt something cold and smooth, like a metal disk. She pulled it out. It was… a frisbee. Literally a *frisbee*.

How did a frisbee get here? she wondered. The group certainly hadn't brought any frisbees with them—especially not a cold, hard, gray one like this one. *Unless… when the serpent died, did its body dissolve into this? If that was the case, does this have a curse on it? Or does it contain the serpent's magic and power?*

"Hey, Andrew!" she called back to her brother. "Look what I found!" She waved the frisbee over her head as she walked back over to him.

Andrew stared at it, then grabbed it for closer inspection. "A *frisbee?*" he asked, scrunching up his nose. "What's *that* doing down here?"

Izzy shrugged. "I don't know. But since you're the obvious one who knows the most about mechanics, can you do anything helpful with it?"

Andrew frowned, a look of concentration on his face. "I think I can… hang on a sec." He kneeled down and grabbed a sharp chip of rock nearby, then started cutting at the frisbee. Soon enough, when he'd chopped about half an inch the way through, he chipped right into a hollow part that had a bunch of wires and gears in it, spinning and twisting in ways that Izzy didn't understand. "Okay… I think I got it…." Andrew tapped a button on part of a small disk inside the frisbee. The frisbee made a *beep* noise, and then a robotic voice started counting down.

"Five...." Andrew quickly shoved the parts he'd carved out of the frisbee back into it.

"Four...." The voice was a little muffled now, but Izzy could still hear it clearly.

"What's going to—"

"Three...."

"—happen?" she cried, backing away from the frisbee in alarm. *Is it going to explode or something?* she wondered.

"Nothing," her brother replied calmly. "Just—"

"Two...."

"Wait, okay?"

Izzy was silent.

"One...."

All of a sudden, the frisbee grew robot wings and flew over to perch on Andrew's shoulder. "An automatic buddy," he said, grinning.

"Why didn't you tell me?" Izzy complained. "*I* could've made a mechanical friend *very* useful!"

Andrew shrugged. "I wanted a robot frisbee. It sounded cool. And look! He's already really smart already. See?" Andrew looked at the frisbee, struggling to restrain a grin. "Robot frisbee mode sixty-three, go and find the same rock that I cut you up with." He threw the pointy rock over his shoulder, and the robot frisbee zoomed away to grab it, then came back. Andrew looked at Izzy expectantly.

"Fine," was all she said, accompanied with a sarcastic sigh. "You can keep it. But is there anything else in here?"

Andrew shrugged. "I don't know." He turned to the robot frisbee. "Activate mode one hundred and five. Detect stuff that appeared after the serpent was destroyed."

The robot frisbee gave an obeying *beep* noise—Izzy didn't actually know if it was obeying-ish, because all the sounds that the robot frisbee emitted where beeps, but she thought beeps could have their own tone—and flapped into the giant cloud of dust. Izzy could see a flashing red light coming from it, along with an unblinking white one.

"That should do the trick," Andrew said, looking at Izzy with a smug expression. Izzy rolled her eyes and glared at him.

"Anyways, I should go alert the others that we're in here," Izzy said. "Be right back." She hurried through the fog, clamping down the urge to cough until her throat was dry and caked with dust.

"Hey! Chloe!" Izzy called. She waved her hand, trying to get the group's leaders' attention. "Over here!"

She was barely a foot away from Chloe, but the dust was like a wall for vision, blocking Chloe's eyesight. "What?"

"*Here!*" Izzy shouted, waving her hand even more rapidly. "*In the dust! Right in front of you!*"

Chloe blinked, like she was seeing the sky for the first time. "Oh, *there*. Sorry. The dust is so hard to see through!" she gushed. "Anyways, what is it?"

"Andrew got a robot frisbee—" she ignored the half-shocked half-annoyed look on Chloe's face "—and we think that there's other stuff from the serpent's d—" She punched herself internally for almost saying 'dead body' "—remains, and we want to see what they are."

Chloe shrugged and twisted her electric spear sideways. Electricity crackled on the spearhead, but Izzy noticed that Chloe was handling the spear almost... *carelessly*. Izzy knew her friend wasn't lazy, not in the least bit.

Is she immune to it somehow? she wondered. *If that's the case, how did she get that power? She definitely hadn't been invincible to electricity before they'd started their path as a questing group. Had she taken the power from her spear, perhaps? Was it enchanted? Or from Lava? Maybe her fire staff? After all, lightning is related to fire... a little bit.* "That's fine with me," she replied, shrugging again.

"Okay, thanks," Izzy said, hurrying away to where the dust clouds were slowly falling apart. "Found anything, Andrew?"

Andrew shrugged. *That has to be the millionth time someone has shrugged today,* Izzy thought. "The frisbee hasn't come back yet," he replied. "But I'm thinking about a name for it. How about Max?"

Izzy gawked at him. "You're thinking of a *name* for it?" she cried in disbelief. "Um, well... oh, here it comes!"

"Here *Max* comes," Andrew corrected. "But yeah, he's coming."

Max the robot frisbee was flying back over to them with something clutched between talons that it had magically sprouted. As it flew closer, Izzy realized it was a book, its pages stained and grayed over time.

"*Beep*," Max beeped. "Beep-beep-beep." Max dropped the book in front of Andrew, making sure not to rip any of the pages or tear the cover accidentally, then flew up a little bit at eye level to stare at Andrew with the unblinking white light.

"Continue mode one hundred and five," Andrew told the frisbee. Max zoomed into the cloud of dust as the boy picked up the ancient book. "Got any idea of what this is?" He squinted at the front cover. "I can't make out the title." He handed the book to Izzy. "See if you can figure it out."

Izzy turned the book over in her hands. *How long has it been here?* she wondered. She could barely make out the title: *The Ancient Guide to the Devil Serpents*. "The old guide," she whispered. "The ancient guide. To devil serpents."

Andrew frowned. "The *what*, exactly?"

"The guide to devil serpents," she explained excitedly. "It probably has all their secrets and stuff in it, because it was written by numerous generations of serpents. The more recent ones are near the back." She flipped to the last page. "Wow! It dates back to the day before yesterday. Wait... it says that the humans *first started* invading the ravine on that day." She looked up from the page with an alarmed expression. "That means we've been underground for, like, *two days!*"

Andrew gasped, then recovered himself. "Well, it isn't *that* bad," he said. "We could've been gone for, like, a week or something."

Izzy sighed. "Well, I'm just going to continue reading this."

"You do you."

Lunch (Breakfast? Dinner?) Break

After about half an hour of skimming, reading, and flipping through *The Ancient Guide to the Devil Serpents,* Izzy finished the book. She closed the book carefully, put it in her backpack, and walked over to where Andrew was standing.

"Found anything?" she asked. "I mean, did Max find anything?"

"Yup," he replied. "Take a look." He gestured towards a pile a few feet away. "A lot of it was junk, but I decided to keep it anyways, just in case it could come in handy. You can keep anything you find, but not *everything*," he added. "Because obviously, you don't have enough space for everything."

Izzy nodded, hurried over to the pile, and began digging. There was a stack of books that looked only slightly younger than *The Ancient Guide to the Devil Serpents,* a pile of old-fashioned papyrus scrolls, large patches of silk and fabric, robot parts, flashlights, ropes, scales, jewels, mini statues, and other items, some valuable, and some worth as much as a year-old loaf of bread.

She recognized a beautiful sapphire with tiny flecks of gold in it as the Cursed Water Gem, a jewel that could summon cursed water. Many people had drowned in the water when they'd tried to unsuccessfully make swimming pools, oases, or an ocean across a dry desert. All this zoomed through her mind, the result of a brutal studying session in the town library.

She was careful to avoid the sapphire, although it looked really shiny. *That's probably just to lure people in,* she reminded herself.

There was also a necklace made of beautiful, pure white pearls, with a large crimson ruby on the chain. *The Lost Queen's Necklace,* Izzy thought. Queen Physia, the queen that was about six generations before Queen Sola's time, had mysteriously disappeared during an attack on her royal palace by the Rebels, a fierce group of dragons. No one knew where she went, and personally, Izzy thought it was pretty creepy. There were rumors that the ruby was cursed in a way that was superior to any other curses, and nobody had confirmed that the rumors were true—or stopped them.

Izzy wondered what had happened to Queen Physia. *Did the dragons capture her? Did they kill her?*

There were a ton of other creepy, cursed items, but the most unsettling thing that Izzy found was a statue of a dragon. The pedestal, which was smooth, white quartz, without a single speck of dust (Izzy found that strange, since dust was all around them in a cloud), was about half as tall as Izzy; it went up to her waist. The dragon was made out of a large block of magenta ruby, and it had gold spheres for eyes. Izzy shivered, thinking how much this statue looked like Firestriker, the dragon they'd fought in their last adventure.

She realized there was some sort of engravement in part of the pedestal underneath the dragon. It read *Opaque, the Dragon of Walls, Last Fire Dragon to Ascend the Royal Molten Rock Throne, Last Queen of the Western Fire Dragons, Mother to Six Fire Dragons*. She shuddered, reading the last line. *Mother to Six Fire Dragons?* One of those six fire dragons could be Firestriker. The two looked so similar that it was easy to believe that they were mother and daughter. Queen Opaque... she must've been quite the dragon.

Izzy picked up the statue of Opaque, the Lost Queen's Necklace, the Cursed Water Gem, and a couple of other items that she'd like to keep, collect, or study. She found a time-worn but sturdy-looking sack nearby and shoved all the items in it. After getting suspicious that the bag didn't weigh anything, even after putting what looked like a sixty-pound dragon statue in it, Izzy realized that it was enchanted so that it was bottomless. *Very useful,* she thought. *But how come there's so much stuff here? I wonder why....*

She spotted her friends over by numerous piles of things that Max had dropped down helpfully. He had also deposited a bag just like hers—probably also a bottomless sack—for each of them. She walked over to where Sara was rummaging through her pile. "Found anything good?" she asked.

"Yes," Sara replied, her eyes on the pile. "I got some books, relics, ancient gems, and things like that."

"Oh, yeah!" Izzy said excitedly. "Guess what, Sara? I found a statue of Opaque! Here, check it out." She took out the statue of Queen Opaque from her bottomless bag, which she'd put a sticker that said 'I' on it (her bag, not the statue, of course), and held it up for Sara to see.

Her friend squinted at it. "Does that remind you of Firestriker?" Sara asked, looking slightly uneasy.

"Yeah," Izzy answered. "She's probably one of Opaque's daughters."

Sara shrugged. "I guess that would make reasonable sense." She went back to looking through her pile.

Izzy watched her for a bit, then asked, "Hey, do you mind if I look through your pile? I already took everything that I liked in mine."

Sara paused. "Sure. Why not?"

Izzy kneeled down beside her and picked up an ancient-looking scroll. It was tied up by a worn red ribbon and looked as valuable as a donut, but sometimes things weren't always as they seemed. Izzy was right this time.

In tall, straight handwriting, the title was: *How to Gain Magical Superpowers*. Izzy didn't really want to read it just then, since she was scouting out things that might help them find out where—or what—was the serpents' 'secret' that the giant serpent had said... or was it a trick? For some reason, Izzy didn't think it was a trap. The serpent had acted too sure that it would win the battle, so it probably was like, *Okay, I'll just kill these dragons and humans, and nobody will know the secret. That won't matter, so who cares?*

Izzy found a few more cool jewels that she wanted to keep, along with a book that listed some rare constellations that she could give Angela. She stuffed a few more scrolls in her sack, said bye to Sara, and headed over to where Angela was.

"Hi, Angela," Izzy said. "I found a book about constellations for you." She took the book out of her bag and handed it to Angela.

She turned it over her hands, examined it, and put it in her bag. "Thanks," she said. "I already took everything I wanted from this pile. Where's yours?"

Izzy pointed over to the pile that she'd taken her first items from. "Over there," she replied. "You can go check it out. I'll do yours."

After rummaging through everybody's piles, everybody checked with each other, and they all had everything they wanted from each of the piles. The dragons weren't really interested in jewels or books, but they took a few scrolls that had ancient myths of powerful dragons.

"So, should we continue on with our journey?" Chloe asked her group.

"Definitely!" Izzy exclaimed excitedly.

"Then are you ready?"

"*Yes,*" Lava said, looking annoyed. "When can we get a move on?" The fire dragon had spent the majority of the time pacing and muttering and occasionally blowing small plumes of fire while the other dragons had been looking for scrolls.

"Be patient, Lava," Chloe huffed, glaring at the fire dragon. "But *fine*. Guys, come on. Let's go."

"Wait!" Andrew exclaimed. "I'm hungry. Is there anything to eat?"

We've been underground for two days, and we've barely eaten anything, Izzy thought, surprised. As soon the shocking realization came to her, her stomach began grumbling like the traitor it was.

"Okay, I guess we're all on the verge of starving," Chloe admitted, clearly ignoring the rumbles coming from Izzy's direction. "Let's sit down and have a bite to eat."

This time, they all ate salads from plastic bowls, which they then gave to Leaf to insta-decompose into soil. Izzy didn't particularly like salads, but she ate it because she was so hungry she was considering going back up to the surface to get a bite to eat. After they'd all gotten their fill, Chloe gathered them up and their adventure resumed.

They hurried through the rock tunnel, not worrying about anything they'd missed in the piles since Max had helpfully scooped up everything they'd left and put it in a bottomless bag. They headed towards the hole, carefully avoiding patches of water where they could possibly slip on the slick rock floor.

"Did the serpent come through here?" Izzy asked, kneeling down to examine the hole carefully. She could hear the steady lapping of calm waves a few yards below her. *At least I won't fall to my doom if I accidentally fall in here,* she thought. She shook her head. *Okay, that's way too far from a comforting thought.*

"Yes," Whirlpool answered. Izzy hadn't seen the water dragon so subdued before. *That's definitely not comforting,* she thought. *Totally a bad sign.* "It just slithered right past us when I was taking a break in a nearby cave with Ice. I asked Lava to guard, but apparently she didn't." Whirlpool glared at Chloe's dragon.

Lava breathed a breath of fire. "*I* was taking a break, too," she snarled. "You just walked up to me and told me I had to be a lookout." She marched over to Whirlpool angrily and spread her wings offensively.

"You could've just *told* me you didn't want to guard," Whirlpool snapped. "I value your opinion, you know?"

"Well, it seems like you *don't*," Lava hissed back, heavy gray smoke rising from her scales. *One wrong move and Lava could burn Whirlpool to ashes,* Izzy thought, her mind paralyzed with fear.

Luckily, Chloe stopped them. "Just come on already," she grumbled, seeming more exasperated than scared. "We have to continue on our journey to find the 'secret'. And if you don't move, I'm going to stab you with my electric spear." Somehow, Chloe managed to make her spear more menacing. Twice as many electric sparks danced up and down the spearhead, far away from Chloe's hands.

Lava and Whirlpool glanced at her spear, then closed their mouths. Izzy felt a flow of satisfaction. *That's it, dragons... Chloe can be dangerous, too,* she thought proudly.

"So, what should we do now?" Izzy asked. They needed to get at least a *piece* of a plan. What else were they supposed to do? A group without a quarter of a plan was as useless as a ninja that could possibly slice off his own arm on accident with a sword.

"Well, first, we should go down that hole," Chloe finally said. "This tunnel ends here, and I'm pretty sure all the other tunnels are dead ends, too. We should go down here when we have the chance, before we get lost."

"Good idea," Angela said with a happy smile. "So... the *real* question is, how do we get down there?"

The Stranger

The plan was that Leaf would hold a rope that Angela had found in her bottomless bag next to the hole, and the others would climb down it. Lava, Ice, Jewel, Whirlpool, and Storm would transform into smaller creatures of their element and climb down in this order: Storm, Lava, Ice, humans, Whirlpool, Jewel. This was the order that the humans would climb down: Chloe, Sara, Izzy, Andrew, Kelsey, Angela. Leaf came last, after everybody had gone. Those orders were in that particular order for a reason. Chloe pointed this out when Andrew protested about his place in the line.

They all went down, one by one (well, Lava and Ice went down at the same time, since Lava became a fire beetle, and Ice became a snow beetle), until they were all safely down on the ground of the cave they'd been trying to fill with water.

"So where should we go next?" Chloe asked. When Sara, Izzy, Kelsey, and Angela gave her puzzled glances, she added, "Take a look around. I did while you guys were coming down."

They were standing in a large cavern. The rocky floor was soaked, thanks to their attempt of filling the cave with water to safely swim down. Izzy now saw that it was impossible, and here was why: the cavern branched off to two different tunnels that were wide enough and looked long enough so that Izzy could believe that they could keep in all the water they would pour in for five days without filling to the brim—possibly even more.

The first tunnel was dark and menacing; there was something about it that said, *Go away or I will kill you.* It was narrow at the beginning, but Izzy could see that it widened quickly. *Maybe it wants to make people believe that it'll come to a dead end?* she guessed. *Well, it's not going to fool me,* she added in her mind confidently.

The second passageway was wide, with even a tiny bit of light pouring inside, but there was no light source, not even a crack in the ceiling where it could've possibly reached back up to the surface. *Why is this place eerily reminding me of Firestriker's cave?* Izzy wondered, shuddering.

"Oh, that's because *I* am here, young one," a cold voice sounded behind them.

Immediately, they sprang into action. Lava and Ice spun around, and as a team, they tackled whoever had spoken until they were a pile of red-hot scales, shimmering, flickering pale blue scales, and... scraps of black fabric? Izzy suddenly had a terrifying flashback of seeing a black cloak in Kelsey's pile of items that the serpent had dropped. It had read *The Royal Cloak of Queen Opaque.*

"Quick! Help them!" Chloe shouted, grabbing her electric spear and racing into the pile. Her eyes were darting back and forth. "It looks like whoever's in that spooky hood is overwhelming them!" She was right. Izzy could slowly see the stranger overpowering Ice and Lava, gaining the upper hand as it did so.

Storm, Leaf, Jewel, and Whirlpool leaped into action. Storm jumped onto the creature and started slashing at its cloak. *Probably so we can see what it is,* Izzy thought. Taking a closer look, Izzy realized that the stranger was almost twice as big as the Withering Wings.

Ripping her eyes off the stranger and back onto the battle, she saw Whirlpool throw herself at the stranger, trying to claw it, but nothing seemed to happen. The stranger was *still* clawing at Ice and Lava, with much more success than Ice and Lava were having themselves.

Izzy felt her heart race. They could very possibly lose Lava and Ice to this stranger in a fight... but what about in a test of wits?

"Wait!" Izzy blurted. "Um, uh—" She hit herself internally. She couldn't scrape up the courage to give a public speech, so why had she decided to do this? "—I—I challenge you to a—a guessing contest."

Lava, Ice, Whirlpool, and Storm immediately stopped once they realized what she was attempting to do. *With probably a brutal punishment if I lose,* she thought sullenly. *Death.*

The stranger snarled. Well, Izzy couldn't actually *see* whatever it was snarl, but it sounded like it was snarling. And viciously, too. With not even a hint of mercy. *Okay, so the punishment will be death,* Izzy thought. "Such a weakling?" it growled. *Could it be a dragon?* Izzy wondered. "Fine. I will accept. Now... what are we guessing about?"

So the stranger is smart, Izzy noted. "We—we're going to guess on—on who the other—other creature is," she stammered. "But you c-can already s-see me, so y-you have to guess who—who the dragons are. I—I have to guess what you are, who you are, and from what line you are."

Izzy could practically feel the stranger considering that. Having to guess the names and types of six dragons? She wouldn't've done that, either.

"I'll do it," the stranger said at last. "But whoever wins gets to do whatever they want with the other."

Izzy took a deep breath and let it out. *Calm, calm, calm,* Izzy thought. "Okay," she said. "Let me list the rules. First person—I mean, *creature*—to guess the other's name, type, and line win. We each get twenty guesses. If none of us guess the other's things in that number of guesses, then we add ten and continue. It goes on like that. The judges will be...." She stopped at that thought. Who would judge fairly, but not cheat? "Angela," she said finally, gesturing to her friend, "and Whirlpool." Those two were a pair, so hopefully they would work together. "They will not cheat," she added, glaring at the two judges.

The stranger nodded slowly. "That makes sense," it said finally. "Let us begin before we dawdle."

"The black-cloaked creature will go first," Whirlpool announced. "Begin."

The stranger eyed Storm. "I believe that *she* is a *storm dragon*," the stranger hissed. "Her name is *Owl*."

Whirlpool nodded patiently. Next to her, Angela was looking like she'd seen a ghost, as pale as the moon. "She is a storm dragon," Whirlpool said. "But her name is not Owl. Please wait your next turn, stranger."

The stranger gave a little growl of frustration but didn't argue. *It shouldn't,* Izzy thought. *This is a game where nobody can cheat.*

"Um...." Suddenly, it occurred to her that the stranger *could* cheat. It could lie to them about what it really was. *But I'm not going to allow that,* Izzy thought with a rush of new strength and confidence. "I think you're a dragon," she announced.

The stranger hissed. "Yes, indeed... I am a dragon," it growled. "What kind of dragon am I? What is my name?" It turned to Whirlpool. "My turn." Whirlpool nodded. Angela opened her mouth to say something, froze, and closed her mouth again. The stranger looked at Storm again. "Your name is Storm," it hissed. Storm stood rigid, her eyes wide but her mouth firmly clamped closed.

"Correct," Whirlpool announced. "Stranger, you have eighteen guesses left. Izzy, you have nineteen. Now it's your turn."

Izzy gulped and said, "You're a... a...." *Think of something, Izzy!* her mind screamed, but her body didn't obey. For a second, it felt like she was trapped in a solid ice block, her body cold to a temperature that should've been extinct in anywhere but Antarctica. And then she was back on the ground again, the stone firm under her feet. "A fire dragon," she said at last.

The stranger made some sort of annoyed noise. "Correct," it huffed, sounding more annoyed than when it had made the noise. It turned towards Whirlpool. "My turn?"

"Yeah," Angela stammered. She looked barely conscious, so frozen from terror. *That's what happened to me,* Izzy realized. *I was frozen by fear.* She narrowed her eyes at the stranger. *Does that strange creature have some kind of scary power? Or is it just natural? Is she spooky naturally?* "It's—it's your turn, stranger."

"Eighteen turns for Izzy," Whirlpool added, shaking out her wings. *How can she keep her cool?* Izzy wondered.

"Very well," the stranger hissed, turning its eyes on Lava this time. Well, Izzy couldn't *see* the black-cloaked figure's eyes, but it certainly *felt* like that. "You are a fire dragon. You are named Lava."

Whirlpool looked slightly surprised. Izzy had no idea how she could keep it together, since she'd been a cheerful, carefree dragon before with a slightly crazy attitude. "Correct," she replied calmly. "Seventeen turns left for you. Izzy, your turn."

Izzy took a deep breath. *Name first, then line,* she told herself, trying to keep calm. The name, in fact, was going to be harder than which dragons the stranger was descended from. "Um... your name is... Flame?" she guessed. Flame was a common fire dragon name. If this dragon's name wasn't Flame, it was probably a much more important dragon, *or* it had a different common name. Izzy *really hoped* it was the last option, because she was thinking about a certain dragon that she and her friends had defeated in their last adventure.

"No," the stranger rumbled. Izzy had heard enough of its voice to determine that it was female, so she was going to call her a 'she' in her mind now instead of an 'it'. *That makes much more sense,* Izzy thought. "My name is *not* Flame."

"Thank you," Whirlpool said. "Seventeen turns left for you, Izzy. Your turn," she added, turning towards the stranger.

This time, the stranger looked at Whirlpool. "You are a water dragon," she hissed. "You are Whirl."

Whirlpool shook her head. "No, unfortunately," she replied. "You have sixteen turns left, stranger. Izzy, it's your turn."

Izzy sucked in a breath, hoping the air could somehow be infected with good luck. *Or at least hope,* she thought wryly. "Your name is Molten," she guessed.

"Nope," the cloaked figure answered, sounding pleased that Izzy failed once again. However, she didn't continue to gloat. *Maybe she feels too sorry for me to rub it in my face?* Izzy wondered. *Well, whatever it is, it's* probably *not pity....*

"Sixteen turns for you, Izzy," Whirlpool said. "Stranger, you have sixteen turns as well. Use this one wisely."

The stranger nodded, a feeling of confidence pulsing from her. "The water dragon's name is Waves," she announced.

"No," was all that Whirlpool said this time, although Izzy could still feel the stranger's confidence wavering. *Good,* she thought. "Fifteen turns left for you. Izzy, it's your turn."

Izzy thought hard. Flame and Molten were both *common* fire dragon names, and they were the only other common names that she knew other than Lava. Fire would be pointless, although Ice *was* an ice dragon, after all. But perhaps things worked differently with fire dragons.

That must mean that this dragon was no *ordinary* dragon. She must be a niece to a former queen, or possibly even a princess herself. However, a *queen* wouldn't live at the bottom of a cave, so that option was scratched out.

What was a princess or niece-to-queen name? There was Queen Opaque... Izzy hadn't read about any other queens of fire dragons before, so she had no idea what they were like. But judging by the meaning of 'opaque,' she could guess that they were all brutal... and there were probably multiple executions in their kingdoms each day.

Maybe Black? Or Scorch? Or Talon? Wait a second... but didn't princesses have the right to have *two* words in their name instead of one? So it would it be Blackfire, or Scorchmark, or Talonclaw instead? She had no idea. *I should've done my homework on fire dragons' queens,* she thought dryly. Not that that was going to help her out of this mess.

"Um... is your name... uh... Scorchwing?" she guessed quickly. It probably wasn't the best name, but—

Her mind exploded when the stranger growled, "Yes."

The Serpent of Tears

It felt like her head was spinning. "But—but—how is that *possible?*" she cried. "There are *millions* of different, unique fire dragon names out there"—she caught Lava's eye and the fire dragon nodded, agreeing—"and I managed to guess what yours *is?*" It was like her mind was a volcano, and the volcano just erupted and blew her mind to bits.

The stranger growled, and Izzy thought she saw her scales *ripple* for a moment, then slide back into place. "Yes, you did," she hissed. "I never thought someone would guess that." Then her scales rippled again. It was like a nightmare and the worst fear combined, freezing Izzy in a way that she didn't understand. *Scales rippling can make someone freeze in fear?* she thought, confused.

Whirlpool looked confused, too, but she managed to say, "Fifteen turns left for Izzy. Scorchwing—" Izzy thought that she saw that Scorchwing was about to say something, but no sound came from the cloaked figure "—you have fifteen turns as well. Your turn."

Scorchwing looked at Whirlpool, as if trying to read the water dragon's expression. "Your name is Whirlpool," Scorchwing hissed.

"Correct," Whirlpool replied. "Fourteen turns left for you. Izzy, your turn."

Izzy thought carefully. *Is she lost royalty?* Izzy wondered. *It's very possible... wait....* She was starting to connect the dots. Firestriker had two words in her name. 'Fire' and 'striker'. Did that mean she was...?

A Battle With A Princess

Izzy shook her head. *No time to think about that,* she told herself. *Focus on Scorchwing.* There were a few lines of royal ancestry that Scorchwing could possibly be part of. *There's Queen Robinmark, King Magmaflow... wait a second. That... that cloak... could it be a clue? That was Queen Opaque's cloak. But Queen Opaque isn't alive anymore. I've got it!*

"You're a daughter of Queen Opaque," Izzy announced.

Scorchwing took off her cloak, revealing a dragon slightly larger than Firestriker, but with the same magenta scales and gold eyes. Izzy was so shocked that she stared straight into those eyes, but luckily, they didn't hypnotize her like they'd done with Andy last time. Her wings were extremely large, about as big as Ice each. A pearl necklace with a large ruby on it hung from her neck, and a bracelet with the same pattern as the necklace adorned each leg and horn.

She looks mean. And bossy. And rude, Izzy thought.

"Correct," Scorchwing growled. "And that's *Princess* Scorchwing to you."

Izzy gulped, slapping her hand over her mouth. "Wha—how—" This dragon just kept amazing her more and more.

"I can read minds," Princess Scorchwing hissed. "I was *pretending* to not know your names... but of course I already know." *So, she's smart,* Izzy thought, feeling terrified. *Note that. Wait. Haven't I already noted that?*

"What do you want with us?" Chloe asked bravely. "We're going to fight you if that's what it takes."

"Oh, I don't want to fight you," Princess Scorchwing hissed. Her eyes flickered from Chloe to the six Withering Wings. "I want your *alliance.*"

Chloe was silent. Izzy could feel that everything around her—even the air—was calculating whether or not Princess Scorchwing was setting a trap for them or not. *Could she?* Izzy wondered. She skimmed her eyes over the fire dragon princess, trying to figure out their odds of beating this dragon in a fight. *Twelve against one... but then again, we're more inexperienced than Scorchwing.* She absolutely refused to call Scorchwing 'Princess' except for in her face.

The fire dragon had scratches all over her body. There was a claw mark on her left back leg that went from the bottom of her foot to the dragon's waist, a scar on her face that went from her right horn to her left cheek, and burn marks where fire had scorched both her wings. *That's probably how she got her name,* Izzy thought wryly.

"No," Chloe finally said. "We're not going to be your allies."

Scorchwing didn't appear shocked, but steam rose from her scales. "How dare you say that?" the princess of the fire dragons hissed. "I have been underground for so long that no one of my kingdom recognizes or remembers me anymore. I want to win back my kingdom, but how can I do that with no army, or even any allies? Three of my sisters are dead, and the other two are not agreeable in the slightest."

"Well?" Chloe retorted. "We're not going to join you. You're related to Queen Opaque. We're not going to help a relative of *her* win the fire dragons' kingdom."

Princess Scorchwing growled at Chloe, steam rising from her magenta scales, and turned back towards Whirlpool and Angela. "Then I will fight you," was all she said before she charged at the pair.

Storm leaped at Princess Scorchwing before she reached Whirlpool, but that barely stopped her. Scorchwing flipped Storm over, thumped her on the rocky ground, and left her lying on the floor like it was nothing. She reached Whirlpool and began slashing at the water dragon, ignoring Whirlpool's shrieks of outrage and screams of pain.

"Get her!" Chloe yelled, brandishing her electric spear and charging at Princess Scorchwing. Chloe bravely jumped (*trying to get onto Scorchwing's back,* Izzy thought) in the air, but Scorchwing probably read her mind and intercepted her, slashing her talons across the hoodie that she was wearing. Chloe yelped in surprise and fell back.

Angela grabbed one of her Starstruck Arrows and stabbed Scorchwing in the neck far too fast for the dragon to intercept her movements. Scorchwing emitted a low growl of pain, spinning around to kick Angela. Angela shrieked and fell back. *How dare Scorchwing do that?*

Izzy grabbed a few of Angela's Starstruck Arrows and began firing arrows at Scorchwing, making sure that each arrow hit the wound Angela had made in the dragon's neck. Scorchwing didn't exactly howl in pain each time one of the arrows hit its mark, but Izzy did see her wince.

Whirlpool and Storm jumped on Scorchwing and started clawing and scratching her, urging the other dragons to join in while they did. Leaf, Lava, Ice, and Jewel all slashed at Scorchwing, using different techniques. Izzy saw

Whirlpool and Storm fighting in close combat with the princess while Leaf and Jewel hung back, circling Scorchwing. Ice and Lava were hovering just out of reach above Scorchwing's head, ready to head into action if that was needed.

Sara was furiously reading a book on the floor, but Izzy didn't see how that was going to help. *Oh well,* she thought. *Maybe that book has some kind of information that can help us defeat Scorchwing?*

Andrew fished something out of his bottomless bag and held it up proudly. Izzy stared at it. It was a *boomerang*. "Hey, Andrew, how is that going to help?" Izzy called over to her brother.

The boy grinned back. "You'll see," was all he said before he threw the boomerang at Scorchwing. "Stand back!"

Whirlpool and Storm quickly backed away from the boomerang as it came in contact with Scorchwing. At first, it didn't seem to do anything, and Izzy wanted to straight-up slap that gleeful smile off Scorchwing's face.

Then it exploded.

It was a pretty small explosion, but it enveloped Scorchwing's face and a quarter of her body in smoke. Izzy could hear Scorchwing roaring in pain (and also, to be honest, some insults at the lifeless boomerang). The boomerang was lying on the floor, looking undented and like it had gone through a beautification appointment instead of a minor explosion, which Izzy was pretty confused about.

Scorchwing screamed and the smoke disappeared, blown away by her powerful breath. Izzy finally got to see what Scorchwing looked like after the boomerang, but it wasn't pretty.

First of all, the lower part of the dragon princess's face was burned and black, but the upper part was only scorched, making it look *super* weird. Scorchwing also had new fire marks on both her wings, which made them look less menacing and more... *run-over*. Her stomach was also charred, making her look like a half-black dragon along with her wings and face.

"Um...." That was all she could think of. The only word that described Scorchwing's new appearance. It was 'um'. Literally. She turned towards Andrew. "Where'd you find that?" she asked.

Her brother rolled his eyes. "Duh. In the weird pile of stuff after we killed the giant serpent," he answered sarcastically, although Izzy didn't get which part of his sentence was sarcastic. *Am I not getting anything anymore?* she wondered.

"Oh," Chloe said, dusting off her hoodie. "Well, that explains that, I guess."

"Have you forgotten about me?" Scorchwing snarled, flapping her wings menacingly. "I will kill you. *After* I leave, of course." She started towards the brighter, more friendly-looking tunnel, looked back at the group, and then hurried in the tunnel in a hustled run.

"What a coward," Lava muttered, stretching her wings. "She didn't even stay here for a proper fight."

Izzy shrugged. *I'm just glad that's over,* she thought. "Well, if it excites you, I'm sure that's not the last time we'll be seeing her," Izzy said helpfully.

Lava paced around the cavern, but she didn't respond.

"We're still trying to find that water serpent, right?" Angela asked. "Just checking."

"Yeah, we are," Chloe replied. "The water serpent probably has all the answers we need, including the answer to the weird writing we found in Angela's notebook."

The prophecy, Izzy thought.

The dawn can bring up the hottest fire,

With their power they grow higher,

But with only those tears can they make,

The following words: the largest lake.

"When are we going to continue?" Lava asked impatiently. "I want to properly fight something. And this time *without* a guessing game," she added, casting an annoyed glance at Izzy, which made her feel bad. *Did I slow the group down?* she wondered, trying to replay the entire scene in her mind again, except with an old-fashioned group fight instead of a guess-your-name game.

"Okay, fine." Chloe sighed. "Come on, guys. Let's go!"

A Lonely Prisoner

After a few minutes of spirited debating (Whirlpool almost drowned Andrew in a crazy wave), the group decided to go the way that Scorchwing *didn't* go through. This way, they'd thought, would give them less of a chance of having a run-in with the fire dragon princess if she backtracked her steps.

As they entered the tunnel, Izzy saw the surprising lushness of the corridor for the first time.

Thick, green vines sprouted from walls in the ceiling, some of them dangling just above their heads. Tiny brown mushrooms appeared from cracks in the ground, angling their tops to the ceiling, their stems a perfect, straight line. Flowers in the colorful shades of orange, pink, and cyan crept down the vines and decorated the thick, branchlike plants. Light streamed from the same crevices the vines appeared from.

"This place is beautiful," Angela whispered.

Izzy had to agree with her. The light lit up the flowers just like a sun, and it reflected off the smooth, shiny rock walls of the tunnel. Izzy expected that the plants would disappear the further they went in the passageway, but instead, there seemed to be more and more instead of less and less.

"Something about this place creeps me out, though," Andrew muttered.

Izzy had to agree with *that* comment, too. Even though it was beautiful, there was the sensation that they were being watched... *closely*. Izzy didn't know *how* or *why* she felt that, because in the smooth, unbroken walls, there was absolutely no place for something—or someone—to watch them... except maybe for a beetle or two.

Soon, they came to a small cavern. *With a dragon sitting on a boulder.*

"Hello," the dragon said as they entered the cave.

Cautiously, Chloe replied, "Hello to you, too."

Izzy studied the dragon. He seemed to be an earth dragon, like Leaf, with splotches of dark green over bright, lime-colored scales. His eyes were solemn and brown, but not cold or selfish. It was like he'd been lonely for a long time, but never had he been pushed by evil or any sort of badness.

"Who are you?" Sara asked, stepping forward bravely. She eyed the dragon warily.

"I'm Reed," he replied, standing up with a sigh. "Let me tell you my story."

Before any of the girls (or Andrew) could protest, he began. "A long time ago—oh, how long ago it was—I was a young dragon, spirited and carefree. I lived in the kingdom of the earth dragons, but one day, we were attacked by a group of ice dragons."

Here, Ice looked a little bit guilty, as if she knew that her ancestors or friends had been part of that, and she'd done nothing to stop them.

"I was carried off as a prisoner while trying to fight for justice.... I only killed a couple of ice dragon soldiers. The only thing I knew of my kingdom after that was that the ice dragons had killed our leader." His shoulders slumped, his eyes flicking to the ground, and Izzy felt a pang of sympathy for him. *Be alert,* she warned herself, catching her kind emotions. *He's still a stranger, even if he got attacked by ice dragons.*

"I was taken to the ice dragons' dungeon, where they kept all their prisoners. There, a friendly fire dragon helped me escape, but I never saw him again." His shoulders slumped even more. "I met Princess Scorchwing, and she offered me sanctuary in exchange of my exploring this cave system and marking it down on a map. The ice dragons were tracking me rapidly, even in the caves, and I was desperate, so I accepted." He paused for a moment.

"Was that a good idea?" Chloe asked, frowning. All of her care had apparently evaporated into politely mild suspicion.

"No," the dragon replied, sighing. "She sent me into the caverns to fend for myself—without any food or water, in fact. I wouldn't've made that a deal if I'd known what trouble I'd get into."

He paused, then continued. "I explored the caves and mapped out the area, like my part of the deal asked. But she betrayed me." His expression grew hateful and angry. Instead of untouched eyes, his orbs flickered from red to brown in a mad manner. "While I was drawing the map, she somehow contacted the kingdom of the ice dragons and told them that I was here. They made a deal. She would imprison me here, and they could come in occasionally to check on me."

"Why can't you get out?" Izzy wondered aloud, eyeing the lush tunnel. She couldn't believe that something so pretty could be the lock to a prison. *Sometimes things aren't what they seem,* she reminded herself.

"Scorchwing put a magic spell on me that created an invisible barrier between me and the world, but other creatures aren't affected by it. The only reason I've survived down here is because of the plants within reach."

"How?" Angela asked, looking curious.

"The berries and small fruits that grow on the vines are edible and non-poisonous, so I can eat them without getting sick," he replied, sighing. "But it just angers me even more. She's keeping me alive deliberately, and I know it. I'd love to rip her throat out." His gleaming silver claws shimmered in the light that the cracks provided.

An image of Reed choking Scorchwing to death appeared in her mind. Izzy forced herself not to gag, instead swallowing so violently that she choked on her saliva.

"So, what do we do now?" Chloe asked, looking straight at Reed. Luckily, the anger had faded from his now once-again lonely brown eyes. *But why did they turn red?* Izzy wondered. *That's a little creepy, not to mention something a bad guy would do....*

"What are you looking for?" Reed returned, curling his thick tail around himself. "I'm not making a deal without knowing if I can trust you."

Chloe frowned, tapping her chin. "If I tell you, will you help us?" she asked slowly.

"That depends," Reed replied, "if it requires me to risk my life."

Chloe took a deep breath. "We're looking for a water serpent down here."

Reed's eyes brightened. "Oh, yes! I know all about that. In exchange for the information, you have to free me. Then I'll tell you."

Chloe frowned. "But how do we know that you'll stick to your side of the promise and not attack us as soon as we break the spell?" she asked. "Plus, we can easily kill you right now."

Reed's eyes twinkled. "I guess so," he replied, pretending to sigh in defeat. "Fine, I'll tell you."

"Get on with it," Lava growled impatiently. Chloe's dragon had started to pace around... *for the* millionth *time today,* Izzy thought, amused.

Reed narrowed his eyes at Lava. "I was *getting* to it," he huffed. "Be *patient*. Anyways, as I was saying, the way to the water serpent is through the other tunnel. You'll reach a place in the path with a boulder in front of you. The boulder's supposed to stop you."

He paused for a moment, his eyes a long way away. "But the trick is to say the words 'ice dragon cannonballs,' and then it'll disappear. Then, you'll come to a fork. For extra caution, the serpents move the water serpent regularly, but they have a way of tracking it. Say the words 'Light will glow, sun will shine,' and a sparkly path should appear under your feet. It'll grow towards the way the serpent was taken."

"How does a path that glows *grow?*" Izzy wondered.

"Magic," Reed answered.

"*Get on with it!*" Lava suddenly shouted.

Reed rolled his eyes but complied. "So you need to go down that passageway, and the serpent you're looking for should be chained down at the end in a *really* big cave. I don't know how to free him, so that's up to you."

"Thanks," Chloe replied, turning to go out and find the serpent.

"Wait, wait! You didn't free me yet!" Reed reminded her, his eyes promising death if they betrayed him.

"Oh, yeah. Sorry," Chloe said, looking embarrassed. "Do you have any idea of how to free yourself?"

"Yes," Reed replied, sighing. "Someone has to climb up there." He pointed to a large crack in the ceiling of the cavern where a small vine was crawling through. "I would do it myself, but Scorchwing enchanted it with a barrier spell so that I can't get past it."

"So we have to break *that* spell, too?" Angela asked, sounding exhausted.

"Yes, but it should be a piece of cake," Reed answered. "Smaller spells take less energy, and since Scorchwing didn't want to waste any of hers, she made the smaller one weaker, but I *still* can't get past it." He sighed a sigh of defeat, this time for real. "I've tried for a week, but the spell doesn't seem to get weaker. In fact, it seems to get stronger."

"How is that possible?" Izzy asked. *This is definitely magic, not physics,* she noted.

"I don't know. But I *do* know how the spell is made. One of you needs to climb up the hole and pull out the shimmering vine up there. That will break the spell," Reed explained. "But there's a guardian beetle."

Izzy nearly fell over laughing. "A guardian *beetle*?" she sputtered. "Can a beetle even fight?"

Reed's dark brown eyes glinted. "Oh, it's no ordinary beetle," he replied. "It can shoot lasers out of its eyes. Its shell is nearly indestructible. Its bite is three times as toxic as a poison serpent's. It is extremely deadly."

Izzy shuddered, quickly rethinking her opinion of this beetle. "That sounds scary," she mumbled, shivering. "I've got the chills."

"So do I," Sara said, eyeing Reed suspiciously. *How is she still suspicious?* Izzy wondered. *He made a deal with us, gave us direction to the water serpent, and is telling us how to free him....*

"Once you defeat the beetle, a red glow will appear. It will then break the barrier. If you capture the red glow in a bottle, however, I will be trapped forever, so be careful with it."

"Sounds hard," Angela muttered, her gaze locked to the floor. "Tell me, why did we have to do this in the first place?"

"I gave you the information, and in exchange, you will free me from this cavern," Reed reminded her firmly.

"I hate bugs," Angela mumbled. "*I. Hate. Bugs.*"

"I know," Chloe said sympathetically. "But we all have to face what we are terrified of *some*time in our lives."

Angela's head snapped up. "*I'm not terrified of beetles!*" she shouted. Chloe stumbled back, looking dazed.

"S-sorry," Chloe spluttered. "I-I didn't know you were pretty sensitive about that."

"No problem," Angela grumbled, adjusting her quiver full of Starstruck Arrows.

"Let's get going," Lava announced.

"Right," Chloe said. "So how do we get up there in the first place? Reed?"

"There's a long vine over there," he explained, pointing, with a talon, to a thick vine that snaked upwards from the bottom of the cavern to the hole that the shimmery vine was supposedly in. "Climb up it, and you'll reach the hole. Then you can climb up a different vine." He paused. "Why do I feel like I'm forgetting something? Ah, I remember now. You also need the shimmery vine to obtain the glow. Place the vine on top of the beetle, and *then* the red glow will appear. But the beetle has to be dead," he added hastily.

Chloe frowned, her face a mask of concentration. "Okay. We got this. Let's go," she said confidently, without a single waver in her voice.

Betrayal

Chloe went first, naturally, and began to ascend the vine. She grabbed a smaller, thicker vine and used that as a handhold as she boosted her feet up onto to two symmetrical vines that were strong enough to support them. She slowly, but surely, climbed up the vine, and made it to the top. She pushed herself onto a rocky ledge that was just big enough for her feet, and for a moment, it seemed like she would fall straight onto Reed's head.

"Don't fall, don't fall, *don't fall*," Izzy muttered to herself.

Luckily, Chloe got the momentum to heave herself onto the ledge, and everybody breathed a sigh of relief—except for Reed. In fact, he was full-out *frowning*.

Why? Izzy wondered. *Is he expecting us to fail? But why? Doesn't he want to get out of his prison? Hm... this is very interesting.*

"Sara, you come up next!" Chloe called. They couldn't see her, but her voice echoed in the dark chamber.

"Okay," Sara answered. She began climbing up the thick, sturdy vine, making sure to put her foot exactly where Chloe had and putting her hand exactly where Chloe had.

Up ahead, Chloe directed her. "Put your hand on the vine that's in front of you! Good! Okay, now put your foot on the one next to your other foot—yeah, that's it... okay, good...."

Carefully, Sara made her way up to the snaking vine. Suddenly, a thick vine that was underneath her right foot snapped in two, and she looked like she was about to fall!

"Ack!" Sara yelped in shock before collecting herself and adjusting her posture so that her foot was safely on a different branch of the vine. "I wonder how that happened."

Yeah, me too, Izzy thought privately. *That vine was too sturdy-looking to break, so somebody must've deliberately broken it....* Her gaze landed on Reed. The earth dragon was staring hard at the vines underneath Sara, his face scrunched up in concentration. *He could be planning to break another vine, or he could be holding her up,* Izzy realized. *There's really no way to tell for sure.*

Soon, Sara reached the top. "Where should I go?" they heard her ask Chloe.

"Stand on that ledge over there, by my hand," Chloe's voice answered. "Yeah, that one—okay, next! Kelsey, you go."

"Okay!" Kelsey shouted enthusiastically, jogging over to the vine. She scaled up the vine safely, without any problems, and this time, Izzy noticed that Reed's expression and posture was *relaxed,* not stony. *Very interesting. Note that,* Izzy told herself.

They heard the footsteps of Kelsey's feet echo on the rocky ledges where Chloe and Sara were perched, guiding her to a safe area. "Put your foot on that rock—no, not *that* one! Okay, yeah, that one. Good. Okay, n—"

She was interrupted when Reed suddenly drew himself up and lunged at Izzy, his face twisting horribly into a mask of evil glee. He spread his wings as he did so, and the brightness of the world was abruptly extinguished by a malicious tarp of green scales. His silver claws flashed, his teeth gleamed, his paws thumped across the stone floor.

"Wha—*what's happening?*" Izzy screamed, too shocked and confused and *scared* to do anything.

"You are foolish to believe my light lies," he hissed. "Now, those will be the last spoken words you will ever hear."

He slashed at the girl, but Leaf was quicker. Leaping in front of her friend, she courageously took the swipes that were meant for Izzy. The injured earth dragon fell to the ground, moaning in pain.

"Leaf!" Izzy cried, frozen in terror as she stared down at the dragon, horrified. "*ANGELA! What's happening?!*"

"What's going on down there?" Chloe's voice echoed from the top of the chamber. "Don't worry, we're coming!" Izzy heard footsteps climbing down narrow rock ledges.

Angela grabbed a handful of Starstruck Arrows and sprinted towards Reed, holding the tips out towards the earth dragon. "You regret that!" she shouted bravely, stabbing him first in the side, then in his neck, all before he knew what was happening.

Once the shock left him, though, he was dangerous.

Howling and screaming, he tore at Angela, racing after her as she jumped over rocks, dodged hanging vines, and ducked under stalactites. "Be careful!" Izzy yelped, her mind filled with fear for her friend.

The Serpent of Tears

"Don't worry, I'm—" Angela was cut off abruptly when she tripped over a rock and Reed caught her.

His evil smile was so smug that Izzy felt encouraged enough to stomp over and slap him in the face. Which she did.

"Ow!" he cried, letting go of Angela, who immediately ran as fast her legs would take her to Sara, Kelsey, and Chloe, who had arrived at the bottom.

"Give up now, dragon," Lava hissed, her fire-colored eyes dark and full of menace, "and we won't kill you. Promise that you will ally with us, and we won't claw your face out and stuff it to put in my room."

Izzy wanted to say that Lava didn't *have* her own room, but her mind was inundated with images of Lava tearing out Reed's face. *Ew, ew, ew,* she thought, revolted.

"Fine," Reed sighed, making sure to glare angrily at each of them. "I'm surrounded anyways."

It was true. Lava, Ice, Jewel, and Storm had made a half circle around Reed, who was backed up against a wall. Whirlpool was tending to Leaf, who was still lying on the rocky ground. Andrew was also with his dragon, pointing the Slicer and the exploding boomerang at Reed. Max hovered above Reed, just out of the earth dragon's reach.

"Good choice," Lava snarled.

Chloe marched over and pointed the head of her electric spear at Reed's face. "Why did you do this?" she demanded. "Tell me, or I'll cut your head off."

Izzy stuck her tongue out in disgust and looked away to prevent the image of Chloe cutting Reed's head off from piercing her mind.

"Scorchwing told me to," Reed explained. "Her plan was to pretend like I was trapped, make up a ridiculous way that would free me and also get rid of some of you, and then I would attack and kill everyone." He glared at the six dragons, Whirlpool and Leaf included. "Looks like she didn't tell me that half of the group was made up of dragons."

"Your fault—or Scorchwing's," Chloe huffed, "not ours. You'll help us navigate these tunnels and help us free the water serpent… or we'll kill you."

On cue, everyone who had a weapon brandished it.

"Fine," Reed grumbled, who didn't really seem *fine* with this particular change of plans. "It's not like I have a choice. Lead on."

Blue Spark

They'd been traveling for a few minutes, enjoying the silence that rested upon their shoulders. Lava, Ice, and Storm surrounded Reed, making sure he wouldn't escape if he decided to bolt for some reason. Whirlpool was letting Leaf lean on her, because when Reed has slashed at the earth dragon, it had made her temporarily lame in her two left legs.

Near Reed, Sara was traveling next to Ice; Angela was walking beside Whirlpool a few feet away from Sara; a foot away from Angela, Kelsey was with Jewel (who was *still* looking for jewels hidden in the walls, floor, and ceiling); Izzy was near Angela and Whirlpool; and Chloe was right next to Izzy. This way, they could pass information on which way to go easily without running back and forth.

Andrew stood faithfully beside his dragon, Storm, guarding Reed with the tip of the Slicer pointed at his neck at all times. (Reed's neck, obviously, not Andrew's neck. Otherwise, that would be absurd.)

They were at the boulder that Reed had told them about, but after determining that all the information he gave them was real, they proceeded to say 'ice dragon cannonballs,' and the boulder magically disappeared. At the fork in the path, they said 'light will glow, sun will shine,' and a shiny magenta trail sparkled into reality under Chloe's feet, moving towards the left-sided tunnel.

The Serpent of Tears

They followed the path until it faded away and then looked up. In front of them was the water serpent they were looking for.

Izzy's first thought was *He looks terrible.* Thick, heavy chains were wrapped around his neck and tail, binding him to the floor with their weight. Unlike the dark green scales that the devil serpents had, this water serpent had deep blue scales that matched the water in the depths of the ocean. His eyes were a unique, magnificent sea-green, clouded with sadness. The water serpent was lying on the ground and seemed to be in pain, and now Izzy was close enough to see why.

Somebody had clawed the water serpent repeatedly until wound marks covered his scales. The fight obviously hadn't been fair because the serpent was chained to the ground; he couldn't fight back easily. The wounds were slash marks that were narrow, caused by long, thin claws. *Definitely the work of a dragon,* Izzy thought. *Scorchwing, by the looks of things. Has she allied with the devil serpents? They're both evil, I guess, so it makes sense....*

The serpent tiredly, and seemingly with as much effort as he could muster, raised his head. Slash-mark wounds were above his eyes, angled slightly downwards, so it looked like he was mad, even though Izzy knew that serpents didn't have eyebrows to express any type of feeling. She wanted to laugh, but she couldn't. *Keeping a prisoner like this is as evil as making a creature unable to eat or drink,* Izzy thought, angered as she had the thought.

"Who are you?" the serpent asked, no strength in his voice. The only thing that Izzy could detect in it was weariness that came from being scarred repeatedly. *He's in too much pain to even fight back,* she realized, sympathy welling up inside of her.

"I'm Chloe, and these are my friends," Chloe said, walking forward and gesturing towards Angela, Sara, Izzy, Kelsey, Andrew, Reed, and the six dragons. "Who are *you?*"

"I was once a normal water serpent, like all the others," the water serpent began, seeming to be revived as he talked. "But my water breath was special. The water sparkled like sunshine was reflecting upon it, even though we lived in underground caves. In fact, *every* kind of water that I produced was bright and glittery, but the most outstanding were my tears. They sparkled like diamonds themselves."

A hungry gleam burned to life in Jewel's eyes.

"Scorchwing told me about a prophecy or something that required a certain creature's tears.... I never thought I would be the one that provided it. She even scratched the prophecy out on the walls so it would forever haunt me." The water serpent sighed.

"What's your name?" Chloe asked, her voice now empty of cautiousness and full of curiosity.

The water serpent blinked, like he didn't expect Chloe to ask that question. "Blue Spark," he replied.

"Where's the supposed 'prophecy' that Scorchwing scratched out?"

"Over there," Blue Spark answered, flicking his tail at the wall behind him. *Maybe that's the serpent equivalent of pointing?* Izzy wondered.

"Come on," Chloe told the group, hurrying over to the marks that Scorchwing had crudely scratched out.

They all saw the letters at the same time, and there it was.

The dawn can bring up the hottest fire,

With their power they grow higher,

But with only those tears can they make,

The following words: the largest lake.

But that wasn't all of it. There was more:

Twelve must travel deep underground,

Escape the fire that continues to hound,

The reed, after a betrayal, can make a choice:

Ally with fire, or with his own voice?

Twelve must stop the powerful three sisters,

One will join three who have before missed her.

The sisters have power; they can fight,

But they follow darkness, not true light.

Twelve must battle armies of fire,

To reach the destiny they desire.

If they don't, the world will be doomed,

Dark, light, all consumed.

After reading the prophecy, Izzy shuddered. "Sounds scary," she mused.

"It must be," Chloe agreed. "And is there any doubt that the twelve are us? And that the reed is Reed?"

"No," Angela said.

"And do you think that it's weird that the prophecy uses *missed her* as a rhyme for *sisters?*" Chloe asked, frowning deeply.

"Yes!" Kelsey shouted enthusiastically.

Izzy rolled her eyes.

"But what are the three sisters?" Chloe asked, frowning *again* in concentration.

Izzy rolled her eyes *again*. "Isn't it obvious?" she complained. "It's *Scorchwing* and her *other two sisters that aren't dead!* How are you guys so slow?"

Chloe huffed at the insult and grumbled, "How do you know there's only three of Queen Opaque's six daughters left?"

"Scorchwing said that two of her sisters died," Izzy reminded her. "That means four left. And I just realized that Firestriker, the dragon that we killed last time, must've been one of Queen Opaque's daughters, too. She had the same magenta scales and gold eyes. In fact, almost *everything* about her was the same with Scorchwing, except that she could hypnotize creatures that looked her in the eye, and Scorchwing can read minds. Then that's three sisters left."

"This is like a math problem," Sara commented.

Leaf suddenly spoke up. "But how can we, six people and six dragons, defeat three daughters of the fire dragons' most powerful queen in history?"

"I don't know," Izzy replied fiercely, "but we're going to do it, no doubt. Reed?"

The earth dragon looked triple-shy. "I—I was considering on joining your side, actually," he confessed.

Chloe looked confused. "Wait. But didn't you already ally with us back in the cavern?"

Reed's eyes glinted. "I *pretended* to. Scorchwing expected that, and she told me that you wouldn't trap me properly, so I should attack when you least expected it, after you thought I was on your side. Luckily, it's up to me now." He paused. "The prophecy said I could choose my own choice, not Scorchwing's."

Angela narrowed her eyes. "How do we know that you're not lying to us right now?" she asked suspiciously.

"I don't know," Reed replied simply. "I guess you're just going to have to trust me."

I don't know about that, earth dragon, Izzy thought.

"Well, let's move on to another topic," Chloe continued hurriedly. "Let's free Blue Spark. We all agree on that, right?"

"Yeah," Lava grumbled, rolling her amber eyes.

Lava used her heat to melt the chains, Jewel moved the chains to Ice, who froze them, then passed them back to Jewel, who gave them to Whirlpool, who washed them to make sure they were bright and shiny (Izzy didn't actually know if that was required for a block of ice with chains in them, but they didn't want Whirlpool to feel left out), then gave them to Leaf, who stacked them as a careful, sturdy ice pyramid.

In no time, all the chains were gone from Blue Spark, and they had transformed into a magnificent ice pyramid that had six blocks for the base, five blocks on the level above that, four blocks on the third level, and so on. There were fifteen blocks in total.

Blue Spark stretched his scaly body. "Thanks," he said, grinning for the first time. *Or what's the equivalent of serpent grinning,* Izzy thought, feeling a little creeped out. His eyes shimmered with relief. "I've been in there for... wow, I even lost track, since there's no sun or moon down here. When are we going back up to the surface?"

Chloe looked at the wall, her face masked in concentration. "I don't know," was the answer she finally came up with. "Our quest was to find the serpent that made the special tears—*you*—and rescue him, but obviously, the prophecy isn't done with us yet."

The serpent took a closer look at the scratched words. "You must be the twelve," he mused. "Free the serpent...." He paused for a moment. "It doesn't look like to *me* that you have a clear part of the prophecy to fulfill this time. It does say *'Twelve must battle armies of fire'*, but it doesn't really say specific armies and a landmark. I think the last two verses have nothing to do with this mission."

Izzy frowned, tapping her chin in concentration. *This serpent is smarter than we think,* she thought. *And he's right. The reed is definitely Reed, and he chose his own voice. The 'fire' that the prophecy speaks about, though...what did we escape from down here? Serpents? That doesn't make sense....* Suddenly, her brain connected the dots, and she got the answer.

"The three sisters!" she shouted, blasting everybody's eardrums slightly.

Angela shook her head in confusion (and to probably shake the piercing sound out of her ears). "Wait, wait. Back up a little there. The three *what?*"

"The fire that's mentioned in the prophecy must be the three remaining daughters of Queen Opaque," Izzy explained excitedly. "It makes sense, because we *escaped* Scorchwing, and she's one of the daughters! Although she really just ran away...."

"I still think she's a coward," Lava muttered under her breath. Izzy didn't know if Lava meant for anyone to hear it, but it looked like everybody did.

"Good job, Izzy," Chloe congratulated, clapping her hands. "Another piece of the puzzle has been solved."

"That doesn't make sense," Jewel observed, her eyes flickering around the cavern.

"It's a *metaphor*," Chloe snapped. "Metaphors *always* makes sense."

"That's not true," Jewel grumbled, but it wasn't loud enough for Chloe to hear it, or she just ignored it.

"I think this quest is over," Chloe said. "We've done what we set out for."

"But what about the serpents?" Angela asked worriedly. "Will they continue to attack builders that wander in the ravine?"

"No." This time it was Reed who spoke up. "Scorchwing told me her next move, which was not very smart. If her plan failed, she'd retreat with the serpents, who have allied with her. Her plan all along was to get the serpents to lure you into the cave system, where she would destroy you. I was just part of a backup plan."

"So we're really done then," Andrew gasped. He sounded like he thought this time would never come. *Very funny,* Izzy thought dryly. "Are we ready to get back up to the surface?"

"We are," Chloe confirmed, sighing. She glanced at Reed. "And *you're* coming with us."

Without another word, they began the long ascent back up to the surface, where the prophecy would still haunt them... just like it had once haunted Blue Spark.

The Land of Flowers

The Land of Flowers

The three remaining daughters of Queen Opaque are out in the world, causing danger and destruction wherever they went. Twelve, from the prophecy, must stop them and the evil they bring.

And those twelve are Izzy and her friends.

A Mysterious Message

"I'm bored," Lava complained, flipping through a book titled *The Top Ten Most Dangerous Volcanos*.

"Stop it," Chloe snapped. "Gaining knowledge is as powerful as taking real action."

Izzy, Leaf, Lava, and Chloe were at one of the town libraries, searching through books that they hoped would shed even a *little* bit of light on the prophecy and the three sisters. Angela, Whirlpool, Sara, Ice, Kelsey, and Jewel were scattered around town, checking the other two libraries for valuable information. So far, they had no luck.

Andrew and Storm were exploring the ravine with the builders, looking for precious gems that could benefit the village. Jewel had complained when she found out that Storm was going instead of her. Kelsey had told her to be quiet.

Leaf flipped to the next page of the book she was reading, *A Guide to Species of Fire*, pausing to say, "Yeah, sure."

Izzy shook her head and continued reading the book that she was currently cruising through. It was about the line of royal fire dragons, and she hoped that it was up to date. Her goal was to find any mention of Queen Opaque's daughters, or even Queen Opaque herself.

The book said that King Firestone, Queen Opaque's father, had been a fantastic ruler, and explained all his royal achievements and major life events. *Yeah, I don't care about that,* Izzy thought, feeling annoyed. *Books can't magically appear with the information we need,* she reminded herself.

Then she blinked. Something was wrong with her reading environment. It was... it was a *noise*. A tinkling noise, like the gentle notes of a fairy's bell or a piano—a noise like the prettiest music, quiet and solemn yet happy and content. Appearing along with it, the smell of fresh lavender bloomed in the library, and Izzy coughed in surprise. Chloe seemed confused, too, and Leaf and Lava looked like they were about to throw up any minute.

Probably because the lavender is too *sweet,* she concluded.

The window closest to them magically opened. With a burst of teal sparkles, a scroll neatly tied with a red ribbon drifted through the opening, flying right through the air, and landed on the table. Izzy stared at it, her mind unable to comprehend what just happened.

The window closed.

Leaf was the first one to speak. "Wha—what just happened?"

"I'm not sure," Chloe replied, shaking her head clear of shock. "Should we read it? Or is it a trap sent by one of the sisters?"

Izzy frowned, recalling the pretty music and the colorful sparkles. *Scorchwing and the other sisters would probably aim for... I don't know... a sinister drumroll? Or a demon face hologram?* "I don't think so," she said. "I think it might be a message."

The Land of Flowers

Chloe leaned forward in her seat to grab the tied-up scroll. She unrolled it and began to read aloud, slowly so they could fully digest it.

"To the twelve: this message is serious, not a joke. We need your help. Our kingdom is in danger, and only you know about the enemy that concerns us. If you wish to help us, there will be a dragon at the dragon stables tomorrow at dawn. It will lead you to where we are, and we will explain ourselves. We are sorry we don't have enough time to write this plea, but we hope that you will come to our rescue. Sincerely, King Sky and Queen Turquoise, the rulers of Ariadnia."

"Wow," Izzy gasped once Chloe had finished. "Do you think this message is a fake?"

Lava frowned. "I don't know. But King Sky and Queen Turquoise, whoever they are, will probably send a dragon at the time they said they would at the dragon stables, so we can just follow it and see where it leads us. It wouldn't hurt," Lava added quickly. Izzy knew that the fire dragon had been itching for a new adventure since... when? *A day after we returned from the caves in the ravine,* Izzy remembered, amused.

"I'm in," Izzy said. "It doesn't sound like this Ariadnia is underground.... I'm up for anything except for going into a cave again. That was a pretty terrifying experience." Izzy shuddered, recalling the serpents' evil red eyes and their slithering dark green scales.

"Yeah," Leaf agreed with a nod.

"Whatever," Lava said. "I'm coming no matter what."

"Wait," Chloe said suddenly. "Do any of you guys even know where Ariadnia *is?*"

Izzy tried to remember. "Um... nope. Well, I'm a failure at geometry, except for the basic coordinate plane." She sighed.

"You're mixing up geometry with geography," Leaf told her.

"I guess I'm more of a failure than I thought I was," Izzy admitted, disappointed by her lack of knowledge.

"Well, I guess we're going to have to trust that dragon and hope that it doesn't lead us into a death trap," Chloe said.

And with that happy thought in their mind, the four left the library with the scroll to tell the others about the message it brought.

Angela shook her head in disbelief. "Wait, you're saying that there were actually teal sparkles?" she asked, looking a little confused.

They were at Izzy's house, briefing the others on what they'd found and the weird things that had happened before that.

"Yeah," Chloe answered promptly. "And the smell of lavender. And this thing." She held up the scroll that she'd tied back together with the red ribbon.

Kelsey squinted at it. "What does it say on the inside?"

Chloe unrolled the scroll again and repeated the mysterious message.

"So we're going?" Sara asked, glancing from Angela to Chloe.

"Yeah," Chloe said, smiling from ear to ear. "Isn't that amazing? Plus, we're not going underground again!"

Sara rolled her eyes.

"So, meet at the dragon stables at dawn tomorrow, alright?" Chloe asked. "How about at... say... five in the morning?"

Angela blinked, looking very shocked. "Okay, then I'd better get to sleep early today," she said hurriedly, seeming to be slightly alarmed. "Bye, guys! See you at two in the morning!"

Without another word, she dashed out the door. Izzy heard the *crunch*es of the girl's feet hitting the pebble path that led up to the front door.

Suddenly, Andrew poked his head in the room that Chloe, Sara, Izzy, and Kelsey were still in. "Planning another adventure?" he asked, a grin slowly spreading across his face. "Without *me*?"

If she was being honest, Izzy *had* really forgotten about Andy. But since they'd brought him along on their last adventure (and he'd proven himself to be very helpful), Izzy thought it wouldn't hurt if he came with them again.

"Fine, fine, you can come, too," she sighed. "Just remember to bring your weapons. And Storm." Pausing for a moment, she added, "I suppose you've been eavesdropping on our private conversation?"

Andy looked a little embarrassed. "Well, yeah," he muttered. "At least you don't need to tell me where you're going now."

Izzy rolled her eyes. "Okay, okay, fine. You win. Come on, let's go. If we're leaving at dawn tomorrow, we need to go to sleep extra early."

Riding Through the Clouds

Izzy yawned as she packed her backpack for the long trip to come. She checked her watch again to make sure she wouldn't be late. It was 4:27 a.m. *Still lots of—yawn—time,* she reassured herself. Waking up early had messed with her sleep schedule. *It doesn't help that I'm bad at sleeping....*

She put the last item in her backpack, a sturdy, handmade rope, and zipped the pocket up, then grabbed her lilac-colored backpack and leaped downstairs, where Andy was supposed to wait for her.

The silky dawn light filtered through the windows, casting an orangish glow in the living room and the kitchen. Outside, Izzy could spot purple and pink clouds beginning to rise from the horizon, so thin that she could see the sun right through them.

Andy was going over the things he'd put in his own blue-and-green backpack, taking everything out, inspecting it, and then putting them back inside the backpack. *Very inconvenient,* Izzy thought wryly.

"You ready?" she asked her little brother, climbing down the stairs and landing on the first floor with a *thump.*

"Yeah," Andy replied, stuffing a book inside his backpack and taking out a yellow flashlight. "Just give me a second to finish organizing this." He examined the flashlight, nodded, and put it back in his backpack.

Izzy waited next to him, casting a shadow over Andy. "Done yet?" she asked in a tone dripping with sarcasm after a literal second.

"No," Andy replied just as sarcastically. "Give me *another* second."

After another literal second, Izzy grumbled, "Done yet?" She was beginning to feel impatient. *How much stuff does Andy need to examine? Three hundred?* she thought, annoyed.

Luckily, Andy zipped up his backpack, slung it over his shoulder, and stood up. "All done," he announced. "Let's go!"

"It's about time," Izzy muttered. "Come on, let's get to the dragon stables before Chloe starts getting impatient." It was only 4:43, but knowing Chloe, she would probably be there already.

She dashed out of the house, Andy right on her heels. Running through the village at dawn gave Izzy a somewhat peaceful feeling, just watching the sun grow closer and closer with each hurried step. Pebbles clattered on the cobblestone pathway, disturbed by the two's footsteps, which echoed slightly in the eerie silence.

A row of wooden houses stood on the path that led to the Peaceful Plains, standing there like tall, solemn sentries. A lamp suddenly began burning in one of the windows of a house, and Izzy grabbed Andy and ducked behind some bushes to avoid being spotted.

When Izzy was sure that nobody had come outside to investigate, she dragged Andy out from the bushes and whispered, "Come on, we have to hurry. It's four fifty."

They ran to the edge of the town, and without looking back once, sprinted towards the dragon stables that stood in the middle of the Peaceful

Plains. They arrived at the dragon stables at 4:53 a.m. The dragons and everybody else were waiting for them.

Izzy gasped for breath, panting, and waved weakly to Chloe. "We're here," she called, walking over with Andy right behind her.

"About time," Chloe grumbled. "All of us are here, and we've been here since...." She glanced at Angela, who was staring at her watch. "Since what time, Angela?"

"Since 4:42," Angela answered.

Izzy frowned. "That was only *eleven* minutes ago!"

"Whatever," Chloe snapped. "It's more than ten minutes. That's what matters."

Izzy rolled her eyes but she didn't say anything.

"Hey, guys?" Sara interrupted quietly. "The dragon's here." She pointed at the dragon stables.

Immediately, everybody's heads swiveled to follow her finger.

There was a beautiful silver dragon standing next to the stables. About two-thirds the size of Lava, the biggest one there, her silver scales glimmered in the pale sunshine, and her eyes were a pretty emerald green. On her head was a thin, silver-speckled teal tiara, the same color as the sparks that had appeared when the mystery scroll had. A precious diamond as big as a walnut shimmered on the top of the tiara.

"Advance," Chloe murmured softly to the group. They slowly began walking forward, trying their best to not alarm the magnificent silver dragon.

The Land of Flowers

Izzy couldn't take her eyes off her. *What a beautiful dragon. I wonder where she lived before she joined King Sky and Queen Turquoise, whoever they are.*

As they grew closer, the silver dragon slowly turned towards them. For a moment, Izzy thought that she was going to breathe fire at them (although she didn't know what type of dragon she was), but all the dragon did was say, "My name is Swift—follow me," before she flew into the air without so much as a flick of her tail.

"Quick! Follow her!" Chloe shouted, climbing on Lava. "Come on! Go, go, go!"

"She's making me nervous," Leaf muttered as Izzy got on her trusty dragon. "Chloe, I mean. Not Swift."

As they ascended into the air to follow their silver-scaled guide, Izzy could definitely see where Swift had gotten her name from. Even the Withering Wings, who were a very fast species, were slow compared to her. Spreading her large silver wings majestically, Swift flapped and soared between wind currents with the grace of a dolphin.

Eventually, Izzy lost track of how high they were in the air and which direction they were going. When they took off for the sky, they'd been heading in the direction of the ocean, but now thick, multicolored clouds hung around them, blocking Izzy's eyesight, and she couldn't even tell if they were heading towards the sun.

All she knew was that they'd been flying for over an hour. At least that's what her *watch* said. It was now approximately six thirty-six, for all Izzy knew. She checked with Angela's watch. Her friend's device read the same time.

The long dragon ride was kind of like an airplane ride, minus the seat belts, bathroom, and snack cart, of course. But the turbulence was still a problem. One time, Leaf lurched so much to the side that Izzy nearly plummeted to her death.

"Careful," she snapped. "I don't want to die during a peaceful dragon ride. Do you realize how *embarrassing* that would be?"

Leaf rolled her eyes but didn't say anything.

They began to descend at precisely seven sixteen a.m., lowering slowly through the puffy clouds, the horizon becoming clearer and clearer the farther they went downwards. *Even the sun's below us,* Izzy thought in amazement. *How high are we really?*

Instead of reaching land in thirty minutes (as Izzy had predicted), there was a strange island in the middle of the sky. *Is there no gravity here?* Izzy wondered. *How can matter float?*

"Land there!" Swift called, looking over her shoulder to gaze at them with her shiny green eyes. "It's safe, I promise," she added when she saw the looks of doubt on everybody's faces.

They landed on the floating island, Lava and Chloe first, Reed last. They'd brought Reed along with them after he moved into the dragon stables because they'd thought he might be helpful along their adventures—kind of like Andrew, now that Izzy thought of it.

Now that she was much closer to the ground, she could see that this wasn't an ordinary place. Of course, the 'floating' part of the floating island was already very unordinary on its own, but the lushness of this… island, place, whatever you wanted to call it, was incredible.

Towering elms, majestic birch trees, sturdy oaks, and many other trees dotted the landscape. The closest tree to her was a young evergreen, only a foot taller than her. As she glanced closer, she noticed that tiny sparkles of magic had been placed upon the branches. *I wonder what's that—some kind of fairy essence, maybe?*

Flowers were also included in the vegetation, of course. Colorful orchids, tulips, and roses were knee-high and showing off their petals, while dahlias, asters, magnolia, and jasmine bloomed, but the flower in most quantity that Izzy noticed was lavender. The stalks of lilac were almost everywhere; there was a patch over there, by that red rose, another over there, by that clump of blue orchids, and so on.

There were ponds scattered all over the place, too. Sacred lotus flowers spread their petals as they floated along the surface of the crystal-clear water, pushed by a silent breeze. Water lilies sprouted in bright colors, yellow, pink, orange. Smooth wooden benches sat next to each pond, almost like a park.

Green hills rose above even the tallest trees and plants, but not casting a single shadow in this early time of day. Izzy glanced at where her *own* shadow would've been, but instead, there was only grass and flowers. *Strange....*

With a flourish of her wings and a low bow, Swift nodded to the landscape in front of them, smiled, and said, "Welcome to Ariadnia."

The Flower Palace

Of course, the first place they asked to go to was to wherever King Sky and Queen Turquoise were. Swift said they were at the palace (obviously) and then they all felt embarrassed that they didn't know that before.

Swift led to them to the palace, which she called the Flower Palace. As they went along, she explained what Ariadnia was and who she *herself* was. According to her, Ariadnia was the magical land of flowers, and the king and queen watched over the kingdom, settled disputes, and did all the ruling stuff. Swift introduced herself as the tour guide of Ariadnia to visitors of all shapes, sizes, and creatures, and she boasted with pride that she'd been a guide for over six years.

The palace was beautiful. It was constructed of smooth quartz, quartz as white as the drifting clouds in the sky. Pale blue diamonds glittered on the tall pillars, each only the size of Izzy's fingernails (the diamonds, not the pillars, of course. If it were the pillars, it would be absolutely absurd). A magnificent garden stood in the front yard of the palace, complete with leafy hedges, a simple gravel path, and three ponds.

Swift led them inside the palace, through a long hallway with a teal carpet, and into the throne room. There, King Sky and Queen Turquoise sat on thrones fit for... well, a king and queen.

The Land of Flowers

King Sky had skin the color of pale peaches and brown hair that matched perfectly with his soft brown eyes. He wore a circular, pointed crown on his head and a diamond-encrusted, sky-blue robe lined with fake white fur. His throne was made out of white quartz, with a light blue cushion on the seat, and it had the symbol of a blue star flower on it.

Queen Turquoise had long, blond hair that tumbled all the way down to her elbows, neatly combed and brushed. She had green eyes—the same shade as Swift's—that sparkled like all the other magical shimmers in this place. She wore an elegant turquoise dress with a soft pink ribbon tied around her waist as a hem. With skin as pale as snow, Izzy thought she resembled Snow White—at least a little bit.

Queen Turquoise's throne was slightly shorter than King Sky's, but hers was also made out of the smooth quartz. However, her cushion was light turquoise, and her symbol was a teal emerald.

Swift immediately fell to her dragon knees and bowed deeply to the king and queen. King Sky blinked at her acceptingly. "*Bow*," she hissed furiously through clenched teeth.

Izzy made sure to give Swift a look but complied, except that she didn't do it on her knees. She watched as her friends (including the dragons) bowed, but Andrew did it even more tentatively than the rest of them, like he wasn't sure he should be following the others' lead. *He looks exactly like how I feel,* Izzy thought.

After just a few moments of staying in a knee-aching pose, King Sky said, "Well, well, Swift. Our visitors have come. Do you mind if you leave the room so we can... *discuss* things with them."

The Land of Flowers

Swift got to her feet and glanced at the Withering Wings nervously. "But, uh, sir," she mumbled, "they can attack you easily. And Queen Turquoise," she added hastily.

King Sky glanced at Izzy, Chloe, Angela, Sara, Kelsey, Andrew, Leaf, Lava, Whirlpool, Ice, Jewel, Storm, and Reed calmly. "Don't worry," he said. "It'll be fine."

Izzy wondered what he meant. *Does he mean that if we attack—but it's only if—he can fight us off? Two to thirteen? I don't believe it. Can I? Who can?*

Izzy stole a look at Queen Turquoise. The queen was staring at King Sky with a stony expression that Izzy couldn't read. *Angry? Embarrassed?*

Swift bowed and left the room, sending Izzy one last trusting look that read, *Please keep my king and queen safe.*

King Sky faced the thirteen (it was thirteen, since Reed was here). "I see that you replied to our message," he said, his eyes scanning Izzy and her friends. "I can now tell you what is the great danger that awakens before us."

Eloquent words, Izzy thought, fighting against the urge to roll her eyes.

"Yes," Queen Turquoise put in, her face expressionless. *What is wrong with her?* Izzy wondered, not intending to be disrespectful. "An army is rising out of the dark mist that is outside the borders of our kingdom." *Wow,* Izzy thought in amazement. *She even* speaks *in a monotonic voice.*

"Literally?" Chloe spoke up.

"No," Queen Turquoise replied even more stonily.

"To start in on the details," King Sky said hurriedly, "we know that one of the daughters of Queen Opaque is going to lead the army. Obviously, the army is a gigantic group of devil serpents that you might've encountered in your last adventure."

Izzy nodded while Angela and Sara shared looks of agreement.

"The daughter is a dragon named Magmastone," King Sky continued. "Our spies have captured the news that she can lift items with her mind, and she can lift more than one thing in the air at once, which makes her extremely deadly. Our spies haven't found out who the third sister is, but they're working on it right now."

Izzy frowned. Magmastone... oh, right. Scorchwing, Magmastone, and question mark. "So, what do you want us to do, uh... sir?" she asked, stumbling a bit on what she could call King Sky.

King Sky frowned, rubbing his chin. "Well, I didn't think that through...," he said slowly, "but I suppose you could help our army prepare for war. We don't know when Magmastone and her army is going to strike, but we want to be prepared."

Izzy glanced at Chloe excitedly. Her eyes were shining with excitement. *Chloe does love good battles,* Izzy reflected.

"Where's your army? And what are they made up of?" Izzy asked, trying not to let herself be swallowed by nervousness. *Come on, put on a brave face,* Izzy willed herself.

"The Royal Army is made up of fairies, unicorns, and dragons, but the majority is phoenixes," King Sky explained. "We have Flower Phoenixes, Water Phoenixes, and Fire Phoenixes. You'll find all of them in the Royal Training Grounds. I'm sure that Swift will lead you there."

"Say, where did you *get* Swift?" Kelsey asked. Izzy could detect a hint of curiosity in her voice. *I've been wondering about that, too,* she thought. *Please answer that question. Please answer that question.*

King Sky smiled. "I'm afraid I can't answer that question," he replied calmly, with no sign of anger or frustration. Beside him, Queen Turquoise turned her stony gaze to Kelsey. "That is too big a secret, and besides, Swift has made me promise to never tell *anyone*... except for the queen, of course." Queen Turquoise nodded, but her face was still monotonic.

"What are you guys waiting for?" Chloe asked impatiently, glaring at Angela, Sara, Izzy, Kelsey, Andrew, Reed, Lava, Whirlpool, Ice, Leaf, Jewel, and Storm. "Let's get going!"

"Um, Swift hasn't come yet," Angela reminded her. "And, well, we don't know the way to the Royal Training Grounds...."

Chloe stopped in her tracks. "Oh, fine," she grumbled, sighing in annoyance.

"Swift!" King Sky called. "Come here, if you will."

Swift quickly hurried into the throne room, although her movements were still graceful. Izzy had almost forgotten about how impressive the dragon was looked. *What kind of dragon is she?* Izzy wondered. *Some kind of rare, unknown species?*

"Yes, King Sky?" Swift asked.

"Take these guests to the Royal Training grounds," King Sky ordered. "And they are *guests*. Keep that in mind," he added when Swift gave the 'guests' a half-suspicious half-doubtful look.

The Land of Flowers

Swift nodded importantly and gestured for them to follow her. Izzy dared to glance over her shoulder, and she saw King Sky staring at them with what could only be described as an... *eerie* expression. *It's like he knows something we don't,* Izzy thought, her temporarily put-to-rest suspicions waking.

Swift's noise broke through her thoughts. "This way," the silver dragon directed, turning down a corner. Izzy followed her, and the scene that was laid in front of her almost made her brain explode.

Phoenixes, unicorns, dragons, and fairies were training quickly and *noisily* in obstacle courses, magic contests, and flying races in a large, grassy area. Izzy watched as a fairy ducked neatly under a metal bar, did a somersault over a pool of water, and flew over a wall—all while facing the wrong way and closing her eyes.

A Flower Phoenix raced against a Water Phoenix in the air through the hardest flying obstacle course that Izzy had ever seen, gliding with elegant loops and ducking under sharp knives that jabbed at them from above.

"Wow," Sara breathed beside her. "Isn't it... *dangerous?*"

Izzy took another good look, and she realized her friend was right. The pool of water that the fairy had jumped over had electric eels zipping and zapping everything that hovered over the water, even clouds. The knives were actually sharp metal swords with blades as sharp as a dragon's claw.

I just got the chills, Izzy thought, shuddering.

"*I want to do an obstacle course!*" Chloe shouted, jumping up and down in excitement. "That looks *awesome!*"

Swift gave her a concerned glance. "Are you sure?" she asked. "You can possibly die a very painful death."

Chloe paused, but only for a moment. *"I'm sure!"* she screamed, sounding more enthusiastic than ever.

Swift backed away, looking a little startled. "O... kay," she stammered. "Over there's an obstacle course for beginners. It should keep you busy for a while. I'm going to check with the fairies, all right? You guys can just hang around. Feel free to try anything, but I'm warning you, everything has the potential to possibly kill you!"

Everyone nodded, and with that warning in mind, they headed over to where Chloe was eyeing the Level 1 obstacle course. For the first part of the obstacle course, swords were moving up and down relatively slowly, but their blades gleamed like fire in the bright sunshine.

"Do you think I have a chance?" Chloe babbled excitedly. "I mean, look at those swords!"

Angela frowned. "I don't know," she murmured slowly. "Look at the next part."

Izzy tore her gaze from the swords and settled it on the second part of the obstacle course. There was a platform at the end of the first part, and there was a wall in front of the platform with a rickety wooden ladder attached to it. Whoever was doing the obstacle course had to climb up it without falling off, and then they... oh.

Tiny blocks of stone drifted in the air in front of the top of the wall, and below them was a pit filled with water. Izzy supposed that Chloe would have to jump from each rock to rock, and if she missed just *one* leap, she would land in the water, have to swim to the top without drowning, and climb *all the way* back up.

Good choice, Chloe, Izzy thought dryly.

Chloe sized up the obstacle course. "Time me!" she shouted, and before Izzy could protest, she was leaping into the obstacle course.

Izzy watched as Chloe weaved nimbly through the swords, ducking low and leaping high. A sword jabbed at her back from above, and Chloe slid onto her stomach to get past it. Right after that one, a sword abruptly poked up from the ground, and Chloe *just* managed to jump over it before it impaled her.

Talk about close calls, Izzy thought, feeling as afraid as she would in a real fight. *Why is she doing this, anyways?*

Now Chloe was at the ladder. "Wish me luck for the next part!" Chloe yelled as she quickly climbed her way up the wall. Once, she almost lost her grip on a rung when she tried to spin while on the ladder. *She's the queen of doing daring things,* Izzy thought jokingly.

She made it safely to the top, then stared at the floating rocks, looking determined. "Let's face this head-on!" she shouted, bracing herself. Then she did a super-quick dash that nearly made her topple over and into the water-filled pit below. "*Ahhh!*" she screamed, leaning back and forth to try and regain her balance. "Wow, that was hard."

Andrew rolled his eyes. "Well, you're only on the first rock!" he yelled up to Chloe. "There's still... um... sixteen more! Better get going!"

Now it was *Chloe's* turn to roll her eyes. "Fine," she grumbled, leaping onto the next rock and almost falling off again.

When Chloe was *finally* done doing the obstacle course (Angela had timed her, and it took exactly forty-six minutes and thirty-five seconds), Swift came back over to them. By then, Chloe was dripping wet; drops of crystal-clear water were falling off her like raindrops.

"Finished the obstacle course?" Swift asked cheerfully. "Unfortunately, you don't have time to do the other nine." She gestured with her silver-scaled paw to nine more obstacle courses that looked even harder and more deadly than the first.

Chloe stared at them, shocked.

"Okay, what are supposed to do next?" Lava asked impatiently, pacing around. She'd been pacing around for most of the time that Chloe had been doing the obstacle course, and Izzy didn't know exactly why. *Probably because she longs for an adventure,* Izzy reasoned with herself.

Swift bowed, not looking the slightest bit ruffled by Lava's rudeness. "Now you need to take weapons, armor—whatever you need—from the Royal Armory and Weaponry. Feel free to take whatever catches your fancy, and keep in mind that you can keep everything you are going to wear."

"Can you lead us there, please?" Izzy asked politely.

"Yes, of course," Swift said. "Follow me."

They followed the shimmering silver-scaled dragon out of the Royal Training Grounds and back into the castle. They went down a long, majestic hallway with soft red carpet that squished under Izzy's feet and down different, winding corridors.

Soon, Izzy had completely lost her sense of direction in the twisting passageways. "Are you sure we're even going the right way?" Izzy asked, feeling slightly dizzy from the feeling that they were traveling around in circles.

"Of course we are," Swift replied. "The castle is magical, but I've memorized every location and room."

"Are you sure?"

Swift rolled her green eyes. "Obviously," she grumbled.

Izzy glanced at Sara. Her friend stared back at her, her eyes seeming to bore into Izzy's head. She shuddered and glanced around. Her other friends were all normal, talking in whispers and mumbles, and looking behind and in front of them nervously like her. *Sara is giving me the creeps,* Izzy thought, shuddering again.

They walked for a few more feet until Swift turned abruptly and opened a door with the symbol of two crossed swords. "Here is the Royal Weaponry. The next door is the Royal Armory," she said simply, holding the door open for them. "Good luck. And go in already!"

The thirteen silently filed in, and Swift gently closed the door behind them. The room seemed to be soundproof, because the echoes of Swift's footsteps that had occurred in the hallway had disappeared, and Izzy thought it wasn't likely that the dragon was still standing outside the weaponry's door.

Inside the Royal Weaponry, it was surprisingly messy, considering that it belonged to a king and queen. It wasn't really that *unorganized,* though. From a quick survey of the room, Izzy saw that a bunch of bows were in woven straw baskets, sharp adamant swords in scaffolds lying all over the floor, and ultra-sharp spears were clasped to the walls. Many other weapons hung on the walls or were lying on the floor.

Chloe walked over to a spear that had a flame at the tip. "Do you think this is effective?" she asked, glancing at it. "More than my electric spear, I mean." Her spear crackled with power, and shockingly (to Izzy, at least), Chloe rested a hand on the spearhead.

"*What?*" Izzy shrieked, nearly exploding in shock. "*Why did you just touch the electric part of your spear? Why are you not hurt?*"

Chloe glanced at her. "Oh, calm down," she said, chuckling and grinning at the same time. "You *do* know that I've been training for a quarter of a day each day before we set off on this mission, right? Lava helped me become immune to electricity, so I don't have to worry about shocking myself!" She smiled, clearly pleased with herself.

Izzy gaped at her, unable to process what she just heard. "Wha... what... *how?*"

Chloe grinned. "Oh, you know."

Izzy sighed. "I want to get going. I also want to find a better bow for myself. I just have a regular one."

"Yeah, me too," Angela added. "I have my Starstruck Arrows, but I don't have a bow equal to them."

"Good point," Sara commented, her eyes normal and totally not creepy. *At least not anymore,* Izzy though suspiciously.

"I'm fine with my Full Moon sword!" Kelsey sang, dancing in circles and swinging her shiny white blade dangerously.

Izzy quickly dodged to the left to avoid the sword that would've pierced her skull if she hadn't moved. "Be more careful with that, okay?" she muttered, although she doubted that Kelsey heard her in the racket she was making.

Izzy walked over to the far side of her room and examined the bows in the baskets there while Chloe was snapping at Kelsey for nearly slicing her head off. She pulled the first one out and took a good look at it. *Nope, nothing,* she thought. *Just a regular one.*

She grabbed the second one and turned it over it in her hands. It was pitch-black, with a dark gray string and yellow stars. Something felt strange about this bow, though. *I think this is what's wrong,* Izzy thought, lifting the bow right above her head. She was right. The bow was heavy—in fact, *much* heavier than any bow that she'd ever held; she almost toppled over! She quickly set the bow down gently and reached for the last bow in the basket, a pale white bow with a nearly invisible bowstring.

She grabbed it and gasped. It felt so light and fragile in her hands that she accidentally dropped it, and it crashed to the floor. She gasped *again,* afraid that she'd broken it, but it was as light as ever, without even a crack in it.

Hm... I wonder if...?

Izzy grabbed the bow and slammed it onto the floor. The force of the hit would've broken a regular bow, but this one stayed intact, and it didn't make a single noise. *This is perfect,* Izzy thought, feeling delighted. *Now, all I need are some arrows....*

She walked over to an entire wall dedicated to arrows. Well, there wasn't an inscription, but it *should've* been. All over the wall, quivers full of arrows hung on nails that had been hammered in the wood. Each quiver had different types of arrows than the other quivers. Labels on each quiver showed which type of arrow was in them.

Izzy rummaged through the quivers, browsing quietly. There was one with Light Arrows, another with Night Arrows, and much, much, more, but Izzy didn't see any Starstruck Arrows. *Hm... are Starstruck Arrows really that rare?* she wondered.

Then she came along a quiver that seemed like an amazing match for the item she'd already picked out. When she slung it over her back, it was as light as the bow. The label on them read *Invisible Arrows*. Personally, Izzy thought it was a good name since the arrows were extremely thin and looked almost invisible, but like the bow, when she tried to crack them, they wouldn't budge. *Perfect,* Izzy thought.

She looked around the room, surveying everyone. Angela was digging through a pile of mismatched bows, Chloe seemed to be picking out a scaffold for her spear, Sara was choosing a new weapon for herself, Kelsey was polishing her Full Moon sword, and Andrew was quietly talking with his robot frisbee friend, Max.

I guess the Slicer is good enough for him, Izzy thought, pleased that her brother had the decency to stick with his sword even though there were more powerful options literally right at his feet.

Lava, Whirlpool, Ice, Leaf, Jewel, Storm, and Reed were standing around and poking each other with rusty sword blades, messing around with the broken bits of bows, and shocking each other with electric weapons.

What a group of clowns, Izzy thought, unable to restrain a grin.

Chloe found a good scaffold—it was electric-proof—and stuffed her spear in it. "Ready, everyone?" she called, picking up a sword and moving it out of her way.

"I am," Sara said, smiling. She held up a metal double-sided battle axe. Izzy *had* to gape at her.

"How can you manage such a weight?" Izzy asked, baffled.

Sara's eyes gleamed. "Tricks on the eyes." She handed it to Izzy. It felt so light—almost as light as her bow. *This is probably like my bow,* she thought, testing its weight.

"Impressive," Izzy muttered, giving the axe back to Sara. "You're sure you can defeat an enemy with it?"

Sara grinned. "Of course!" she exclaimed. "Here, watch this." She backed away from Izzy to avoid slashing her to bits and jumped into the air, swinging the axe wildly. For some reason, the movement reminded Izzy that Kelsey had been slashing air enemies with her sword a few minutes ago. So Sara *did* know how to use it.

"Um, nice," Izzy said. "Are you guys ready?"

"Yup!" Angela exclaimed, holding up her prize. "This is a Starstruck Bow!"

The bow that she was clutching was golden and shimmered in the light beautifully, and stars swirled around it like they were orbiting. Izzy took a quick glance at Angela's quiver full of Starstruck Arrows, and sure enough, the two weapons looked like they matched.

"Awesome," Chloe congratulated her. "Kelsey, you ready?"

Kelsey dabbed the handle of her Full Moon sword one final time. "Yup!" she announced cheerfully. "Totally ready!"

Chloe's gaze flew over to Andrew. "Are *you* ready?"

Andy whispered something to Max, who *beep*ed obediently, then walked over to where the others were, the Slicer in its gray scaffold, as usual. "Yeah," he said, not-so-accidentally bumping into Izzy.

"Stop it," she hissed. "Not funny. Plus, that just gave me a minor bruise."

Smiling mischievously, Andrew nudged Izzy again and walked over to Storm.

"Alright, so I guess we're ready to go to the Royal Armory," Chloe announced.

King Sky's Speech

They all walked out of the Royal Weaponry and into the Royal Armory silently, not speaking a word, but their minds were subways of thoughts. Well, *Izzy's,* anyways.

We don't have a lot of armor, she thought worriedly. *But then again, armor weighs us down. I like being quick on my feet, even though I don't do close-ranged combat. Is that the same for Angela and sometimes Sara? How do Chloe, Kelsey, and Andrew feel about this? What about the dragons? Including Reed?* Her mind was buzzing with questions as they entered in the Royal Armory.

Much like the Royal Weaponry, the Royal Armory was messy, but it was organized. A *bit,* anyways. Sturdy-looking armor hung on the walls, but about a quarter of all the armor in here was on the floor. Just as Izzy thought about it, Andrew kicked an adamant helmet like a bowling ball away from them and sent it into a boot made of gold, making a large *crash* sound.

"Can you keep quiet?" she hissed to Andrew. "We don't want to draw attention to ourselves."

"There's no one in here," he grumbled, but he didn't do anything else that included a loud, disruptive noise.

I want some boots, Izzy thought, walking over to a wall that displayed only boots. *Some light ones, like my Invisible Bow and my Invisible Arrows.*

The Land of Flowers

She picked up a promising-looking pair of pale blue boots, then dropped them. They were *so cold* that she bet that only Ice (or maybe Sara) could hold them without feeling too much cold.

Her eyes scanned the other boots, taking in all the details. There were some red boots with flames flickering around the ankles that looked cool, except that Izzy bet it was just like the blue boots—but it was scorching instead of freezing. Sitting next to the fire shoes were a pair of boots that seemed to be made out of dark, nighttime clouds, small yellow stars decorating the sides as tiny pinpricks of light. However, since clouds were extremely heavy, Izzy guessed that she probably wouldn't be able to walk once she put them on—kind of like the heavy bow back in the Royal Weaponry.

Finally, she found what looked like exactly what she was looking for. The pair of boots that her eyes rested upon was nearly transparent—Izzy could almost clearly see the other side—but, like before, it didn't break when Izzy tossed it high in the air and it landed on the ground without a single *clunk*. *This might be perfect,* Izzy thought hopefully, trying them on. They were the perfect size, and they were light, too. Izzy bet they were awesome for dodging and running around in a battle with a lot of action.

That battle is going to come soon, Izzy realized, facing reality for the first time. *Magmastone and her army of devil serpents are coming.*

Everyone had taken the armor that appealed to them most, and personally, Izzy thought that they all looked just as heroes should in their choices. Chloe wore an adamant helmet and boots—both crackled with electricity—that looked heavy, but from Chloe's easy stance Izzy supposed it didn't weigh that much; Angela got a helmet that had stars circling around it like her Starstruck Bow, Quiver, and Arrows; Sara had a dark gray metal helmet that matched with her axe; Kelsey had shiny white boots and a white helmet that had a pale gray visor (that obviously matched with her Full Moon sword); and Andy had a full set of adamant armor that Izzy could probably call the Slicer gear.

So, in short, they were ready.

Chloe stalked out of the Royal Armory, and everyone followed her. Surprisingly, they met Swift outside, who only bowed and said curtly, "King Sky and Queen Turquoise wish to speak to you."

The thirteen followed Swift to the throne room for the second time in the same day, where King Sky and Queen Turquoise sat on their thrones with grim expressions. Well, *King Sky* had a grim expression, anyways. Queen Turquoise's face was the same: stony and expressionless. Her face seemed to always be still. In fact, it seemed *too* still....

Is she a robot? Izzy wondered.

"Our spies have spotted a gigantic shape moving in the distance." King Sky spoke gravely, like it was the last time he would ever talk to them. "We are convinced that they are the army of devil serpents. The spies have also spotted an unmistakable shape flying over them: Magmastone."

Izzy gulped nervously, swallowing a large lump in her throat. *Maybe we underestimated Magmastone's army,* she thought fearfully. *It's just us against millions of them... do we even stand a chance?*

"Of course, my army will assist you," King Sky assured them, seeing the looks of worry on everyone's faces. "We stand more than a chance. We can possibly win—if we use the right tactic."

Chloe stared at King Sky, but Izzy was too nervous to tell her that staring was supposed to be rude during times of formality. "What kind of tactic are you talking about?" she asked slowly. "A logical sneak attack? An ambush?"

"Yes, exactly," King Sky replied, smiling. "You've got it. Swift!"

Swift hurried into the room, stretching her wings quickly. "Yes, sir?"

"Bring me the map," King Sky ordered. And before Izzy could inquire about how Swift knew exactly *which* map it was, since King Sky had just said *the* map, the silver-scaled dragon was hurrying out the doorway.

"She should be back in a few minutes," King Sky said, giving the others a reassuring smile. As for Queen Turquoise, she was staring straight at Izzy, totally creeping her out.

But something—something Izzy just couldn't place—about the queen's face read, *Go! Run while you can, little girl. Something is coming. Something big. It will shock you like lightning. Go now! Run!*

Izzy shuddered and looked away. *Do I trust Queen Turquoise more than I trust my own instincts?*

Swift hurried through the doorway, holding a map with a carefulness Izzy had never seen. It was like the torn, stained page was the brightest, shiniest jewel instead of... well, what it really was.

"Here it is, sir," Swift mumbled, handing the map to King Sky before she left the room abruptly.

"Strange," Angela muttered under her breath, nudging Sara, who glanced at her, and looking at Izzy.

Izzy silently agreed with her as King Sky got off his throne, walked over to a table, unrolled the map, and beckoned for the other girls (and Andrew, of course) to join him and Chloe.

Izzy came over and carefully studied the map. The paper was filled with extremely detailed drawings of the entire kingdom of Ariadnia—well, Izzy didn't know that, but there was a label at the top that read *Ariadnia*, anyways. She found the castle and the Royal Training Grounds on the map.

"Here's where the army of serpents and Magmastone are going to attack," King Sky said, gesturing to a place with high hills that was right behind the palace. "They're going to climb onto the palace and attack it from the inside. We need to get to them from the back garden and surprise them while they're still getting up on the palace walls."

Izzy frowned. "Doesn't seem much like a sneaky ambush to me, but I'll go with it, I guess."

"Same here," Angela added, while Sara and Kelsey nodded. Chloe narrowed her eyes, not agreeing or disagreeing, but she said nothing.

King Sky nodded approvingly. "All right," he said, smiling confidently. "Next task for you: check on the Royal Army."

After summoning Swift and having her lead the thirteen travelers to where most of the Royal Army was assembled, King Sky went back to his throne and nodded to them as they left the throne room.

They followed Swift to the Royal Army's Preparation Room, where most of the Royal Army had been gathered. Izzy was impressed when Swift explained that many underground tunnels were installed under the Flower

Palace so that the entire Army could file into the Preparation Room without the hallways getting crowded and noisy with pushing and shoving.

The Royal Army's large Preparation Room was shaped like a dome, with smooth, polished white quartz for the walls and arching ceiling. The dome's top was far higher than any of the creatures in the Royal Army—there was space for a Gigantic Giant or two in the dome along with the Royal Army. A skylight the size of two large dragons let sunlight pour in, drenching the quartz walls in brightness so intense that Izzy had to shield her eyes for a few minutes. Filled to the brim, the room was incredibly noisy; hundreds of creatures were chatting about the big battle ahead of them.

"What should we do?" Angela asked, moving out of the way of a Flower Phoenix.

"Just mingle with the crowd, I guess," Chloe replied, shrugging. "I mean, we're all here for the same reason, so why not chat? Let's meet back at...." Her eyes scanned the room, and she finally pointed at a flowerpot with white orchids. "... those flowers over there in...." She checked her watch. "... at eight o'clock sharp, okay?"

"Sure," Andrew answered, tapping his foot impatient. "Bye!"

As soon as the words flew out of his mouth, he vanished into the crowd, Max whizzing after him.

Izzy rolled her eyes. "I guess that's the end of that," she said. "Anyways, I want to go with Sara, because I get super nervous when I'm among strangers and I'm by myself."

"Come on!" Sara complained. "Is that *really* the case?"

"Yeah," Izzy muttered, grabbing Sara's arm. "Now come on, let's go."

They wandered through the crowd until a unicorn spotted them, decided they looked friendly, and trotted over. She had a magnificent lilac mane with silver stars sparkling in them (not a decoration, Izzy supposed, just how she was) and a body so pale that Izzy almost thought it was ghostlike. Her eyes were a deep violet, a large contrast to the other parts of herself.

"Hi!" she greeted them. "I'm Berry! Who are *you*? I've never seen you around here before."

"I'm Izzy," Izzy introduced herself. "This is my friend, Sara." She waved her hand at Sara, who blinked and nodded. "We—and some of our other friends—were summoned here by King Sky and Queen Turquoise to, um... aid them in the battle."

Berry smiled. "Well, nice to meet you, Izzy and Sara!"

Seeing her chance, Izzy blurted out, "Um, uh... do you... d'you think you can show us what you can do with, um, your... magic?"

"Of course!" Pressing her mouth into a straight line in concentration, Berry directed her horn towards a sword lying randomly on the floor and closed her eyes. The sword suddenly shot up and jabbed sideways, just like it would've if a real person had been holding it!

"Wow!" Sara exclaimed. "That looks awesome! So, how are you going to be positioned in the battle?"

Berry frowned, lifting her head up. The sword clattered back onto the ground. "I'm not sure," she replied carefully. "I think that all the unicorns are going to be given three swords, then we're going to go behind some kind of *barrier*, and then we're going to lift the swords and pretend that they're being held by ghosts that want to attack the enemy." She paused and giggled. "Well, not *really,* but you get the point."

Izzy frowned. *Where is a wall that the unicorns could be stationed behind in the area that King Sky pointed out to us?* she wondered. *On the hills? No, that couldn't be possible, because that's where the* enemy *is coming from.... Wait... are they going to be positioned on the* palace roof? *I think that might be the case... but then won't they be in danger, since the enemy is going to try and climb onto the roof? Did King Sky plan this through correctly?*

Izzy shook her head and nodded politely to Berry. "Thanks," she told the unicorn, doing her best to muster a genuine smile and knowing she probably had a ridiculous grin plastered across her face. "Um, I should really be getting back to my, um... other friends now. Bye!" She waved at Berry, grabbed Sara's arm, and dragged her to where the flowering orchids were.

"What's the *meaning* of this?" Sara gasped, snatching her arm out of Izzy's grasp. "You almost *strangled* me!"

"Sorry," Izzy muttered. "But I just realized something. You know what Berry said? Where *are* they going to put all the unicorns?"

Sara scrunched up her face for a moment before realization struck her. "Oh... but why would King Sky and Queen Turquoise decide to put them *there*?"

Izzy shrugged. "I don't know." She paused, surveying the area. "Oh, hi, Chloe! And Angela. And Andrew. And Kelsey."

Choe, Angela, Kelsey, and Andrew had all come, Max flying above Andrew's head like a mechanical halo. "Hi!" Kelsey greeted them. "Ready to *fight?*" She hefted her Full Moon sword.

"Yeah," Chloe agreed with her. "I've been itching for a battle since, like, our last adventure!"

"I thought our last adventure *had* a lot of battles in it," Izzy grumbled. *Has Chloe suddenly morphed into a human version of Lava or something?*

"Well, I really want to test out my new electricity abilities," Chloe admitted.

"Come on!" Andrew huffed, rolling his eyes obnoxiously.

"But it isn't every day that you see a person who's immune to electricity," Angela pointed out helpfully.

"Yeah!" Kelsey agreed enthusiastically. *She's always enthusiastic. Or excited,* Izzy noted, smiling.

Andrew rolled his eyes again but didn't say anything more. Going to talk to Max a few feet away, he walked a couple of steps, his back to Izzy, until he was out of earshot.

What's he saying to that flying drone of his? Izzy wondered. *Can Max hear him? Does he have ears? Is he even intelligent enough to process what Andrew's telling him?*

Suddenly, the crowd became quiet, and Andrew hurried back to the girls. The seven dragons joined the group, too, and everybody stared at the figure that was coming onto the stage. It was King Sky.

King Sky smiled as he took the microphone from its stand and boomed in a loud, regal voice, "I assume that all of you know about the fight that awaits us, but do not worry, my friends. We will hold strong, and we will not let a single enemy escape us. The other side is a wicked fire, burning and swallowing everything that crosses its path, but we are the courageous waves of the majestic sea, splashing across their raging inferno. We will fight them. We will end them. We *will* hold strong—*for Ariadnia!*"

"*For Aradnia!*" the Royal Army shouted back at him, clapping and shouting streams of encouragement. Phoenixes waved their wings enthusiastically, unicorns reared up in excitement, and fairies flapped their wings.

However, Izzy was more than a little suspicious of King Sky. *He sounds so confident,* she noticed. *He doesn't even seem nervous when he's not giving a speech—like in the throne room. I mean, you can't be completely, utterly unafraid of a big battle, right?* She didn't want to suspect King Sky of being a traitor or a spy, but she couldn't avoid the memory of Queen Turquoise's almost *pleading* gaze. Another part of her, a part that was trying to think about what her friends thought, said, *King Sky is a friend! Totally! Besides, he's probably been on the throne for, like, what? Years? You should be ashamed of yourself, Izzy! How dare you even THINK about such a thought!*

Those two parts of her argued and fought and snapped at each other, unwilling to let each other win. If Izzy chose a side, what if she was *wrong*? What if she thought he was a traitor when really, he was just a king trying to cheer his troops up?

King Sky smiled and waved at the crowd. "Exit through the back door," he boomed, surprising Izzy with the loudness of his voice. "Use the tunnels as well. We will defeat this enemy in no time, crushing it just like the others that have dared to attack our home!"

With that, he exited the stage, placing the microphone back on its stand.

The Royal Army streamed through a pair of large glass double doors. Some of them went down into staircases that probably went low enough to reach the stone layers of the world underneath.

Izzy motioned to her friends. "Let's go through the underground tunnels," she said. "I want to see what they look like."

Invisible Arrows and Serpents

In the end, only Sara, Andrew, Leaf, Jewel, and Max decided to go with her. (Well, Max didn't really *decide;* he went because Andrew went.) Those who weren't traveling through the underground tunnels assured them that they would meet up with them back at the other end of the palace walls, but as Izzy watched the crowd sweep the sight of her other friends away, she felt a rush of loneliness mixed with mild panic.

When's the last time I went on an adventure and didn't bring my friends? She realized they'd never been on one without any missing members of their group. Or member.

Izzy shook those thoughts out of her head and followed Sara, Leaf, and Jewel into the tunnel. Andrew and Max trailed after her, casting looks at everyone. Izzy wanted to tell them that staring wasn't polite, but she decided not to, for multiple reasons. Reason number one was that Andrew would get mad at her. No more reasons needed.

They went into the underground tunnel, which was surprisingly large, considering that it was an *underground tunnel.* Quartz made up the ceiling, walls, and floor, like the other parts of the palace, and the walls had multiple doors, switches, and furnishings, like paintings. Izzy began to realize that instead of just a few tunnels underground, the Flower Palace had a whole different building.

They exited the tunnel through some smooth white stairs (made from quartz, obviously) and met up with Chloe, Angela, Kelsey, Lava, Whirlpool, Ice, Storm, and Reed at the other side of the palace walls.

"Hi," Izzy greeted them. "What's going on?"

"I'm looking for signs of the enemy," Chloe said, her eyes scanning the horizon. "I want to *fight!*"

"You look like you're on a sugar rush," Angela observed.

Chloe rolled her eyes. "Whatever. Humph."

"Bunny!" Angela suddenly shouted, dashing after a small white creature in the bushes. "Come back, bunny!"

Sara sighed. "I almost forgot Angela's obsession with bunnies," she told Izzy, who nodded good-naturedly in agreement.

An enormous clearing spread out in front of them was the only obstacle between Izzy and her friends and the beginning of a large, seemingly endless mass of tall, rolling hills. *I can see why Magmastone chose this place to launch her attack,* Izzy thought, taking a few steps away from her friends and turning around to look at the palace. *Tall serpents and a flying dragon can easily climb on the roof of the Flower Palace.*

King Sky walked out of a door Izzy hadn't noticed before, stared at the hills, and called, "Army lines, quick! The enemy is approaching!"

Izzy's eyes flew over to the hills. Indeed, the enemy was coming.

Hundreds and hundreds of serpents were climbing over the hills, getting nearer and nearer by the second. The unmistakable shape of Magmastone's magenta-scaled body hovered over the army, shouting commands and occasionally swooping down to claw a serpent that was distracted or idle.

Izzy shuddered and ducked behind Sara. "Leaf!" she called, waiting for her earth dragon.

Thumping over, Leaf growled, "When are we going to fight?"

Izzy rolled her eyes. "You're sounding like Lava," she told her.

Leaf stopped. "Oh. Okay." She squinted towards the serpents against the western horizon. "I guess King Sky's going to give us orders?"

"Yeah," Izzy replied. She watched King Sky carefully, like all the other creatures in the Royal Army.

"Rank one, Flower Phoenixes!" King Sky yelled, his eyes flickering back and forth between the approaching enemy army and his own. "Run to the top of that hill"—he motioned towards the hill closest to them, between them and Magmastone's army—"and inform us when they come close enough to attack! Rank two, unicorns, go on the roof!"

Izzy was shocked. It was how she'd imagined it!

Izzy spotted the pale figure of Berry in the crowd giving her a confused and worried look. She tried to send a look back that said, *Don't worry. You'll be safe.* The unicorns ran onto a good angle of the hills and leaped onto the castle roof, where they got a good view of everything.

"Do you think this is a coincidence, or...?" she whispered to Sara.

"I don't know," Sara replied, looking puzzled. "I'm going to get the others." She hurried away into the crowd, then came back a few seconds later with everyone else trailing behind her.

Lava was opening her mouth to speak when King Sky walked over to them. "Hello," he greeted them, smiling despite that there was the beginning of a battle going on. "Would anybody want to lead some of my soldiers?"

Immediately, Chloe and Lava brightened. "Really?" Chloe squealed, which convinced Izzy that this was an exciting occasion for her, because Chloe *hardly ever* squealed.

"Yes," King Sky confirmed, nodding.

"And me too," Lava added quickly. "I'm Chloe's dragon."

King Sky frowned. "You're a fire dragon, right?" he asked. When Lava nodded, he continued. "Are you sure that you're not loyal to any of the daughters of Queen Opaque?"

Lava gasped, looking very insulted. "Of *course* not!" she snapped. Izzy could practically see coming out of her ears. *Now, was that a fire pun?* she thought.

King Sky looked taken aback (Izzy was pretty sure he flinched), but he replied with enough calm to sound in control. "Okay. You can go with Chloe, then." He gestured towards a group of sixteen majestic fairies that were near some flowering bushes. "You can lead them. They'll follow your commands."

With that, he walked away towards the hill where the Flower Phoenixes were perched.

Chloe and Lava nodded and went over to the fairies, gesturing for the others to follow them. Izzy hurried after the two, her other friends following her quickly.

Upon closer examination, all the fairies had gentle, light brown eyes and light brown hair that went down to their elbows. Seemingly fragile wings flapped on their backs, flashing bright colors.

Chloe approached them and introduced herself. "I'm Chloe. King Sky told me to lead you, so here I am." When Lava shot her an annoyed look, she added, "And this is my dragon, Lava. She's here to, um...." She coughed. "*Assist* me."

Lava glowered at her.

The fairies all nodded, not speaking a word, obviously waiting for orders from this strange girl.

Just then, King Sky yelled, in a little bit of a panicked voice, "*Attack!*"

Izzy's head snapped swiftly to the direction that the shout had come from. King Sky was standing on top of a hill. The serpents were so close that Izzy could distinguish each and every pair of glowing red eyes that belonged the serpents. Magmastone's brightly colored silhouette, red and orange with the colors of fire, was hovering above the serpents near the back of her soldiers, surveying her enemy—the Royal Army.

"You heard him!" Chloe shouted, gripping her electric spear firmly. "Attack them!"

Immediately, seven of the fairies pulled out gleaming silver swords out of nowhere, darted into the air, and swiftly glided forward, heading toward the serpents. Other fairies also armed with swords and melee weapons followed their lead, while the rest of the fairies had bows and quivers full of arrows. Those ones flew away, landed on nearby trees, and began raining arrows down on the serpents, aiming and launching with deadly precision. Serpents instantaneously started falling, just dropping dead in front of their fellow comrades.

Meanwhile, Chloe had hopped on Lava, and they were currently flying to the back of the army, where the powerful duo could get a hundred serpents *and* Magmastone all to herself. Izzy wasn't really on board with the idea of Chloe battling a load of serpents and a daughter of Queen Opaque with nobody but a fire dragon, though. She called for Leaf, and they flew after her friend.

Looking back and trying not to fall off, Izzy saw that Angela was riding Whirlpool in the air behind them; Sara, Kelsey, and Andrew were running to the hills, where they could fight the approaching serpents. Ice, Jewel, and Storm were right behind them, casting some long-ranged attacks with their dragon powers. Max was flying above Andrew, shooting silver bullets that made minor explosions wherever they made contact with something. Reed was hovering above the serpent army, making trap-vines pop up everywhere. Sometimes, the trap-vines caught a surprised serpent in it, and then the vines would strangle its unlucky victim to death.

Izzy's gaze flew ahead of them when Leaf landed on the ground a considerable distance away from where they'd taken off. Chloe and Lava were already fighting, slashing at devil serpents and setting them on fire. Magmastone was nowhere in sight. *Time to see what these can do,* Izzy thought, taking out her Invisible Bow.

She notched an Invisible Arrow in the bowstring, lined up carefully with her target, and shot one devil serpent. Immediately, the serpent flinched; a good-sized wound ravaged its underbelly, but Izzy couldn't see the cause of all that pain. *I guess that's why those arrows are so... invisible,* she thought, feeling satisfied.

Her thoughts changed abruptly as the injured serpent hissed something inaudible to a few other serpents, and suddenly, they were all coming after her, slithering and snapping and snarling with the ferocity that came from seeing a hurt friend. Izzy froze, a tidal wave of fear washing over her. The serpents came closer and closer, spreading out to all around her....

And then those agonizing, heart-pounding seconds ticked by in what seemed like an eternity. Once she regained the ability to move, her first instinct was to get help. "*Leaf!*" she screamed, but her dragon was locked in claw-to-claw combat with a fire dragon far away—*too* far away. She watched, terrified for herself and her dragon and all of her friends, as Leaf turned towards her with an equally horrified expression, but it was too late. Her opponent took advantage of the earth dragon's distracted state and puffed out a billowing breath of fire that nearly caught Leaf in its grasp. The dragon had to counterattack, and the time it took for her to do so made her helpless to improve Izzy's dire situation.

The serpents were coming closer, and closer, and closer....

When one bold serpent came at her, intending to bite the girl with its wickedly sharp teeth, a star-streaked arrow whizzed out from somewhere behind Izzy and struck it right in the eye. The serpent howled in pain and retreated, giving way for six more.

Izzy turned around to see Angela climbing down from Whirlpool, a grin across the other archer's face. "I should've known," Izzy said, rolling her eyes.

Angela shrugged, seeming to be not bothered at all. Suddenly, her eyes went wide. "*Behind you!*"

Izzy spun around to find herself face-to-face with yet another serpent, its eyes glowing hypnotizingly at her an inch away from her face. She couldn't move. Her breath came in short gasps. *I'm about to die!* Her heart froze in terror.

Then Angela shot another Starstruck Arrow, pierced the serpent's scales, and sent it to its death. Izzy gagged and held her throat exaggeratedly.

"Let's help Chloe!" Angela shouted as she ran past Izzy and a few shocked serpents and towards the clump of dark-green-scaled tails where Chloe and Lava were fighting for their lives. "Whirlpool, Leaf, guard us and make sure no more serpents come at us. It'll really help. Thanks!"

Leaving her with no choice, Izzy ran to help Chloe, too. *Short-range combat time,* she thought miserably. It didn't help that the memory of her report card popped into her mind. *I don't need that, Mr. Brain!* She shoved it out of her head and pulled out two Invisible Arrows to use as weapons.

Seeing that Angela had already joined the fray, Izzy charged forward and jabbed a serpent for each arrow. Both flinched like the one Izzy had initially shot, and the arrows left them with wounds too large to have been caused by small projectiles themselves. *That must wait for later,* Izzy told herself, stabbing the serpents again and sending them to their deaths.

As she sprinted and ducked around the oversized reptiles to get closer to Chloe, Lava, and Angela, her Invisible Boots seemed to aid her, giving her a little extra speed and making her run the fastest she'd ever ran. *This is awesome,* she thought as she whizzed past a serpent, much to its utter shock and bewilderment.

Izzy reached Angela, who had a Starstruck Arrow in each hand, and yelled, "How are you holding up?"

Angela dodged to the left, quickly avoiding a serpent that lunged forward with its sharp fangs. "I'm doing okay! Hey, why don't you go help Chloe and Lava? I can't get close enough." Her gaze flicked from her enemies to Izzy, then back again; both of them knew that not watching your opponent was a dangerous thing to do when fighting. "With those super-speed boots, maybe you can get past them."

Izzy jumped over a serpent that was trying to do a not-so-sneaky sneak attack from behind the bush next to her. "I don't know," she replied, choosing her words carefully so that her friend wouldn't be disappointed if she didn't succeed. "But I'll try."

Angela gave her a halfheartedly relieved glance. "Okay. Just *hurry!*" She ducked under a serpent and stabbed it in the stomach, making it emit a hiss of pain.

Izzy nodded and leaped onto a serpent that was coming up behind Angela, squashing its head flat. Three serpents stopped in confusion when Izzy ran past them. They were probably thinking, *Hey, wait, our prey is that girl with the star arrows over there. Does that mean* this *girl is* not *prey?*

'This girl' skidded to a stop in front of Chloe, making her jump. "Ah!" Chloe shrieked, then realized that it was *Izzy* that had almost smashed into her, not a serpent. "Oh, hi, Izzy. What are you doing here?" She kicked a serpent in the neck and slashed at another with her spear. Beside her, Lava *thwack*ed a serpent with her long, spiked tail and hit a serpent with each of her front paws. Her jaw, full of knife-sharp teeth, lashed out at each serpent that reared up and tried to overpower her with height.

Izzy rolled her eyes, ducking to avoid a serpent that lunged for her head and to spin around and kick it in the underbelly with her foot. The serpent recoiled in pain and slithered away. "To help you, obviously," she grumbled, annoyed. She shot a serpent with an Invisible Arrow, and like all the other times, a large wound opened immediately.

"I don't need any help," Chloe insisted, stabbing a serpent in its evil red eye with her electric spear, then turning the spearhead around and jabbing at another.

"Yeah," Lava added, kicking a serpent, clawing at another, and *thwack*ing a serpent all at the same time. "We can *totally* manage this by ourselves."

Izzy gave a skeptical glance to all the serpents that were surrounding them, giving a quick count of *at least* thirty, very likely more. "I don't think so."

Chloe groaned dramatically. "Fine," she admitted, sighing as she slashed at two more serpents. "You can help." She paused to duck. "But I've noticed that the serpents have a tactic when it comes to fighting like this."

"Wanna tell me what it is?" Izzy panted, throwing an Invisible Arrow at a serpent like a pale, thin dagger and using another arrow to block another serpent's fang attacks.

"Sure," Chloe replied, slashing at a pair of serpents with her electric spear. Izzy watched out of the corner of her eye as the electricity crackled up and down the spearhead. "So, like, the serpents go in by themselves or in pairs, but once we get 'em, they go back again. Why do you think they're doing that?"

Izzy thought about that while she slammed a serpent into tomorrow. "I'm not sure. Wait a second...." She gave it a little more thought while embedding two Invisible Arrows in a serpent's scales, making two large wounds that formed into one *giant* one.

"Hey, Lava, do you need any help?" Chloe called to her dragon. Izzy's head swiveled around to look at Lava. The fire dragon was bravely battling against four serpents, earning scratches and bruises too quickly to count.

"No—eek! Yes, yes, *yes!*" Lava yelped as the serpents piled onto her. A couple of serpents that were in the ring that was surrounding them gave hisses of interest and slithered forward to get a closer look.

Chloe spun around and deftly hit three serpents with her electric spearhead, infecting them with shocking electricity. Izzy threw six Invisible Arrows with rapid panic; two entirely missed their mark, but the other four each landed on a serpent each, immediately opening large wounds. Those four serpents slithered away like the three that Chloe had hit.

"We need help!" Izzy yelled, feeling like walls were closing in on her throat as she spotted eight more serpents coming their way. Six more were slithering towards them from the other side of the serpent ring.

Immediately, three Starstruck Arrows whizzed past Izzy, just grazing her ear. Making a breezy whistling sound as they zipped through the air, they each hit one serpent, causing them to retreat.

"Angela?" Izzy heard Chloe call hopefully.

Angela was zooming in on them from the sky, riding on Whirlpool. "*Coming through!*" she yelled as her water dragon landed heavily on the ground with a gasped *oof* that startled four serpents away on its own.

When Angela landed, Izzy had the satisfaction of watching her friend's baffled expression as she rolled her eyes. "Why do you have to make such a weird entrance?"

Angela gave her an insulted look. "*Somebody* called for help, so I came to *help*."

Izzy rolled her eyes again.

"Anyways," Chloe interrupted hurriedly, "thirteen—no, fourteen—serpents are coming our way. We could *really* use your help, Angela!"

Angela smirked and shot a look at Izzy. "Told ya."

Izzy sighed, but she couldn't help grinning. It felt so good to smile when they were surrounded by enemy serpents. "Fine, fine, you win. Just don't tell anyone."

Angela shrugged, pulling three more Starstruck Arrows from her quiver. "Sure."

As the fourteen serpents neared, a realization struck Izzy in the same way amazement strikes a person when they catch a tennis ball from a football field away. "I think I know why they're coming close to attack, and then retreating when we land one hit!" she exclaimed. "The serpents, I mean."

Chloe impaled her electric spear in a serpent, then quickly pulled it out as the serpent flopped to the ground, dead. She proceeded hit another serpent. *That's only been the fourth serpent killed since I've been here to help fight,* Izzy noticed, worried. "What is it?" Chloe demanded, watching with narrowed eyes as the serpent she'd just shocked slinked back to the ring of its comrades.

"They're saving their numbers," Izzy explained, throwing four Invisible Arrows and watching as they each landed on one serpent in the ring. Those serpents quickly moved to the back of the crowd. "They're toying with us. But why? It's almost like they're trying to buy time for some—" Suddenly, she stopped talking as a thought hit her like a brick to the back of her head. *Well, an idea, anyways,* she told herself, desperately trying to calm down.

"Buying time for *what?*" Chloe demanded, hacking through a mini wall of three serpents with her spear. Lava grabbed one serpent in each of her front paws, mauling them with her sharp claws.

"I'm not sure," Angela replied, frowning. She shot two Starstruck Arrows in the crowd of serpents, and Izzy watched, almost in a trance, as they pierced the serpent's armor.

"I didn't ask you, silly," Chloe huffed as she jumped up, slammed her electric spear straight through a serpent, dug the tip of her spear into the ground, and did a twirl.

"Not what—*who*. I—I think their idea is to keep us busy until Magmastone arrives," Izzy explained, her hand trembling so hard that her next throw with an Invisible Arrow missed a serpent by a foot. She frowned and pulled out her bow. *I've always failed at throwing things,* she recalled.

Angela looked suddenly alarmed, and not just because of Chloe's scornful comment. "Oh no," she said, her face turning as pale as a white bunny's (minus the furry texture). "Should we try and escape now instead of trying to defeat all these serpents? Which seems impossible, by the way?"

"We definitely should," Chloe piped up.

"Yeah, I guess so," Izzy answered, choosing not to waste another second of thought. "Leaf!"

Immediately, she spotted the long figure of her earth dragon dive through the air and land next to her. "Good," the girl said, smiling approvingly. "But you could be faster."

Leaf grumbled and glared at her. "Whatever," she mumbled. "Why'd you call me, anyways?"

The Land of Flowers

"We need to get out of here before Magmastone arrives," Izzy explained. "The leader behind all of this scheming." She nodded at Chloe and Angela. "Come on, guys!"

She hopped on Leaf, made sure she was in a comfortable position, and soared away into the sky on the back of her dragon. She turned her neck around to see Chloe on Lava and Angela on Whirlpool, flying right behind her and Leaf. She looked back forward and told the earth dragon, "Go to where Kelsey, Andrew, and Sara are."

"Say please," Leaf muttered.

"*Please?*"

Leaf nodded, seeming satisfied, and flew over to the empty space above Andrew, Kelsey, and Sara. She swooped down low, waited for a few seconds as Izzy clambered off, and then launched herself into the air again.

Izzy watched as Whirlpool and Lava landed, Angela and Chloe dismounting their dragons and hurrying over to her. "Where're Kelsey and Sara?" Chloe asked, squinting as she peered into the crowd that was filled with phoenixes, fairies, and serpents battling.

Suddenly, the group of fairies that King Sky had told Chloe to command earlier drifted over. They already looked much less majestic after only fifteen minutes of fighting, but Izzy took them seriously anyways because of their solemn brown eyes. "We saw your friends over in that direction," a fairy told them in a slow, melodic voice, pointing a finger over to where the fighting was most intense.

That fairy sounds so… peaceful, Izzy thought. *Like she isn't fighting a battle that will cost her her home and her life if she loses.*

Izzy nodded politely in thanks to the fairies as Chloe rushed away, her crackling helmet, boots, and spear the only signs of her as she fought towards her friends. Momentarily stressed about losing her friends in the rush of action, Izzy dashed after Chloe, Angela trailing her. *One can't take down many enemies at once,* she told herself, reminding herself of a moral of one of the books she'd read over and over again.

She skidded to a stop when she was about three or four feet away from the serpents and two away from Chloe. Regaining her balance and hoping that her breath would come back soon, she notched an Invisible Arrow in her Invisible Bow and fired, making a grotesque wound right on a serpent's scaly face. Izzy shuddered and looked away.

A few steps to her left, Angela was shooting arrow after arrow in an attempt to get all the serpents away from Chloe. *Two long-ranged fighters and one melee fighter isn't the best force to charge straight into a bunch of serpents,* Izzy reflected.

"Come on!" Angela shouted to Izzy, getting her attention by poking her in the arm. "The coast is clear!" Without waiting for a response, she ran ahead, leaving Izzy with no choice but to follow.

Izzy sprinted as fast as she could, stopping in her tracks so abruptly she almost crashed into Angela and Chloe. If she had, they would've toppled over like human dominos. Luckily, she didn't. (She didn't crash into them because it would've been absolutely absurd to watch them fall over like dominos.)

"What's the problem?" Izzy asked, dusting herself off and pretending that she hadn't almost made them fall over.

Chloe was staring at where Kelsey, Sara, and Andrew were most likely going to be, her face pale. "That," she whispered, lifting a finger to point.

Izzy followed her gaze to see the biggest crowd of serpents yet... right where Chloe was pointing. She gasped, her lungs already constricting with fear. "Come on!" she yelled, already running towards the serpents, barely thinking straight. "We've got to save them!"

She was running so fast she couldn't look behind her, but she was certain that Angela and Chloe had both rolled their eyes at her and then ran off after her. *Deal with that later,* she told herself. *Our friends are in trouble. Andrew's in trouble.*

She reached the serpents, then stopped. *Why am I here, anyways? I use a bow, not a sword... but I can still make this work.* She pulled out four Invisible Arrows, armed her hands with two each, and threw them in the air, hoping that it was her lucky day.

And it seemed like it was.

Two arrows, the ones from her left hand, whistled through the air towards the three serpents that were slithering towards Sara, who only had a metal axe and a metal helmet. One of the arrows sliced a serpent clean through and continued in the air to impale a second serpent. The other Invisible Arrow pierced the third serpent's scales, and they all snarled in pain and retreated at the same time.

Simultaneously, the other arrows from her *right* hand zoomed past those three serpents, flying faster than any arrow that Izzy had ever seen. Each of the two projectiles landed on a serpent that was going to ambush Kelsey. Kelsey, alerted by the whistling noise of the arrows, swung around and stabbed her Full Moon sword into the not-so-sneaky serpents to end their lives.

Meanwhile, Izzy saw that Andrew was doing just fine by himself. *He even looks like he's having fun,* Izzy thought, feeling a little envious that he could be happy in this kind of situation. When she walked closer, she saw why. Max was dropping bombs on top of serpents right and left that were slithering closer to Andrew, and he was cutting them down with the Slicer. Max would occasionally let a few serpents slip through so that Andrew wouldn't get bored.

Another one of his 'modes,' I suppose, Izzy thought, amused.

She shook her head and raced towards Sara, skidding to a stop as she nearly crashed into her friend. "Eek!" Sara gasped in surprise, hopping away. "Be more careful, okay?"

Izzy sighed as she stabbed three Invisible Arrows in the scales of a serpent that was coming towards them. "Fine," she grumbled, giving the serpent a fierce kick as it tried to bite her in the leg. "Let's go over to Kelsey. Andrew's doing fine."

"Since he has that robot frisbee to help him," she heard Sara mutter under her breath. She ignored it and ran over to Kelsey, jumping over serpents and sticking an Invisible Arrow in them as she passed.

"How're you doing, Kelsey?" Izzy called as she neared her friend.

"Hi! And *great!*" Kelsey replied cheerfully, just like she always did. Suddenly, her eyes grew as wide as moons and her mouth dropped from its smile as she pointed at something.

"Look at *that!*"

A Confusing Mess

Izzy followed Kelsey's finger—and saw the most stunning, shocking, and appalling sight ever.

King Sky was battling against three Flower Phoenixes and five fairies—part of his *own army*. The expression on his face was determined, scrunched up in concentration, but Izzy didn't understand why he was fighting the good guys' side; that was the side he was supposed to be loyal to!

"A betrayal," Izzy whispered, barely daring to breathe. Queen Turquoise's more-than-serious looks all made sense now. They *were* warning her of dangers to come—and of a betrayal. *But why didn't she come and say it out loud?* Izzy wondered, then punched herself for not realizing sooner. *Obviously, King Sky would attack her and deny it, and we wouldn't believe it... so she waited for later. But surely his subjects aren't allied with the enemy, too.... He's a good fighter.*

Indeed, King Sky was holding off well against the phoenixes and the fairies. He even seemed to be gaining the upper hand. *How?* It was possible that he'd done something to himself that made him more powerful.

As Izzy pondered this, her mind wandered back to King Sky's betrayal. *But surely Queen Turquoise could've talked to us privately... so why didn't she?* Then it occurred to her that maybe *Queen Turquoise herself* had been under a spell that didn't allow her to make expressions with strong emotions—or maybe a more powerful spell that didn't allow her to even talk. *And the traitor's probably shared those spells with Magmastone, too. And maybe the other sisters.*

She shuddered at that last thought, afraid that then they would be more powerful and harder to defeat than ever. Because what if they were invincible, and Izzy and her friends would all be killed trying to fight for good?

"Come on!" Kelsey's voice interrupted her thoughts. "We have to help them!"

Izzy's gaze landed on the phoenixes and fairies. King Sky had made a large dent in his opponents' energy, forcing them to resort to slower attacks that were easier to dodge, and had also managed to injure each of them.

Apparently deciding that she was going in whether or not anybody else was, Kelsey ran for the commotion nobody else had noticed, brought her Full Moon sword up like a baseball bat, and swung at King Sky as soon as she was close enough. King Sky was too quick and ducked under the attack. However, a Flower Phoenix took advantage of his momentary distraction and, with a huff and a puff and a choked-out wheeze, trapped him in a cage of sturdy vines.

"*Why?!*" King Sky wailed, suddenly dropping to his knees. "What did I ever do to *deserve* this?"

"Well, for starters, you turned on your own army," Kelsey offered.

"*For starters*," Izzy added, nervous that King Sky was going to lash out and cut her arm off with that sharp sword he was holding. *What even is that sword?* she wondered. *Some kind of ancient weapon that can slice through fairies and phoenixes?*

"I suppose I did deserve *that* part," King Sky admitted, glancing at his sword as if already planning his escape. "But… but Magmastone did the rest. I only allied with her. She... she somehow forced me into betraying my subjects."

I didn't do it, his eyes seemed to plead.

"Why was Queen Turquoise acting so weird?" was Sara's first question, the one that Izzy was dying to ask.

King Sky was confused. "What do you mean?" he asked. "Queen Turquoise is perfectly normal."

He isn't faking it, Izzy thought, though she wasn't particularly good at reading expressions and telling truths from lies. *He thinks that Queen Turquoise was being normal, but she wasn't. So who* actually *started this mess?*

To her, the answer was clear.

"Guys, we need to find Magmastone *right now*," Izzy said nervously, glancing at the fairies and the phoenixes who had fought King Sky. They were now walking slowly towards the Flower Palace, some limping painfully, others supporting their comrades with wings and shoulders. "She's got to be the one behind all of this, right?"

"Probably," Chloe said slowly, her eyes drifting past Izzy, as if she were already scouting for their target. Then she brightened. "Well, that means fighting against a dragon with telekinesis! Sounds exciting! Let's go!"

Before Izzy could say anything to stop her, Chloe had run ten feet back into the confusing craziness of friends and foes. "Ugh," Izzy moaned dramatically. "I guess we're going to have to go after her. Come on, people!"

The Land of Flowers

Then she took off after Chloe. Being a little faster than her, she caught up in a minute. "Next time, give us a warning before you shoot off, okay?" Izzy asked her. "I can't do all of this running about. My legs are going to fall off. Literally."

"Yeah, got it, got it," Chloe said distractedly. She was scanning the battlefield, her brow furrowed; Izzy wasn't really sure if she'd actually heard her. "So where do you think Magmastone will be?"

"Maybe in the forest. You know, on those hills," Sara's voice suggested from behind Izzy. Izzy spun around and nearly screamed when she came face-to-face with Sara.

"Jeez," Izzy said.

"What did I say about *being more careful?*" Sara complained, backing away a little. "Anyways, she really *could* be hiding in the forest, right?"

Chloe tapped her chin thoughtfully as she swung her electric spear around with her other hand, deep in thought. Izzy backed away, standing beside Sara, to avoid getting slashed to bits by the crackling spearhead. She was still a little in awe of her friend's immunity to her very impressive weapon.

"Hi!" Kelsey's cheerful voice rang out from behind her. "What are we doing?"

Izzy shifted to the side a little before mumbling, "Um, I'm not sure. I think we're discussing where Magmastone could, uh, be."

"Oh," Kelsey said, sounding disappointed. "I want to *do* something! But I guess talking is also doing something, so maybe it's okay? I don't know. Hey, maybe Magamstone's hiding in the forest?"

"That's exactly what *I* said," Sara complained with a sigh of exasperation.

"Oops. Sorry!" Kelsey said cheerfully. "I… wasn't here!"

Angela caught up to them. "What are we doing now?"

"That's the same question that Kelsey here just asked a second ago," Chloe said. She too seemed to be getting tired of repeating everything. "We're going to be searching for Magmastone now. If she made King Sky turn against his people and if she was the one who did something to Queen Turquoise, who knows what she'll do next to all of these poor fairies and phoenixes and unicorns."

When Chloe said *unicorns*, Izzy immediately thought of Berry, the horned creature she'd met at the Royal Army's Preparation Room. Although their talk had been nothing but the briefest of brief, she'd gotten the feeling that Berry was determined to help her land. *But will she die for it?* Izzy wondered, then shook the thought out of her head. Now wasn't exactly the best time to think about dying for your home.

"Good idea," Angela responded to Chloe, glancing behind her to make sure all her Starstruck Arrows were safe in her quiver. She'd slung her Starstruck Bow over her shoulder, and Izzy had to admit that it looked pretty amazing with her golden helmet and magically flying stars. "So where do you guys think she's at?"

"Kelsey and Sara both said that she could be hiding in the forest," Chloe said. "But there *must* be other places for her to go."

"I saw a lot of big boulders over there," Angela offered, waving in a vague direction. "*Ginormous* boulders. She could be hiding behind those."

"Good idea, Angela," Chloe said, grinning. "What about you, Izzy? Got anything in that brain of yours?"

Izzy had been thinking about the underground tunnels and how they eased up the traffic. "Those tunnels are nice," she said distantly. "They seem cool."

Sara's eyes widened. "You're a genius, Izzy!" she exclaimed.

"I am?" Izzy asked. "I mean, um, yeah, of course I am!"

"Magmastone could be hiding underground, in one of the many tunnels under the Flower Palace!" Chloe cried, catching on. "Come on! Let's go ask King Sky where we can see all of those tunnels!"

Before any of them could say anything, Chloe ran towards King Sky's vine cage again. As they took off after her, Izzy heard Kelsey mutter under her breath, "Oh, yay. More running. Less fighting. How exciting."

Izzy understood Kelsey. She didn't really like fighting, but that was *way* more exciting than running around after their friend. *This is, like, the second time today. Or the third? I don't remember anymore.*

"Where can we find a map of the underground tunnels under the Flower Palace?" Chloe was asking King Sky. The man was sitting on the ground, looking as miserable as, well, a king trapped in a cage.

"In the map room," he answered. "The second level. Queen Turquoise can lead you there."

"But isn't she, like, frozen or something?" Kelsey blurted out. Seeing King Sky's concerned look, she quickly added, "Uh, to us, anyways."

The king frowned. "Really?" he mused, seeming to be dwelling it over. "It must've been another one of Magmastone's trick spells." He pounded his fist on the ground and then winced. "Queen Turquoise has been the subject of many of Magamastone's spells before."

Or has she? Izzy still wasn't sure whether King Sky was a traitor or not. Part of her wanted to believe what he said, but another part of her, the more suspicious part, told herself that he was just making up lies.

"Nice to know," Angela said. "*That's* why she looked so, er, funky."

"*Funky* is an outdated word," Izzy complained, shooing her thoughts away. They were taking up so much brain space that if she kept thinking them over, she'd start believing that she had wings. "Nowadays the word for 'funky' is 'weird.'"

"*Nowadays* is an outdated word," Chloe shot back.

"Oh," Izzy said, not finding a good comeback for the retort. "Okay, fine, fine. Can we just get on already, please?" *This is taking too much time,* she thought, annoyed with herself for starting to talk about outdated words.

Chloe shrugged. "Sure. Race you guys to the throne room! Last one there is a rotten egg!" Chloe took off for the Flower Palace's entrance, dodging battling fairies, ducking under fighting phoenixes, and weaving through galloping unicorns.

Izzy had no idea how she had a single sense of direction in the whirl of battle, but she followed Chloe, trusting her friend with, well, her life. If Chloe led them into a mud pit or something with a bunch of devil serpents inside, they were totally doomed.

Luckily, it turned out that Chloe *did* have a sense of direction.

She led them to the back of the palace where they'd exited, and they all grouped back together to discuss their next move.

"What should we do now?" Sara asked.

Chloe rolled her eyes. "Duh! Go to the throne room now!" she answered, sighing. "How clueless *are* you?"

"A lot?" Angela guessed.

"Correct," Chloe said. "Congratulations! You're not clueless anymore! Okay, did anybody remember the way to the throne room?"

"*You* didn't?" Izzy asked, a little surprised.

"Duh," Chloe huffed. "But did *anyone?*"

"No," Sara said. "But I drew a route in my notebook. It *should* work."

"Show me," Chloe said. "Or else I'm going to pull it outta your backpack."

"It's not *in* my backpack," Sara retorted, smirking. "That's the problem."

Chloe glared at her. "Well, *show it* already! We're pressed for time here, you know!"

"Gee, cool down a little," Sara said. She took off her backpack and unzipped it, then pulled out a soft-looking gray pouch and zipped up her backpack again. She slung the straps over her shoulder like before.

"I thought you said it wasn't in your backpack!" Izzy blurted out.

"Yeah!" Chloe exclaimed indignantly.

Sara grinned. "It was *inside* something *inside* my backpack," she explained. "That doesn't mean it's *inside* the backpack, really, because the *pouch* is its own backpack. So basically, it's inside a *backpack*, but *that* backpack is inside *another* backpack."

Kelsey rubbed her forehead. "My brain just got tied in knots."

"In other words, it wasn't inside my backpack—it was inside the pouch," Sara clarified.

"Whatever," Chloe huffed, rolling her eyes and clearly even more annoyed, which Izzy didn't think was possible. "Just give it already."

"Please ask nicely," Sara replied cheekily, but she tugged open the pouch, took out a rose-shaped hair clip, and closed the pouch again.

"What's the hair clip for?" Izzy asked curiously.

"Um... doing something?" Angela suggested.

Izzy scrunched up her face. "I'm not so sure," she decided slowly. "But let's see. Come *on,* Sara! Please get going... we don't have all day."

"That's what I'm trying to say," Chloe snapped.

"This hair clip is my notebook," Sara explained, rolling the rose pin over in her hands. "When I click *this* thing"—she tapped an unnoticeable pink button on the back of the hair pin lightly—"it transforms into my red notebook."

"Cool!" Kelsey exclaimed. *She's always so excited about everything new,* Izzy thought, smiling to herself. "Where did you get it?"

Sara grinned. "From the time when we defeated the giant serpent," she said. "And when Andrew thought he lost the Slicer."

"Oh, yeah...." Izzy recalled the time in their last adventure, down in the caves of the ravine, when the giant serpent had snapped the Slicer with its teeth, and they'd thought that it was destroyed forever.

"Can we just get on?" Chloe asked impatiently. "I'm itching for action. Like, I'm not even fighting anything!" She glared at a random tree that was unfortunate enough to be the target of her displeasure. Izzy tried—and failed—to stifle her giggles.

Sara smiled. She clicked the button on the rose clip, and it immediately sprung into a red notebook and the words *Private, Do Not Read (Or You'll Regret It)* in glittery silver letters on the cover. Sara flipped to a page marked with a neon green sticky note and showed it to them.

"Here's where we are right now," she explained, tapping the end of a pen that she'd somehow gotten out of nowhere. "Here's the throne room." She pointed at a square that represented the room. It was about six inches away from the area that resembled the place they were right now. "See, we go through the door, then down *that* hall, then we turn a left, then we—"

"We get it, we get it," Chloe interrupted. "We've got this. As long as we follow it, we can't go wrong. Right?"

Sara scratched her head sheepishly. "Well... er... I might have drawn a left instead of a right, and a forward instead of a backward, but... I guess so?"

Chloe nodded importantly. "Okay," she said. "Let's go!"

Magmastone

Izzy really didn't like gigantic devil serpents that held six swords in their mouths like very sharp teeth. And also serpents whose heads reached the ten-foot ceiling of the Flower Palace.

That was the reason that she screamed when they found an enormous serpent that possessed *both* of those horrifying qualities. After they rounded a corner, confident that they'd reach the throne room without any confrontations, they came across the cursed creature, which, unfortunately, proved them wrong.

"AIEEEE!" Izzy shrieked, stumbling back into Sara.

"Hey!" Sara cried indignantly. "What did I say before about *not running into me?*"

"S-sorry," Izzy stammered, backing away. "It's just that, er, that serpent kind of scared me."

Sara frowned at the serpent, whose red eyes were gleaming like evil rubies. "Not good," she huffed at the serpent. "I'm angry."

You don't want to get on the bad side of Sara when she's angry, Izzy concluded, grabbing her Invisible Bow and carefully notching an Invisible Arrow.

She saw Chloe bringing out her electric spear, Angela notching a Starstruck Arrow on her Starstruck Bow, and Kelsey unsheathing her Full Moon sword. It suddenly became five girls armed with dangerous weapons against a single serpent with six sharp sword-teeth.

"So," Sara said, continuing to glare at the serpent, "what do you have to say for yourself?"

To Izzy's surprise, the serpent actually responded. "Nothing," it growled. "But be aware that the reinforcementsss of my team are coming. They *will* find you. You ssshould be very afraid of them...."

"Team?" Kelsey wondered aloud, momentarily forgetting that they were trying to get to the throne room. "What *team?*"

"I don't know what *that* means, serpent, but there's one place you're going," Sara muttered, glaring at the serpent as she gritted her teeth and gave her metal axe a few test swings. Izzy noticed Kelsey dodging wildly to the left to avoid having her right leg cut off by Sara's weapon. *The irony,* she thought wryly. *I've always been trying to get out of the way of* Kelsey's *sword.*

"And where might that be? Care to tell me, little girl?" the serpent hissed, talking with a funny accent so that it pronounced *little* as *leetle*. Its red eyes seemed almost... *amused* to Izzy. *Why?* she wondered. *Do Magmastone's troops have more tricks up their sleeves than I thought? Even though serpents don't have sleeves?*

"No," Sara responded, her voice determined. "You're going *down.*"

"Dark words, sister," Chloe muttered beside her. A second later, Sara charged. The sight before Izzy's eyes was what her friend could do on her own, and it just... *amazed* her.

First, Sara zipped over to the serpent and, faster than any mind could process, climbed her way up its scaly neck by wedging one side of her double-bladed battle axe into the serpent, getting a foothold and a sturdy handhold in the scales, and then ripping out her axe and wedging it a little higher up, climbing up to get a handhold and foothold, and doing the same thing all over again.

That was also probably the most dangerous way of climbing up an evil, red-eyed devil serpent.

Izzy's theory about the dangerous climbing was proved correct when Sara hacked her axe into the jawbone of the serpent and it roared in pain, accidentally swallowing her axe and nearly making her fall six feet to the ground.

"Ack!" Sara yelped. "Uh, can you guys help me instead of standing there and staring at me?!"

"Right!" Chloe said, snapping out of her awed silence. "Guys, let's go!"

Without another word—or at least a confident grin—Chloe charged into battle, her electric helmet, electric boots, and electric spear crackling with thepowerful energy that she herself was immune to.

She embedded the tip of her spear in the serpent's thick tail, causing another powerful howl of pain from the monster's mouth. The monstrous sound echoed in the corridors of the Flower Palace and almost made Sara fall off again. Now she was just hanging by one of her hands, and Izzy could see that it was slipping.

Thinking quickly, Izzy took off her backpack, dropped her Invisible Bow on the floor, and rummaged through the contents of her backpack. *Flashlight... book... pencil... YES! Found it!*

She took out the sturdy, handmade rope that she'd packed at the beginning of their adventure and tied it to the fletching of the arrow that was already loaded in the Invisible Bow. *I can make this work,* she told herself.

Aiming carefully at a spot on the serpent above Sara, Izzy shot the arrow, and it flew straight and true. Unfortunately, the arrow bonked Sara on the head, nearly causing her to fall off again. "Oops," Izzy mumbled to herself as the arrow fell down to the ground.

"Hey!" Sara yelled from above, her voice flooded with fear. "Be careful, okay?"

"Got it!" Izzy called. She spied the arrow, with the rope still tied to the end, lying near the front of the thrashing serpent. Kelsey was stabbing the serpent's tail energetically, darting here and there and that way and this way. The serpent was too busy trying to stab Chloe with the six swords it had in its mouth to fight Kelsey.

Can I get it? Izzy wondered. *I might have a chance... if Chloe keeps distracting that serpent, that is. Also, how does it even speak around those swords?*

"Hey, Angela," Izzy said to her friend, "I'm going to go get that arrow down there. Can you shoot at the serpent to keep it distracted while I retrieve it?"

Angela glanced at the arrow, her hands still on her bow. "Sure," she replied. "Go get it!"

Izzy nodded and ran towards the arrow, not even trying to get out of the serpent's vision. Her Invisible Boots made her run swiftly, and when the serpent lunged towards her, baring its sharp sword teeth, she dodged nimbly to the left and kept running until she reached the arrow.

The Land of Flowers

She quickly unslung her bow, picked up the arrow, and notched it in her bow. Then she shot it again, this time with success. It latched itself onto the serpent's scales on the part above Sara, who was just holding on now by two fingers. Izzy was close enough to see the expression of relief on her friend's face as she took hold of the sturdy rope. *At least Sara won't fall to her doom now,* Izzy thought.

The serpent roared in pain as Angela made a magnificent shot with her Starstruck Bow and knocked three of the six swords it had in its mouth to the ground, scraping the serpent's scales as it went. "Reinforcementsss will arrive sssoon!" it hissed menacingly, turning abruptly to attempt to bite Kelsey. "Even if I die, it will not be the end of the battle! The three daughtersss are powerful, and they will ssstop at nothing to rule the world! You will all die, sssooner or later!"

The serpent gave one final roar before it collapsed and nearly crushed Chloe and Kelsey with its scaly green body. The two ran over to where Angela and Sara were standing. Izzy shook her head to get herself back in reality before she joined them. Sara had found her metal axe in the remnants of the serpent, had picked it up, and was now carrying it over her shoulder.

"How was it like, hanging from a giant devil serpent?" Chloe was questioning Sara. "Was it fun? How hard where the scales? What was the main thought running through your mind?"

"Hold yer questions," Sara said. "We have something we need to do, Coco. Remember? We have to get to the throne room where Queen Turquoise can give us directions."

"Oh, yeah," Chloe remembered. "I just forgot. Sorry."

Angela smiled. "It's fine," she reassured her. Izzy liked her easygoing nature. "Besides, we still have plenty of time."

Suddenly, a large *thump* noise was heard overheard, like somebody had just dropped a huge rock on the Flower Palace's roof, and the palace began to cave in.

"*Run!*" was the first thing that came out of Izzy's mouth. The walls that could be described as sturdy just a second ago were now crumbling, cracks spreading through them at an unbelievably rapid pace. Izzy's slow-thinking brain calculated that at this rate, it would take about half a minute for the ceiling to collapse and squash her and her friends underneath it, which wasn't helping her. "We've got to get out of here!"

Well, I hope I can get out of here alive, Izzy thought. Her heart was beating about a million times a second; she was trying to locate her friends while also going down the passageway that they'd entered through. It had taken about two minutes to get to this place in the palace, so it would probably take about a minute to exit. Izzy didn't want to believe her calculations.

"Angela!" she heard Chloe call. "Where are you?"

"Here!" Angela's voice was farther away than Chloe's was. *Where're Kelsey and Sara?* Izzy wondered. *I hope they're somewhere safe and not crushed by rubble. But where* is *safe in this place? It's literally falling apart!*

A large chunk of glass dropped from above Izzy, but luckily, she dove to forward just in time to avoid the shattering pieces of glass flying everywhere. Izzy coughed, trying to get the dust to exit her lungs. Her throat felt dry, and she suddenly craved water.

Fresh water, she told herself. *That's what I'll get after I get out of this place.* Around her, the Flower Palace was almost in ruins. It was a miracle she'd survived, but pieces of the structure were still falling around her. *I've got to get out of here,* Izzy thought as she dodged to the left to narrowly avoid a leaning wall that had just collapsed. *I could totally die here, and my friends would never find me.* The thought made her sad.

Hoping to find someone by sound, Izzy called, "Is anyone here?" She waited for a response. No one. "Hello?" Again, nobody responded.

I guess I have to get out of here by myself, she thought. *At least I've still got some supplies to work with.* She ran down the hall. The ceiling had collapsed and now showed the blue sky overhead. Chunks of the roof lay among the ruined red carpet, half-submerged in dust. The sharp bits poked and jabbed at Izzy's legs as she ran past them.

She ran until she came to a dead end, stopped by a looming golden wall. This part of the palace was slightly intact, and the hallway ended here, which meant that Izzy had gone the wrong way. *Ugh,* she thought, frustrated. *I can't even find my way in a destroyed palace. I would be absolutely* hopeless *in those hay maze things.*

She decided to double back and head to the corridor. There, the walls had collapsed, and she could see the destruction of whatever had landed on the roof. Rubble completely covered the grass next to the palace, and dust piled two feet high blanketed the ground, hiding the remains of the Flower Palace.

I wonder what caused this, Izzy thought as she gazed over the area. *It must've been very powerful. Or just really heavy.*

"Izzy!" a voice called from behind her. "There you are!"

She spun around to find Kelsey and Sara running towards here. "You guys!" she cried. "You have *no idea* how powerful that thing that landed on the roof must've been! Like, it must've been *ginormous!*"

"Yeah," Sara said. Her eyes looked far away, like she wasn't even there anymore. "I can sense it around. It's prowling... for us." Then she grinned. "Did I scare you?"

Izzy blinked. Then blinked again. "Wait, what? Um… yes?"

"When can we fight some stuff?" Kelsey asked excitedly, jumping around and swinging her sword wildly. Sara raised an eyebrow while Izzy tried to restrain herself from giggling.

"Soon," Izzy said. "Once we find Chloe and Angela, I suspect."

Suddenly, there was a wild crashing noise behind them, and Chloe and Angela burst into view from behind the crumbling remains of the corridor walls. "Ferocious—dragon—on—the way," Angela gasped, stumbling towards the three.

Sara's eyes lit up. "Do you think it might be Magmastone?" she asked excitedly, who were apparently so out of breath that they couldn't speak.

"*The* Magmastone?" Izzy asked, her eyes growing wide. "You think *she* landed on the roof? Oh, no...."

"It isn't as bad as it looks," Chloe encouraged. "We've finally found out where she is, so we don't need to get directions! Plus, I get to slay another dragon!"

"We didn't exactly slay Scorchwing," Sara recalled. "More like she slunk away."

"We killed Firestriker," Kelsey observed. "I think *that's* what Chloe means."

"Yeah," Chloe agreed. "*That's* what I mean."

"Thanks for the clarification," Izzy said sarcastically, "but we should really get going. You said that Magmastone might be coming after us, right?"

Before Chloe or Angela could even open their mouths to respond, a smashing noise much louder than the one the two had made sounded behind them, and then the most magnificent dragon Izzy had ever seen came into view.

She was about three times as tall as Chloe's electric spear from the tip to the bottom of its grip and three times as wide as Izzy. She had red, orange, yellow, and rose-dawn-colored scales. With a regal head, fiery golden eyes, and sharp, curved claws, the most descriptive word Izzy could think of to describe her was simply *scary*.

This must be Magmastone, she thought, her heart pounding in fear. *Is it too late to back out? Or can I still leave and get some battle fairies the few moments before Magmastone kills us all?*

The stunning dragon roared, then spoke the following words: "You are part of the twelve that shall destroy my sisters and me, and I cannot allow that. I will give you one chance to surrender and serve as a prisoner; will you accept?"

"Never!" Chloe replied fiercely, speaking for all of them.

Magmastone growled in acknowledgement. "I appreciate your bravery," she snarled, "but alas, I have to kill you. Good luck with not dying!" With a final battle roar, she charged.

Chloe ran to meet the dragon head-on, brandishing her electric spear and screaming, *"Thanks for the good luck!"* as loud as she could. Angela had unslung her bow and was carefully notching an arrow. Sara was eyeing the ferocious dragon while the sturdy wooden handle of her metal axe rested in her clenched fist, and Kelsey was looking on the scene with fascination through her white helmet's visor, her Full Moon sword in her hand.

"Don't stand there and do nothing!" Angela exclaimed at Sara, Izzy, and Kelsey. "Attack already!"

Izzy rolled her eyes. "Got it," she replied. Izzy got her bow off of her shoulder, dropped her quiver, picked out an arrow, and notched it in the bowstring of her weapon. Sara and Kelsey charged, axe and sword swinging, helmets over heads.

As far as Izzy could tell, Chloe was doing okay in the fight, considering the fact that she was battling against an opponent ten times her size. Her helmet and boots had the same properties as her spear; they both radiated the neon-yellowish light of electricity, which Chloe herself was immune to. Magmastone, although being a fire dragon, could be harmed by the crackling, almost *alive* energy.

As Izzy watched, Chloe thrust her spear to Magmastone's right shoulder, but the dragon swiftly ducked, dodged to the left, and breathed a gigantic breath of fire that consumed Chloe. Izzy knew that Chloe was too tough to be taken down by a single breath of dragon fire, and her friend emerged from the smoke of the fire unscathed, just like Izzy predicted that she would.

"Was that fire a challenge?" Chloe asked, her eyes narrowing as she approached the now still dragon. *Is Magmastone going to leap out and crush Chloe?* Izzy wondered, a hundred different scenarios leaping through her head.

"No," Magmastone replied smoothly, her gleaming gaze fixed on Chloe. "It is not a challenge, although I can certainly see that you are strong enough to stand up to it."

Flattery, Izzy thought.

The Land of Flowers

"Then we continue to battle," was Chloe's reply, and then she was charging again with her spear pointed straight at Magmastone's throat. Izzy caught her breath.

Magmastone calmly stepped to the left as Chloe's spear narrowly missed her right arm, then slapped her tail over the electric weapon, making it fall flat on the ground and out of Chloe's grasp. "Hey!" she yelped in alarm, skidding to a stop a few feet in front of the magnificent dragon. "Not fair!"

The multicolored dragon cackled, her golden eyes glittering with evil. Those eyes reminded Izzy of the devil serpents. "Who said I would play fair?" Magmastone snickered. "Then it wouldn't be any *fun!*"

"Don't *stand* there and watch me get fried!" Chloe snapped at her friends. "*Do* something!"

Kelsey blinked. Then she sprinted full-on at Magmastone with her Full Moon sword glinting in the sun. For a fraction of a second, her white blade reflected a patch of sunlight that completely blinded Izzy's eyes, and that moment just turned... *magical.*

Magmastone stood where she was and ducked at the last second, when Kelsey swung her sword in a way that would've cut the dragon's head off. Then, rising up to her full self, Magamstone threw an expertly aimed punch, but Izzy's friend blocked it with her Full Moon sword.

Magmastone roared again and was going to knock Kelsey off balance with her massive tail, but Chloe intervened. While Magmastone had been distracted with Kelsey, Chloe had taken her weapon back and was ready to reenter the fight. With a yell that sounded more than a little like a battle cry, she threw her electric spear as hard as she could from where she was standing behind Magmastone.

The glowing bolt of metal struck her right in the neck.

The fiery dragon shrieked—in outrage or pain, Izzy couldn't tell. "This is not over!" she roared, twisting around to clamp her jaw around the spear's grip, remove it, and flick it away. "I will be back someday to kill you all!"

Magmastone spread her wings and lifted into the sky with a loud *whoosh* of air, her golden scales flashing in the sunlight. Izzy shielded her eyes, watching Magmastone fly into the distance until she became a speck, then disappeared altogether.

There was a long, heavy silence.

"Well, that was terrifying," Chloe finally said. She walked over to where her electric spear lay on the ground, doing nothing but crackling and alarming a few startled caterpillars, and picked it up. "You guys okay?"

"S-shocked," Izzy stuttered. "Um—uh—I mean, you did a *great* job making Magmastone fly away!"

"Right," Sara muttered, staring at the blue sky. "Except that the Flower Palace is now in ruins, who knows where Queen Turquoise is, and this Ariadnia place is just chaos."

Izzy turned around and climbed on top of a solid brick, gazing in the other direction to see what Sara was talking about. Her friend was right. Now that Magmastone had left, the devil serpents were retreating, but the army of unicorns, fairies, and phoenixes were still fighting against them. The serpents' speed was nothing compared to the unicorns' magic, the fairies' swords and bows, or the phoenixes' top-notch flying.

"Yikes," Angela said. Izzy jumped, spinning around. "That looks... bad."

"Yeah," Izzy agreed, nodding. "Although that *might* be an understatement."

Angela shrugged in response. "Come on!" she said, turning away and looking back over her shoulder at Izzy. "We have to go *righten* everything."

"Jeez," Izzy muttered as she followed Angela back to Chloe, Sara, and Kelsey and they all started walked back to where the battle was an ember of the fire that had once burned. "This is going to be *so* unexciting."

She was right. They rounded up the rest of the stampeding unicorns, Flower Phoenixes, and mysterious fairies that hadn't been destroyed and drove back the devil serpents until the ranks of Magmastone's army receded past the hills in the distance. They helped clear the bodies of the phoenixes, unicorns, and fairies that had fallen and moved them to the graveyard, where a team of medics were waiting to do the rest. They scouted among the forests, valleys, and hills for any sign that the devil serpent army had come back until their feet ached and their legs screamed for a rest break.

In all, it was tiring, exhausting, and tedious, and tiring all over again.

It especially hurt Izzy to remember that so many lives had been lost, all because the three daughters of Queen Opaque had decided to target an innocent area. *But that means this place can't be innocent after all. There has to be a reason that they did this. So what is it?*

Izzy knew that Queen Turquoise could answer her question. She had come back to where they were at the graveyard, cheerful instead of monotonic, so for *some* reason, the spell must've been destroyed. To be honest, Izzy liked this side of Queen Turquoise *much* better than the other one, the one that King Sky had no idea about.

The Land of Flowers

Speaking of King Sky, he had been tossed in the Flower Palace's prison, which was the most comfortable prison Izzy had ever seen. She could count the number of prisons she'd seen before on one hand, but this one *definitely* topped the list. But so people won't try to get in there *on purpose*, she didn't talk about what she'd seen in it.

After all of the clean-up had been taken care of, Izzy and Sara took a seat on a hill topped with dew-speckled green grass and colorful, blooming flowers of all sizes and shapes. They were savoring a few minutes of just nature's peace, hanging out together and enjoying the picturesque view.

"This is great," Izzy sighed, leaning against a tall oak tree. Its bark was surprisingly smooth. "I wonder if we'll ever be able to visit Ariadnia again."

"Queen Turquoise could send us an invitation on Swift," Sara suggested. "If she wanted to. Just saying."

"I know," Izzy said, gazing at the blue sky, which had faint wisps of white clouds drifting slowly around. "It just feels like... like there's something *missing* from this puzzle, and I can't find the piece until I rest."

Sara smiled. "Metaphorically speaking, huh?"

"Yeah," Izzy said. She got up, dusting off her pants and unscrewing the cap of her bottled water to take a sip. "I just feel like I *have* to find that piece."

"I'll go with you," Sara offered.

Izzy grinned. "I'm not going to say no. C'mon!"

She ran down the hill and towards the demolished palace, where a group of official-looking fairies was carefully writing out the blueprints for a new and better building that would be more resistant to a-dragon-landed-on-the-roof-help-the-palace-is-collapsing attacks. Izzy jogged past them, Sara on her heels (not literally; metaphorically speaking again), and headed towards the main area of the palace that hadn't been destroyed: the throne room.

The Hope Flower

Queen Turquoise was there, sitting on her white quartz throne, along with a long line of subjects that had problems waiting to be solved, problems all caused by the battle. King Sky's throne had been suffocated under an iron beam until it was utterly unrecognizable. Now, Izzy saw it in the form of a pile of white rubble to the left of Queen Turquoise's throne.

Izzy settled into place in the line after a tall Flower Phoenix, who didn't seem as badly injured as the rest of the phoenixes in the army; his feathers only sported a few small wounds and a slightly larger one on one wing. All had been wrapped in white cloth. *Maybe this is just an ordinary phoenix,* Izzy reasoned, although it didn't seem true. This phoenix had the hard, silent look of a warrior, and his straight posture suggested military training.

"This is boring," she whispered to Sara. "What can I do?"

Her friend shrugged, holding up her hands. "We can play rock-paper-scissors," she offered. "Or chopsticks. Or… what's that pat-your-lap game called?"

"No thanks," Izzy said. "Hand games are boring."

"Thumb wrestling?" her friend asked.

"Nah."

The Land of Flowers

"I dare you to ask that phoenix in front of us what he's here for," Sara countered. "And get at least 50 words out of him."

Izzy gulped. "How am I supposed to count the words?" she tried.

"I'll write them down on my notebook," Sara said. "I can put it on my knee and write it there. I'm good at *that*."

Izzy groaned. "Alright, fine. You win."

Sara grinned and took out her notebook, angling on her knee so that when she bent over, she could write on it uncomfortably (obviously it was that when she *bent over* it was uncomfortable, not *writing!* Otherwise, it would be completely absurd). "Go ahead."

Izzy nervously tapped the tall Flower Phoenix on the shoulder, feeling the cold feathers briefly before she flinched her hand away from them. "*What?!*" the Flower Phoenix snapped, spinning around to glare at her.

"Um—m-my friend dared me to talk to you and a-ask you w-why you're here," Izzy stammered, momentarily forgetting how to speak without stuttering under the soldier's piercing gaze, pointing at Sara, who was looking at her casually.

Surprisingly, the Flower Phoenix's posture relaxed instantly. "If you must know," he said, "I am here to ask for a position in the royal healers' room for my brother. He's badly wounded, unable to walk, but nobody was around except for me to deliver the message, and he's too heavy to carry by myself. I didn't see anyone on the way in, either."

"Thanks!" Izzy said hurriedly. "Um, sorry for sticking my nose into your business. Uh... we're done now. Thank you." The Flower Phoenix nodded stiffly and turned back around.

"Only 38 words," Sara said, glancing up from her notebook.

Izzy could almost *certainly* tell when somebody was fudging with *that* tone of voice. "Wrong," she said. "He said 55 words." *Hey, I knew what I was doing when I was counting,* she thought proudly. *And guess what? It paid off!*

"Alright, you win," Sara grumbled, closing her notebook and standing back up. "Hey, look. The line moved forward."

Izzy turned back around quickly and stepped forward to her place in the line. Sara followed her example.

"This is *so* boring," Izzy complained, peeking around the tall phoenix. "I wanna go find Andrew, 'kay?"

"Okay," Sara replied, glancing around. "Just don't be gone for too long or else I'm going to leave and not hold a spot for you in line."

"Sounds great!" Izzy replied cheerfully and jogged away, her eyes roaming the green, grassy hills for a telltale sign of Andrew's red shirt, the gleam of his sword, or perhaps his little robot drone friend buzzing above his head, the one he'd named Max.

No luck.

Where is he? Izzy kept thinking. *Did he go into the forest and run into some serpents?* Despite the fact that Magmastone's army had retreated, Izzy still felt uneasy, like it was the calm before a wicked storm.

Then, with much relief, she spotted Andrew over on a lofty hill, lounging in the shade of the pair of trees on it, with Max buzzing around the leaves, and occasionally making obnoxious noises. Izzy didn't know how Andrew was managing to relax while hearing all the sound.

The Land of Flowers

Izzy jogged to the hill, ran up it, and almost tripped over him. "Hey!" her younger brother yelped, springing up on his feet. "Watch it!" Max buzzed in annoyance. Izzy never knew that robot drones could be annoyed. *Well, there's always a first time for everything,* she thought.

"Sorry," Izzy apologized. "I got bored waiting in line for Queen Turquoise, so I thought I would come see you."

"Well, Max is blaring nonstop," Andrew complained. "It's *so annoying*. Why can't he stop? I told him to sound his alarm if enemies are nearby, but it's not *supposed* to be *going off* when I can *very clearly* see that there are *no* serpents or dragons whatsoever around us!"

"There *might* be serpents or dragons," Izzy offered, "lurking in the forest, waiting for a chance to snap your neck and drag you back to... well, wherever they're supposed to live."

Andrew shuddered. "That's creepy."

"Yeah," Izzy replied. "That's what I was aiming for."

Andrew slapped her on the arm.

"Ow!" she complained. "That *hurt!*"

Andrew shrugged. "Well, how would *you* like it if *I* told you that there could be serpents or dragons in the forest, waiting for a chance to snap your neck and drag you back to their base?"

Izzy paused. "Well, if you put it *that* way, I guess I wouldn't enjoy it very much," she admitted. "Well, we're getting off track. I felt like there was a piece of the puzzle missing, you know, so Sara and I went to Queen Turquoise, but there's, like, a *bunch* of dudes waiting in a line to meet her! It's going to take *so* long!"

"Yeah, yeah," Andrew replied, lying back down on the grass again. "Now, can you leave me in peace? I really can't—MAX, STOP THAT INFERNAL BUZZING!"

Max's buzzing paused for a second, then resumed. Izzy didn't know if it was her imagination, but it seemed louder and more insistent this time. "Looks like Max isn't taking your orders anymore," Izzy joked.

Before Andrew could respond, a loud roar echoed through the seemingly peaceful hills. Andy sat up and twisted his head around, looking for a potential threat. Izzy took a step back in shock and glanced around, trying to spot an enemy.

"It must've come from the woods," Izzy whispered, eyeing the patch of trees distrustfully. "Did that sound like a dragon or a serpent?"

"Um... a dragon?" Andrew offered. "Considering the fact that serpents don't roar?"

"Very helpful, Andrew," Izzy grumbled sarcastically. "Can we leave this hill now? And, you know, go to someplace safer? That's *not* in earshot of terrifying dragon roars?"

"Sure," Andrew said, standing up. "Max, come on. We're going to go to...." His eyes swept over to the hills. "The... uh...."

"The Flower Palace," Izzy suggested quickly. "Sara's waiting for me there, anyways. We should go there. Before a dragon comes bursting out of the woods and gobbles us up."

"Good idea," Andrew agreed nervously. "Max, follow me. To the Flower Palace!"

The run there wasn't so great.

Not mentioning the fact that they were in constant terror of everything because of the possible dragon in the woods, Izzy also wanted to sneak up on Sara, who was still the last person in the line for Queen Turquoise's advice, but in her vibrant-colored shirt, she stuck out like a seagull in a murder of crows.

So Sara ended up keeping her back to Izzy while she zoomed in on her friend and yelled, "BOO!" really loudly. Sara had seen what was going to happen; she didn't even flinch.

"Hey!" Izzy complained. "You're supposed to whirl around and scream, '*What are YOU doing here?!*'"

Sara shrugged. "You asked for it. Why'd you bring Andrew and his annoying flying drone over here?"

"His name is *Max*, and he's *not* annoying," Andrew interrupted.

Izzy shot him a look.

"Okay, maybe he *is* a little annoying," Andrew relented reluctantly.

"As I was saying," Sara continued, "why did you bring them here, Izzy?"

"We heard something in the forest," Izzy explained. "I thought it wouldn't be safe for me to leave him in the open on the hill with only, you know, Max for defense. I thought he'd get a better chance at staying alive if I brought him here."

Sara nodded. "Good thinking," she approved. "He might've been chomped up by a dragon if you hadn't done that."

Andrew rolled his eyes. "Thanks for making me feel so cheerful," he said sarcastically. "You *totally* made my day."

"So, did the line move forward?" Izzy asked, trying to ignore Andrew's comment. "You're still last in line."

"Well, you weren't gone for *that* long," Sara retorted, turning red. "And plus, three phoenixes, a person, and four fairies left the line while you were absent."

"Absent." Izzy snorted. "What a fancy word." *Fancy?* she thought in her mind, shocked at herself. That's *an old-fashioned word!*

"So, yeah," Sara said. She glanced ahead of her. "There's still two phoenixes and a fairy in line before us." Just as she finished her sentence, a tall fairy joined the line behind Andrew, who looked a little startled. Max gave a beep and decided to settle down in a patch of grass that hadn't been mowed for so long that Izzy couldn't see even a glimpse of the little flying drone hiding in it.

The phoenix at the very front of the line left, leaving only a fairy and the tall phoenix in front of Sara, Izzy, and Andrew. Now they were close enough to hear what the fairy was saying to Queen Turquoise, and although Izzy didn't particularly enjoy eavesdropping, she couldn't really do anything about it.

"—many resources," the fairy was telling Queen Turquoise, "so we'll have to organize a team to get more. May we have permission?"

"Of course," Queen Turquoise replied in a quietly weary voice. "I have no objections."

The fairy bowed and left.

The Land of Flowers

Next up was the tall phoenix in front of them. Izzy wasn't really paying attention, though. She was more focused on how to word her question for Queen Turquoise to answer.

"Hi... is there anything that Magmastone or her troops took?" Maybe that would work, Izzy thought. *But what if she takes offense because King Sky could technically be called 'part of Magmastone's troops.' What about "Did the serpents take anything?"*

The tall phoenix left the line. Izzy took a deep breath and stepped up.

"W-was there a-anything that Magmastone or the s-serpents t-took?" she asked. *Hopefully I'm not stammering,* Izzy thought. *But that's just a wishful thought. I probably* am *stammering. Well, I specifically heard* myself stammering, so....

Queen Turquoise looked puzzled. "I believe so," she said slowly and carefully, as if selecting her words like pieces of candy from a basket. "They took the Hope Flower."

"Is it important?" Izzy asked anxiously. She glanced at Sara and Andrew. Sara was intently watching her and Queen Turquoise's conversation while Andrew was holding Max—probably deactivated—in his hands and fidgeting with some buttons.

Queen Turquoise nodded solemnly. "Very," she replied gravely. "It is the flower of hope. If it stays intact, hope stays. If it is crushed, hope vanishes, and despair will fill that void."

Sara furrowed her brow. "I still have hope," she said, looking as confused as a seal in a flock of sheep. "If they took it, why haven't they crushed it already?"

The queen shrugged. "No one knows," she answered. "I suppose that they are making a trap for you. You may leave whenever you want to—as in, Swift will guide you back as soon as you ask her to—but I give you the following warning: Scorchwing, Magmastone, and their other sister are all smarter than they look. You must be careful. Do not be arrogant, thinking that you can take them down as easily as you took down Firestriker."

Izzy promptly overflowed with curiosity. "You know that we killed Firestriker?" she inquired.

Queen Turquoise smiled. "Every queen has her secrets."

"I think it's time to go," Izzy said to Sara once they'd left what remained of the Flower Palace. "There's not much left to do around here. I mean, we *could* help with the rebuilding, but I think it's more important to go after the Hope Flower."

"You know what Queen Turquoise said," Sara replied. "Those three fire dragons could be luring us into a trap with it."

Izzy shrugged. "We still have to get it," she countered. "What happens if they crush the flower and hope is lost forever? Nobody will even give a good fight, and the world will be *doomed!*"

Sara sighed. "Never mind about that. But I do agree that we should get home soon. I want some ice cream."

They found everyone else at the obstacle courses, watching Chloe do loop after twirl after twist after jump-over-a-chainsaw after—well, you get the idea.

When Izzy and Sara arrived, Chloe was ducking under slicing swords, leaping over jabbing points of stone, and walking sideways between walls of lava that were somehow held in place by magic.

Overall, it looked terrifying.

"It's time to go home!" Izzy yelled. "Also, Chloe, get down before you fall in the lava! That's *really dangerous!*"

"What do you—ouch!" Chloe yelped as she jumped back from the lava with a new burn on her hand. "Okay, okay, fine. But I'm putting this on my list of places I want to go."

Izzy sighed. "Let's just go before I get impatient," Izzy grumbled. "And by that, I mean even *more* impatient."

A long story made short, they flew back with Swift as their guide. After exchanging goodbyes, Swift left to return to the Flower Palace, and the girls (and Andrew) settled Lava, Whirlpool, Ice, Leaf, Jewel, Storm, and Reed in the dragon stables.

The six kids walked back to the village, chatting all the way. When they reached the town, they split up to go do what they wanted to. Angela was going to accompany Sara to the butchers' house to go purchase some food for the dragons, Chloe left to attend dance class, Kelsey went to practice gymnastics, Andrew ran to the soccer field to play a game with whoever was there, and Izzy hurried to the library, where their latest adventure had first begun.

As Izzy seated herself in a plush, comfortable armchair, she thought about everything she and her friends had experienced today. Swift the mysterious dragon. The Flower Palace, home to the rulers of a new place. King Sky's betrayal. The stolen Hope Flower.

There's always something going wrong, Izzy thought, a smile beginning to form on her face. *But as long as we have hope, we can fight.*

Made in the USA
Columbia, SC
16 June 2022